Finding
Mr. Gorgeous

Stella MacLean

Finding Mr. Gorgeous
Print Edition

Copyright 2019 by Ruth Stella MacLean

Cataloguing and Publication information is available from The Canadian ISBN Service System, Library and Archives Canada.

ISBN: 978-0-9952968-3-1

Website: **www.stellamaclean.com**
Facebook: facebook.com/**stella.maclean.3**
Twitter: @Stella_MacLean

Editor Services provided by Patricia Thomas:
http//patthomaseditor.webs.com

Formatting Services provided by Jaycee DeLorenzo:
https://www.sweetnspicydesigns.com

Cover Artist: Angella Jacobs

This book is dedicated to the

fantastic group of writers I met at

Vancouver Public Library

where I was Writer in Residence during

during the fall of 2018

Being writer in residence was one of the most rewarding

experiences of my writing career.

Thank you.

PROLOGUE

Promises made.

"This is the most beautiful place in the world to me," Lisa said, matching her stride to Herbert Stackhouse's uneven gait. The sun had just risen as they walked along the edge of the field that formed part of the boundary line of Harmony Farm. She loved this walk with its sweeping vista of green that led to a stand of towering oak trees nestled along a babbling brook. Willow Brook formed the boundary between the trees and the open field.

This farm and everything in it had been her salvation since the day she'd decided to strike out on her own away from the drama of her mother's past. After years of turmoil her life had become a pleasant experience when Herbert offered her a place to stay. She'd been on her own, a new graduate from the local agriculture college, looking for purpose in her life when she met Herbert at the local Nature Trust meeting in Middleborough.

"We have shared so many things since you came to live on the farm. All of them good," Herbert said as he followed the narrow path to the edge of the stream. "I know you're wondering why I've been so insistent that you walk with me this morning… I brought you out here so we could talk for a little bit."

Her heart stuttered. *Was he going to ask her to move on?* She lifted her jaw and asked: "About what,

Herbert? Are we still going to meet with the town about offering tours of the farm? Or have you changed your mind? It would be a nice source of money for the work we need to do on the wetland area below the meadow."

Carefully Herbert made his way across the stream and up to a small rise in front of the oak trees. "Sit down here with me for a few minutes," he said, taking his Barbour jacket off and placing it along the grassy verge. "There is something else. Something I've been meaning to talk to you about for a couple of weeks."

"Sure," Lisa said, suddenly anxious that something was wrong in her friend's life, something that could impact their plans for the farm. Lisa dropped to her knees and made herself comfortable on the edge of Herbert's jacket. The scent of the wax used to waterproof it wafted around her. That smell would forever remind her of the kind gentleman settling down beside her. She had never known anyone quite like him. She had heard of people described as those who led with their heart, but Herbert was the first person she'd ever met who did just that. Every decision he made was from the heart.

"Lisa, you've been like a daughter to me these past months. You've done so many small chores around the farm, included me in all the Nature Trust events, shared information and proven to me that you love this farm as much as I do. I don't know if I ever said this to you but I haven't enjoyed life this way since my wife Elsa died two years ago." He took her hand, his gnarled fingers pressing into hers. "Having you here has made a real difference in my life."

Lisa could feel tears starting at his words. "Herbert, I'm the lucky one. I can't imagine ever being away from this farm." She sighed looking up into the canopy created by the wide expanse of branches and the thousands of oak leaves creating a beautiful umbrella of green.

He leaned back, his gaze following hers as he

sighed. "That's what I wanted to talk to you about. I am going to change my will. I want this farm to go to the Nature Trust when I pass, and I want to leave you in charge, to carry out my wishes to have this lovely bit of heaven forever protected from anyone wanting to harm the trees or destroy the peace and quiet of this place." He glanced around, and as he turned toward her she saw the shimmer of tears in his eyes.

"Herbert, you're not ill, are you?" she asked suddenly concerned that he might have gotten bad news at his medical appointment last week.

"No! I'm fine. I just want to make plans for this place that will protect it for future generations..."

"How wonderful, Herbert." She offered him a reassuring smile as relief washed through her. In that instant she realized that she didn't want anything to change and that she was truly happy for the first time in years. She loved working alongside this visionary of a man.

"That would be wonderful. But are you sure you want to do this? What will your nephew say?" she asked, remembering the last time she'd seen Sam Jackson—the day, years before when she'd cancelled their date for a school dance. She still blushed at the memory of how naïve she'd been where Sam was concerned.

"Sam doesn't come here anymore. He's off doing his thing as an airline pilot, living a life that seems to suit him. He has started his own business and that's all he talks about when he calls. I'm sure he won't care one way or the other about what I do with the farm. Even during the summers he spent here when his mother was alive he always seemed to be waiting to leave."

"I'm sorry, Herbert," was all she could think of to say as her own thoughts around Sam continued to confuse her. Despite the date that hadn't happened and her embarrassment over it she found herself hoping that one day she and Sam might at least be friends. In those days he'd seemed perfect in so many ways. She'd walked away because she didn't have the courage to go to the dance once she learned that Sam really wanted to go with someone else.

Samantha Mitchell, the classmate voted most likely to succeed, and the most attractive girl in her high school class, was the one Sam wanted to invite. When Lisa overheard Samantha and her friends lamenting that Sam had accepted Lisa's invitation to the dance though he regretted that and would prefer to attend with Samantha, Lisa let him off the hook and told him she was ill. It had been the coward's way out but it was better than being humiliated at the dance by being with someone who wanted to be with someone else.

The memory still haunted her, and now interrupted her pleasant thoughts and the conversation with the caring gentleman who sat staring at the beauty surrounding them. Out over the vista of green as the soft whir of the leaves moving in trees above their heads provided a winsome feeling in the moment. "Elsa and I lived a good life here. We never had kids, but if we had had a daughter I'd want her to be just like you."

She clutched his hand. "Herbert, that's the sweetest thing anyone has said to me in a long time. I would be honored to spend my life here with you, and to look after your legacy."

His smile crinkled his eyes, lifting the corners of his handlebar mustache. "You deserve a good life, Lisa. I want to be part of that, to have you enjoy this place for as long as you live."

There was a catch in his voice, as his gaze searched the horizon with such intensity that Lisa wondered if Herbert *was* hiding something. "Herbert, are you sure you're okay?"

He stared at her face for a long moment as if he had more to say, then squeezed her hand and smiled at her with watery eyes. "I'm doing just fine now that I know you're willing to stay here and care for Harmony Farm. You won't regret it. I promise."

CHAPTER ONE

There are times when it's hard to tell a snake from a prince.

Three months later, under darkening skies, gravel pinged against the rusted body of Lisa O'Neill's pickup as she braked hard and pushed the reluctant gearshift into park. She rubbed her eyes to wipe the tears away. Herbert had passed away two weeks before, and she was still in shock. She'd found him unconscious on the floor of his kitchen, his eyes closed. The ambulance came, but by the time they got him to the hospital it was too late.

He hadn't wanted a funeral, only a small tree-planting ceremony on the farm, in his memory. Due to a week of heavy rain the ceremony had been postponed until today. Willing herself not to think about the loss of her friend, Lisa stared out over the open fields of Harmony Farm, along the sloping pasture to where a group of mourners gathered at the edge of Willow Brook.

She remembered the last time she and Herbert had walked there together...

Herbert's nephew, Sam Jackson was supposed to attend the service today. Sam had decided not to come right away when he was informed of his uncle's death. He had sent word that he would arrive today. She couldn't say she was surprised, given that Herbert had told her Sam seemed disinterested in the farm and hadn't kept in touch with his uncle much.

There was so much to do on the farm. It would be good that she'd be busy for a long time straightening things out and dealing with the challenges of running the farm.

Trying to concentrate on anything but the loss of her friend, Lisa pulled her rearview mirror toward her and did a quick check. Her pale face, framed by tight rust-colored curls, stared back at her. She couldn't go down there looking like this.

"Darn!" she muttered as she moved the empty animal cage out of the way and fished a stray tube of lipstick out of the ashtray. With quick strokes, she applied bronze color, her hand shaking because of the stress she was feeling.

She focused on her face, rather than the ceremony being held in a few minutes. Rubbing her lips together, she peered at herself in the dust-covered mirror and pulled a couple of spring-loaded curls down to cover her ears. *What I wouldn't give for straight hair again.*

The bronze tone highlighted her gray eyes but her pale cheeks reminded her of the Pillsbury Dough Boy. She knew she was beating up on herself but she also had to face facts. She had struggled with her weight all her life, convinced that every extra pound that didn't land on her hips appeared on her cheeks. She gave them a pinch and points of color flared.

This will have to do. She sighed as she popped the door open with a nudge of her shoulder and leaped to the ground.

Lisa smoothed her too-tight skirt across her hips and sucked in her stomach, peering at her feet. Dirt-streaked, black rubber boots reaching halfway to her black skirt were testament to her morning. She'd been over at the wildlife refuge helping to rescue a fawn separated from its mother and mired in a mudslide. Without quick action on their part the sweet little creature might have died. It had taken longer than she'd expected to move the fawn to higher ground but it had been worth the time and the sore muscles.

In a rush to make it back to Harmony Farm for the ceremony, Lisa had used the restroom at the local gas station to clean up and change into her skirt and blouse. Because she'd left the house in such a rush, she'd forgotten her shoes.

It would have been nice to be able to dress up a little more, but who would be there to notice? Herbert's friends wouldn't be dressed up—not with the threat of rain. That left Sam. He hadn't noticed her again after that day five years ago when she'd bowed out gracefully instead of making a complete fool of herself. And there wasn't much reason to think he'd notice her now, other than as a mess.

She started across the field to the group gathered at the brook. Clambering over the rocky outcropping she made her way down the wet path to the edge of the stream.

Herbert had offered her the apartment over the garage, rent-free, in return for her help with the Bald Eagles Observation Program at Harmony Farm. She intended to honor that charge as well as his last wish that his farm would become part of the Nature Trust. She owed him that, and a lot more. She couldn't let him down.

Her rubber boots slipped on the damp ground as she approached the group. "Whoops!" She skidded into Kenny Appleby and had to grab his arm for support.

"Well, if it isn't the late Miss O'Neill. Did your old truck have another seizure?" Kenny asked as he held his arm steady to support her and planted his black-framed glasses back on the bridge of his nose.

"Have a heart, will you, Kenny?" She swiped at the new drops of rain on her cheeks. "I know I'm late.

Where's the reverend?" she asked, fighting the urge to search the crowd for Sam's handsome face after thinking about him on her way to the ceremony.

Kenny gave her a half-grin. "He's waiting for you. You did say you'd do the official shovel thing, didn't you?"

"Yeah." She took note of the mist clinging to the oak trees across the brook and the low, rain-swollen clouds hovering on the horizon. The dark day made the loss of her friend even more poignant.

"Reverend Willie will be pleased to know you're finally here."

"If he's a reverend I'm a monkey's uncle," she said, instantly wishing she'd kept her sarcasm to herself. Kenny was a friend and she was being mean spirited. "Sorry Kenny." She let go of his arm and slid along the rain-slicked path ahead of him.

Lisa edged toward several groups of people, nodding to them as she walked to the front of the group. Reverend Willie Anderson stood near the edge of the brook, beside the memorial tree perched uncertainly in its newly dug hole. Space had been left for the shovelfuls of earth needed for the ceremony.

Lisa focused on standing straight and squaring her shoulders while deep in her heart she wished Herbert were there. He'd have been pleased that Sam showed up. But that was how Herbert treated life. He only saw the good in people.

At the thought of her friend, her throat thickened. She couldn't cry here and now. Herbert wouldn't have wanted tears. To ease her feelings of loss, she stared at Willie. A huge pewter peace symbol swayed over his tummy. A once-thick ponytail, reduced to a fringe, was pulled back and tied at the nape of his neck. His bald crown glistened in the faltering light. What Willie lacked in formal preacher training he made up for by being pleasant and caring.

"My child," Willie intoned, taking her hand, "we've been waiting for you."

In an attempt to cover her embarrassment at being late, Lisa assumed a solemn expression. "I'm ready when you are."

He pulled her to him in a bear hug and his peace symbol dug into her chest. "I have someone here I know you'll want to meet before I begin. He's Herbert's nephew and he's come all the way from New York."

Anticipation leaped through her. *Had Sam asked for her? Had he recognized her name? Or did he want to apologize for not being there for his uncle?* "He wants to meet me?"

"See for yourself." Willie pointed toward a tall man in a tailored suit, his dark hair hugging his head, his broad shoulders hinting at an athletic frame. Nothing had changed. Sam Jackson was still the most gorgeous man Lisa had ever seen. She waited, holding her breath, licking her lips as she willed him to meet her gaze across the group of people crowded around him.

He continued his conversation with an old friend of Herbert's, never once glancing her way. When Sam's gaze finally drifted toward her, she felt her pulse quicken. His glance hesitated; then slid past her, confirming his lack of interest.

Why did she torture herself this way? He hadn't wanted her that long ago summer, when she had paid lots of money to have her hair straightened and was pounds lighter, and had asked him out. *Why would he want her now?*

Fighting the anxiety that made her heart hammer, she gazed around at the motley collection of friends gathered along the brook, and forced a smile to her lips. "I'm ready," she said as she edged into position just to the left of where the reverend stood.

She lowered her eyes and watched Sam from under her eyelashes. Gold cufflinks winked where his sleeves met his wrist. Even from her safe distance he exuded sensuality like thick molasses. The way he smoothed his silk tie against his shirt made her want to lick her lips. Then she realized what she'd been doing...

Why was she mooning over this man when she should be concentrating on Herbert's memorial service? She took a deep fortifying breath and planted her feet carefully in the soft earth.

She watched Reverend Anderson as he hitched his pants up to where his waist had resided years ago and then looked out at the mourners. "Friends, we're gathered here to pay our last respects—"

"So you're the one we've been waiting for," a deep male voice whispered near her ear, making her heart jump in her chest. Unable to bring herself to look his way, Lisa suddenly was fixated on her rubber boots and felt the color rush to her cheeks.

The man who had been the inspiration for more sexual fantasies than she cared to remember was standing next to her, his polished leather shoes nearly touching her rubber boots. Her mind raced back to the horrible smelling eau de hand soap from the garage rest room. *Could he smell it?* And her vigorous efforts to rescue the fawn hadn't been entirely cleaned away by her quick scrub in the pint-sized sink.

She should have spent the time to clean up properly. She could have dashed up to the apartment for a quick shower. She had planned to, until she'd been delayed. But the greatest question of all was *why did Sam matter?* Why couldn't she focus on the service?

Resisting the urge to put her hand over her pounding heart, she knit her fingers together and stepped away from him.

He moved with her.

Was he really following her? she wondered. She moved again.

"Is this a new dance?" he whispered, his gaze meeting hers without so much as a flicker of recognition.

What was wrong with this man? His uncle's service was about to start and he was acting like he didn't care, like he had no respect for his uncle. "Why don't you simply stand quietly while the service begins?" she asked, annoyed at his behavior.

Sam glanced up at the sky. "We'd better get a move on or we'll be soaked."

"Do you not care about your uncle?" she fired back.

"Of course I do." His tone was light, breezy and just a little too cocky.

Sam's closeness made her even more aware of the ten pounds she'd accumulated after university. She sucked in her breath and felt her waistband loosen a little. *Why was she worrying about her waist when she was at the funeral of a dear friend?* "Well then why don't you move over a little?"

"As the chief mourners, aren't we supposed to stand together?"

She gave him what she hoped was a withering stare. "May I remind you this is supposed to be a solemn occasion?"

"I'm looking after my uncle's affairs once the ceremony is over." He tipped one eyebrow at her. "And you?"

"You're confused. Herbert asked *me* to look after things for him," she whispered as she glanced from Willie to Sam.

He edged closer, his thigh brushing hers. "This should prove interesting."

"I'm sure we can discuss your interests later."

Sam clearly did not remember her or he would have said something about high school. Annoyed and a little embarrassed, she struggled to maintain her composure.

Willie's voice dropped like a blanket over the collection of people standing around the tree. "Our brother has left us for a better place."

"Any place would be better than this," Sam whispered.

"Will you be quiet?" Lisa forced the words out of the corner of her mouth.

Willie Anderson spread a smile like peanut butter in the Sam's direction. "We have with us today Herbert's nephew, Sam Jackson. He's here to pay his last respects as well."

Willie gazed out over the people assembled there. "Herbert Stackhouse had one last request. He wanted an oak tree planted in his memory." Willie filled the shovel with earth and spoke to the gathering: "I ask you to join in this moment..."

Sam made eye contact with Willie and moved forward.

"Thank you," Sam said as he reached for the handle of the shovel.

What was going on?

She had been asked to put the earth around the tree in Herbert's memory. She'd come here to say a few words about Herbert before dropping the soil into place. After the way Sam had behaved he had no right to take any part in the ceremony, and especially not her part.

"I'll take that," she said. She grabbed for the handle of the shovel and at that second her boots skidded on the slippery ground.

Sam looked at her; surprise traced across his handsome face. "Sure, if you'd like," Sam said, holding the shovel out to her.

"I—" Lisa's feet slipped on the rain-soaked earth as she grabbed the shovel from his hands. The movement pulled her sideways, tipping the shovel at a dangerous angle. She struggled to steady herself as her rear end raced toward the ground. In a vain attempt to stop her rush toward the mud, she grabbed Sam and that pulled him down with her.

They landed together, Sam's shoulder bumping hers as he settled beside her in the mud.

Sam stared in disbelief at the woman sitting on the ground next to him, inches from the toes of his ruined shoes. For some reason she had taken an instant dislike to him.

He'd been delayed by bad weather in New York when he learned of his uncle's death. He had to deal with urgent issues involving his air-freight company, a company he'd started three years ago with a friend. So even when the weather finally cleared he had decided to wait until the memorial service before coming to Harmony Farm.

"Quite a performance. Will there be an encore?" he muttered into the mass of mud-sprinkled red curls that hid her face.

The woman shifted, glanced in his general direction before returning to her intense examination of the overturned shovel.

Should he help her up? He sure wasn't going to spend another minute in the mud. His shoes were a mess and it didn't look good for his only suit. And he gathered she probably would not welcome any help from him, given the way she'd made a grab for the shovel and the fact she hadn't apologized for that or dragging him down into the mud with her.

Easing to his feet, he wiped his hands on his trousers as he stared at Reverend Anderson. The reverend stood Sphinx still, his stare directed somewhere over the mourners. "Let's remain calm, folks," he said, a startled expression on his face.

Although Sam had no intention of remaining in the mud with the redhead, he was just a little curious about her. Anyone who would fight that hard for a shovelful of earth had to have a very good reason. "Are you okay?" he asked, glancing down at her.

The only visible response was a tightening of her shoulders.

He could understand a little of what she must be going through. People did strange things under stress and this lady was definitely stressed. Relenting, he offered his hand to her, and she took it grudgingly.

Who was she? All he knew was that the service couldn't start without this woman. Obviously, she'd been very important to Herbert. *Did she live on the farm?* Uncle Herbert often invited the men working for him to stay in the apartment over the garage, but as far as Sam knew, his uncle had never invited a woman. *So, if she was living at the farm, did that mean she was staying in the house?*

An unsavory thought went through his mind: Had she been having an affair with his uncle? Uncle Herbert wasn't that kind, but was she? A vulnerable widower might be tempted, he supposed.

The quickest way to find out was to ask someone named O'Neill. His name was on the apartment mailbox. Knowing his uncle, the tenant, the O'Neill person, was probably some absent-minded birder from some bird observation station. In his last phone conversation, his uncle had been full of the excitement over the increased number of the American Bald Eagles at Harmony Farm.

Sam understood little of what his uncle did, and for the most part he wasn't interested. He hadn't visited the farm in years—not since his mother's death three years ago. She had moved home to the farm after receiving her diagnosis of terminal cancer. Sam had fought hard to have his mother get the medical help she needed to fight the disease.

She'd refused, saying that she wanted to live what time she had left in the one place that meant something to her. Sam hadn't understood, and to this day he still didn't understand why she'd done what she did. But when his Uncle Herbert took her side against Sam, there was little left for him to say or do. He had attended his mother's funeral and hadn't returned to Harmony Farm until today.

He had called his uncle occasionally, but nothing more. *Did he regret that?* In a way, but he didn't love the farm the way his mother and uncle had. He'd spent summers in Middleborough during high school, where he'd divided his time between riding in his uncle's pickup along the rough trails that wound their way through the acreage, and going into the local pool hall to relieve the boredom.

The woman's rubber boots made a strange sucking noise as she moved away from him and passed the shovel to Willie. "I'm sorry. I should have been more careful." Her voice was low, with a catch in it.

Reverend Anderson said soothing words and the tension in the woman's shoulders seemed to ease slightly.

Feeling the damp spot on his rear through the wool of his suit, Sam did his best to smile.

"I guess we both made a mistake."

The woman glanced at him, meeting his gaze head-on, and a jolt of something resembling awareness darted through him. *It couldn't be.* With her Anne-of-Green-Gables hair and her touch-me-not attitude, she was the last woman on earth that should appeal to him.

"I didn't mean—" Tears pooled in her eyes as she held his gaze.

Why was this woman crying? Perhaps he was right in assuming that Herbert had been having an affair with her. It might explain the disastrous state of his uncle's finances. All the more reason for him to find Mr. O'Neill and get the lowdown on what this woman was doing in his uncle's life. Sam didn't relish pounding over the countryside looking for the man in some observation blind. It made more sense to leave a note on the apartment door.

"We will continue, shall we?" Willie asked as the woman turned her attention away from Sam.

"Would you like to do the honors?" Sam asked.

She glanced Sam's way, her eyes shining with unshed tears and her cheeks a bright pink in contrast to her red hair.

"Yes." She took the shovel from him and placed earth around the root ball of the tree.

Sam moved away from her and watched the proceedings, listening to her eloquent words reminding him of his uncle's kindness over the years. Every hour he spent in the house he expected to see his uncle come in through the back door, toss his boots at the boot box, come into the kitchen and wash his hands before regaling him with a story about something he'd been doing outside. He felt like a kid again and there was a level of disappointment in his thoughts.

Reality was, he missed his uncle...and being here reminded him of his mother in a way that filled him with yearning to recover the time he'd lost.

After the ceremony he turned to follow the other mourners away from the site, feeling sad and strangely alone at the prospect of going back to the house to begin his executor responsibilities.

"Wait. We need to talk."

The urgency of her words nearly made Sam turn around. Then he thought better of if. Whatever she wanted could wait. He needed to get back to the house and out of his mud-spattered suit and shoes.

"We can talk later," he said as he walked up the hill toward the house.

"I didn't mean—"

He heard the squeegee sound of her rubber boots as she hurried along behind him. "Look, I'm sorry. It was an accident."

He answered her by lengthening his stride as he approached the crest of the knoll. The tall, cedar-shingled barn that had once held his uncle's prized Percheron draft horses, lay just to his left. Back in the days before Uncle Herbert had given up trying to make Harmony Farm a working farm, he had a barn full of the big, gentle animals.

"Will you stop running away?" Her words held a sharp edge of exasperation.

He turned and stared at her. The pink flush of her cheeks was in stark contrast to the fiery red of her hair. Her fists were firmly planted on her hips, her feet spread wide apart in a stance that forced her skirt farther up her well-muscled thighs.

The sun had just tipped over the side of a puffy cloud and was spreading warmth over everything, including the air swirling between them. "I will, if you tell me who you are and what you're doing here?"

Her glance shifted. "I'm a friend of Herbert's. I was—"

"You were what? What *were you* to my uncle?"

"Herbert Stackhouse was my friend. He was very good to me." Her eyes glowed, her lips softened and curved upward.

Care to explain what you mean? My uncle never mentioned you."

The warmth of her eyes cooled. She pushed a mass of stubborn curls behind her ears. "I don't have to explain anything to you."

"What's your connection to my uncle?" Sam asked again as he eyed her, trying to make up his mind about what to do. She had intentionally avoided his veiled suggestion of an affair by going on the offensive. Smart move for someone who had something to hide and perhaps with an agenda to go with it. "And why the sudden change of heart?"

"What change of heart?" she said, sniffing as she searched for a tissue in the pocket of her jacket.

Annoyed, and a little tired after the long drive, he said, "A few minutes ago you didn't want to talk to me, and suddenly now you want to talk. So what's your story?"

"I need to explain something. I was shocked when Herbert died suddenly of a heart attack. No one knew he was ill, and things between us were sort of day to day."

Was she trying to make amends for her behavior, or was she testing him to see what he knew? He hadn't noticed any signs of a woman living there when he'd gone to the house before the service; no nesting materials like fancy placemats or decorator towels.

Whatever was going on, he would play his cards one at a time until he knew what this firebrand wanted. "Why don't we put this discussion off for a while, until we're both feeling more in the mood?"

"And what mood would that be?" She furled her brows.

"I just think we need a little time to calm down before we discuss anything."

"Suit yourself. I'm sure you know where to find me when you're ready." She hurled the words at him as she stomped away.

"I do?" So she assumed that he knew she'd been cohabiting with his uncle. He groaned. That meant he had to spend the next two weeks sharing the house with

Frosty the Snow Woman.

He strode along behind her, watching the intriguing way her legs coped with the chunky rubber boots. "I was wondering if you knew the man who lived in the apartment over the garage? I see the name O'Neill on the mailbox. Do you know him?"

She stopped suddenly, forcing him to dig his dirt-soaked shoes into the earth to keep from barreling into her. Her sidelong glance rained suspicion. "So, you think *Mister* O'Neill might help you while I can't?"

He rushed to smooth the expression on his face, to hide just how close she'd come to the truth. "No. I want to meet him. He must have an arrangement with my uncle concerning the apartment. I'd like to know what that is. I may also need his help to make arrangements to sell the farm."

"Sell the farm!" Fire leaped into her eyes, setting off a wave of flat white across her cheeks. "You can't sell the farm! Herbert promised me—"

So that was it. She thought she'd been left the farm in his will. "My Uncle Herbert had no business promising you anything."

With her fists clenched, her head high, she glared at him. "We'll see, won't we?"

Surprised at her outburst, Sam considered his options. This woman had no claim on his uncle's farm. Uncle Herbert had left no indication as to her role in his life… He strode toward the garage and the side entrance that led to the apartment, pulling his cell phone from the inside pocket of his suit jacket as he went.

"I look forward to it," he said as he walked ahead of her.

The woman caught up with him. "Best of luck finding *Mister* O'Neill."

She tossed a triumphant grin over her shoulder as she opened the door to the apartment and went in, slamming the dead bolt in place behind her.

CHAPTER TWO

You can fool some of the people some of the time.

L ater that day, Lisa opened the back door of the apartment. "There you go, Barney." She eased the raccoon off her shoulders and onto the concrete step. The furry little creature shuffled off toward the brook, his body rocking and rolling as he made his way over the gravel.

As she bent over to knot the laces in her running shoes she remembered Sam's behavior toward her. In a way she was relieved he didn't remember her from high school. After her stunned behavior over the shovel, and the rush she'd felt when Sam had helped her up, Lisa didn't want him to link her to another embarrassing incident.

She intended to keep herself under control until Sam Jackson left. It wouldn't be very long. When the will was read and Sam realized that there was nothing left to him, she anticipated he'd quickly return to his life in New York.

She thanked her lucky stars there had been no sign of him since the embarrassing episode at the ceremony and her return to the apartment. He was probably in the house buffing his nails or calling his broker. Her earlier encounter with him left her in need of a heart-pounding run to clear her head and calm her temper.

His casual remark about putting the farm up for sale

had sent her blood pressure over the top. After she and Herbert had talked about him leaving the farm to the local Nature Trust, and from what he'd said to her the week before he died, she was certain Herbert had made the change in his will.

What would have made Sam think he could sell the farm? Did he plan to contest the will?

If Sam did and he won, she was certain he would pass the farm to the logging company on a silver platter and pocket his reward. She needed a plan to put a crimp in Sam's style until she could find out what was going on with Herbert's estate.

Sam's poorly disguised belief that she was romantically involved with Herbert also burned her. She yanked the knot on her sneaker tighter. But when she had gone into the apartment instead of the house what had he thought?

"Was that a raccoon I saw?" Sam's voice oozed disgust.

Lisa's stomach tossed about at the sound of his voice. She vigorously retied her other running shoe while she kept her back to him. "Yes. That was a baby raccoon. I rescue injured animals as part of my job."

"And make them house guests?" he asked.

She kept her eyes on her shoes and struggled to remain calm. "Sometimes, if circumstances require it, I keep animals I rescue. Barney's just about ready to go back into the wild."

"I should hope so. A pest like that doesn't belong around the house."

Sam was now Captain Know-it-all. She stood up. "You don't have to worry about Barney. I'll look after him."

He looked her up and down, his glance cool, assessing.

She returned his inquisitive gaze full measure. "Do

you size every woman up that way?"

He laughed. "I wondered where you were going."

"I'm out for a run. I'd invite you along, but I assume you have other plans." She flicked a glance in the general direction of his suede loafers and the cotton twill pants with the knife-like crease.

"Yes. As a matter of fact, I do. After I'm finished in town, I want to talk to Mr. O'Neill."

That did it for Lisa. Sam Jackson never considered that she might be the tenant. And he wasn't even interested enough in her to ask her name. If ever a man needed a whack with a reality stick it was the male chauvinist standing too close to her.

It was bad enough that he'd thought she was romantically involved with an older man like Herbert, or that she was shacking up over the garage with another man... After what she'd seen of Sam today it was obvious nothing had changed.

"Why do you assume it's a man?"

"I-I... My uncle always rented his apartment out to men—naturalists working with the local efforts to save something or other."

How could a nephew of Herbert's be so clueless? "You haven't been around here recently, have you?" she asked.

"No. Not in years."

"Then you don't know what a big contribution your uncle made to protecting endangered wetlands or wildlife."

"No. You're right." Sam gave her a contrite glance.

Lisa really, really wanted to confront Sam on his chauvinist behavior, but she had bigger worries than that. "Did I understand you to say you were going to sell the farm?"

"Yes. I've got two weeks off to put my uncle's affairs in order. I'm listing the property tomorrow."

She could feel her heart thudding. "*Tomorrow?* Are you the executor?" she asked, waiting…

"Yes. And his will was clear. He left no heirs other than me. I am to have the farm. But I don't want it, and have decided to sell."

"You know that Herbert planned to leave the farm to the local Nature Trust?" she asked, feeling acute disappointment and the loss of her friend Herbert all over again.

"No. But that's not a problem. The Nature Trust can make an offer if they like."

"They don't have that kind of money… Herbert promised me that he would make the necessary arrangements to have the farm transferred to the Trust upon his death—"

"I hate to disappoint you, but my uncle didn't make any special arrangements for the sale of the farm."

That couldn't be true. Herbert had been very clear about what he wanted. There had to be some mistake. *If Herbert had changed the will, where was it?* There were two places Herbert kept documents: One was the kitchen and the other was in his office upstairs.

Sam checked his watch as he pulled his car keys from his pocket. "I'm late for an appointment in town. Do you know if my uncle had any contractual arrangements with the Nature Trust?"

She hesitated. "I don't know. That information is probably in his office." She nodded toward the house.

He hadn't questioned why she was leaving the apartment so he must have assumed that she lived upstairs. *But why did it matter what Sam thought?* He'd be returning to New York the minute he realized there was nothing in the will for him.

She told herself it didn't even matter that he didn't recognize her. Nothing mattered except finding a way to save the farm from the logging company. She'd promised Herbert that she would do what he wished. And she believed he had made the necessary provisions in an updated will. What she needed to do was find it.

With the new will in her hands she could stop Sam from selling the farm. All she needed was a few minutes inside the house.

"I'm pretty familiar with your uncle's filing system." Herbert didn't have a filing system, just a filing cabinet full of papers. But searching for the contract was the perfect excuse to search for the new will. "Why don't I see if I can find any record of the contract in your uncle's office?"

"Great." He smiled at her and for just a nanosecond she experienced a jarring nudge of attraction.

She shrugged it off. When she was through with Sam Jackson, he'd be run out of town in his flashy sex machine, never to be heard from again. "I'll let you know if I find anything."

"What *is* your job here?" His surprised tone matched the expression on his face. "I don't think you told me what you did for my uncle."

"I did a lot of things," she hedged, feeling an odd sense of determination and a need to control what she shared. She had to see for herself whether or not Herbert had made any provisions for the Nature Trust in his will, and clearly Sam had no intention of showing the will to her.

"We'll talk when I get back from town," he said.

"Works for me," Lisa said, amazed that Sam still didn't seem to have a clue about what went on at the farm. No wonder he didn't have a problem selling it.

Sam glanced up at the windows of the apartment and back at her. "I assume you live upstairs."

"Yes."

My uncle must have thought a great deal of you to rent the apartment to you"

Memories of the day Herbert Stackhouse had taken her in and offered her a place to live made her throat tighten. She never understood why Herbert had done it, but she would always be grateful for his help when she needed it most.

Lisa glanced away, looking for anything to focus on other than the man standing so near her.

"We were close," she said as she pulled her sweat top down over her hips and adjusted her ear buds before cranking up the music. She told herself the man standing beside her didn't matter to her in the slightest. What mattered was saving Harmony Farm from being sold to the wrong people.

Determination gave wings to her thoughts as she started down the driveway. She could easily get in the house and search for the will. She had a key. If Sam thought he was executor it was because Herbert's new will was still in the house. "This one's for you, Herbert," she whispered as she broke into a run.

Two hours later, sweaty from her run, she arrived back at the apartment to find her best friend Annie Thomson waiting for her. "What are you doing here?"

"I came by to see if you wanted to go to a movie tonight. My mother-in-law is willing to babysit the boys while I go out." Annie followed Lisa into the tiny kitchen.

"I'd love to, but I have to find Herbert's new will." Lisa went on to explain her conversation with Sam.

"You're assuming Sam hasn't taken the will with him into town," Lisa said as she poured two cups of steaming coffee and settled into the chair across the table from Annie.

"He couldn't have or he would know he was no

longer the executor, wouldn't he?"

"I suppose…"

Annie had been there in their senior year when the embarrassment with Sam occurred. She'd consoled Lisa, taken her out for pizza, and done all the things a best friend would do under the circumstances.

It hadn't been until today, after she'd seen him at the tree planting, that it hit her. She *wanted* Sam to remember her, and give them both a chance to set the record straight. She had wanted to explain to him why she'd not gone to the dance with him.

"All I have to do is take my key, go into the house and find what I'm looking for," Lisa said as butterflies fluttered in her tummy.

"Maybe we can go to a movie when you've finished looking for the will. I'll go home, get supper on and come back to pick you up," Annie offered.

I'd like that, but first I need to know where the new will is. I'll have to call you after I go over to the house."

Annie filled their cups and came back to the table. "I don't believe for one minute that Herbert didn't change his will to include the Nature Trust. He was always a man of his word. Everyone knows that. Perhaps it's just that you're the only one who knows a new will exists, right?"

"That's possible."

"Besides since you have a key and you worked there while Herbert was alive, you could hardly be accused of break and enter. Anyway Sam thinks you're going in to look for a contract with the Nature Trust, right?"

"Right." Lisa watched her friend's expression turn serious.

Annie stirred her coffee slowly. "Lisa, I know how hard this is for you to see Sam again and not to have him even recognize you. But you have to give up this fantasy about him."

"Fantasy? I don't fantasize about him," Lisa protested.

"You do," Annie said, one eyebrow cocked. "You have, ever since you first met him." Annie rested her elbows on the table. "You know what I hope comes out of this? That you get over your feelings for Sam and get on with your life. You don't have to spend all your time rescuing animals. You need a life and a relationship with a man who loves and respects you."

"And Sam Jackson would never have a relationship with someone like me."

"Then why can't you forget about him?"

"I don't know," she admitted.

"You know what I think it is? You're the kind of person who wants what she can't have, a woman who fantasizes about forbidden fruit, so to speak."

Shocked that her friend thought that of her, Lisa gathered her things. "You're wrong about that, and I'll prove it."

"I look forward to it."

Minutes later Lisa slipped the key into the lock and entered the farmhouse via the back door. If Herbert hadn't taken the new will to the lawyer's office before his heart attack, the will had to be at the desk in the kitchen or upstairs in the office.

There wasn't one scrap of paper anywhere on the desk. Maybe he put the will in the drawer, she mused as she pulled it open to a chorus of squeaking wood on wood. Rummaging around she found Herbert's usual clutter, but no official-looking documents.

It must be upstairs in Herbert's office. If she couldn't find the new will perhaps she could find a copy of the will Sam claimed to have in his possession. She moved down the hall toward the stairs, her attention turning to the antique coat rack. There was a jacket hanging from one of the hooks, and it wasn't Herbert's. It had to be Sam's.

She went through the pockets just in case the will was there, but came up empty.

Glancing toward the upstairs landing she knew what she had to do. She climbed the stairs to the rumble and creak of the old wood under her feet. At the top she turned, undecided as to which bedroom Sam was using while he stayed there.

Surely he wouldn't have chosen Herbert's room. Maybe the room nearest the bathroom that faced out toward the garage. She slipped inside. This was definitely Sam's room. There was a suitcase in the corner, and several shirts folded neatly on the dresser. But there was not a scrap of paper to be seen.

She moved into the hall, heading toward Herbert's office. As she stood in the doorway memories assailed her. *How many times had she and Herbert sat in this tiny space and talked about the farm, and their plans for it?* From the time she became part of his life Herbert had sought her advice on everything related to the farm.

On the tiny desk near the window she spotted a folder with white pages sticking out.

"*Ahh,*" she said aloud, rushing to the desk and flipping the file open. Turning on the desk lamp she looked carefully at every page in the file labeled "will." It was clear that Herbert had begun putting together his information and necessary documents for the changes he wanted...

She checked carefully for any sign of an actual will. The only thing she found was a brown envelope nestled against the old-fashioned blotter covering the desk.

CHAPTER THREE

Opposition can be intriguing.

Sam drove slowly around the long turn in the road leading to the driveway of his uncle's house. As he thought back to his afternoon and evening in town it had been less than what he'd hoped for on several fronts and he'd decided to come home early. He'd call Allen Burch, one of the few kids he'd hung out with during his summers here, and invited him to join him at the local pub. Allen had called about twenty minutes after he was supposed to show, saying that something had come up and he wouldn't be there.

For some unfathomable reason his friend not showing up reminded him of the woman he'd met at his uncle's memorial ceremony. He couldn't remember meeting a woman who'd annoyed him more than she did. Their conversation earlier today had seemed really strange and her open hostility was very evident in her behavior. But worrying about a woman he didn't know and wouldn't see again once his business there was wrapped up, was pointless.

Yet, there was something about her... Something he couldn't quite put his finger on...

Feeling a little let down, he'd decided to eat and go back to the farm to work on the cost projections for his air-freight company. After he ordered and glanced around the wide wood-lined room, he noticed a few fac-

31

es he remembered from the memorial service, but he hadn't known them by name. Most just ignored him or glanced away when their gazes met.

It had taken a long time to get his meal at the pub, leaving him with time to think about and plan what he had to do. Morgan lumber had contacted him, wanting to meet with him about the farm. They were prepared to make an offer, and the money they'd mentioned would clear up all his uncle's debts including the remainder of the mortgage. At first he'd wanted to sign right away, but then something made him hang back a little. He didn't know what that was exactly, and put it down to his exhaustion. He knew from his own business experience that no decision should be made in a state of exhaustion, and that's what he'd been feeling all day.

Regardless of his concerns all he wanted to do was have a long, hot shower and relax a little. Then he'd go over to the apartment above the garage and see if... *What was her name? And why hadn't he asked her what it was?*

He walked to the house, feeling conflicted about things. When he reached the door he slid the key in. There was no resistance when he turned it, though he was certain he'd locked the door before going to town. Entering quietly, he made his way to the hall and hung up his jacket, putting his briefcase on the steps leading upstairs.

Mumbled words could be heard coming from somewhere over his head. The woman was supposed to have checked the filing cabinet hours ago... *Why was she still up there?* With his hand on the bannister he eased his way up the steps, careful not to step on the squeaky part of each tread—a slow process. Once on the landing he went to the door of his uncle's office and quietly stepped inside.

"What are you still doing here? I thought you were

going to search the filing cabinet..." The woman was not looking in the filing cabinet. She had a file folder in her hand. "What did you find?"

"Nothing, just paperwork I need," she said, not meeting his gaze.

He felt it again—that feeling, that sense of recognition or connection he couldn't explain. "No contract with the Nature Trust?"

"What?"

"You were here looking for the contract we talked about, weren't you?"

"Oh. Yes." She glanced toward the filing cabinet and back at him.

He sensed she hadn't been anywhere near the filing cabinet.

He moved closer. The scent of her skin, the warmth of her body captured him, and for just a few seconds he wished the circumstances were different. That he'd come home to find a woman who loved him working at the desk, not a woman who clearly disliked him. Sighing he asked, "When did you start working for my uncle?"

"I don't. I work for the Nature Trust doing bird observations," she said, her voice strong with just a hint of something he couldn't identify.

"What's in that file you're holding?" he asked.

"Nothing. Just notes... I helped your uncle with some of his paperwork. This is something I need to take care of for him," she said, slipping the file under her arm.

"Well, if you didn't find a contract, I guess I'll talk to the people in the Nature Trust. They must have it."

"I thought about what you said. I'm not aware of any contract between your uncle and the Nature Trust, and I'm sure I would have known. Besides, why do you need the contract?"

"I want to know what was involved. What sort of

financial commitment, if any, the Nature Trust had made to my uncle."

She shrugged. "I guess that's your business."

An hour later, after safely placing the file on the top shelf of her bedroom closet, Lisa called Annie and told her what had happened.

"If Herbert didn't change his will, Sam will sell the farm. Maybe as early as tomorrow," Lisa explained.

"That's awful. Then I guess you're not up for a show tonight," Annie said.

"No. I'm exhausted. It's been a long and disappointing day."

"Lisa, why don't you try to get along with Sam? Put aside your personal feelings and see if you can work with him? It's the only way you'll be able to have any influence on how the sale of the farm is handled."

"I don't know if I can do that. He is so…so impossible."

"Are you sure?" Annie asked. "Or are you basing your opinion about him on your unhappy contact with him years ago?"

"I…I guess I am. But if he's the only chance I've got to have any say in what is going on, I suppose I'll have to change my approach."

"If I were you, I'd sit down over a cup of coffee and talk with him. Yes, it sounds like he's planning to sell the farm, but maybe he could be persuaded to consider the Nature Trust."

"I suppose… Besides what choice do I have?"

"None that I can think of," Annie said.

"Then I'd better get to work on a plan. I'll find a way to have coffee with Sam," she said grudgingly, while her body warmed at the thought of sitting anywhere near the man.

The next morning Lisa stood in front of the sink watching from the kitchen window, waiting for Sam to appear while she fed table scraps to Barney. The man was a late riser and his car was in the driveway—meaning he hadn't left.

During the night she'd decided that she had to apologize for being in the house so long. Explain she'd gone jogging and only arrived home shortly before he found her in his grandfather's office. She didn't want to apologize or explain, but that was likely the best way to start a conversation and move forward. She'd do it.

She had always found apologizing difficult, but this apology would take all her resolve, mostly because she didn't really feel she had anything to apologize for. She had told him the truth.

Her breath caught in her throat when she saw the back door open.

"There boy. Time's up. We've got work to do." She hurried Barney down the stairs and out the back door.

Rushing back upstairs she opened the window over the kitchen sink. "Good morning," she called down to Sam, hoping she sounded upbeat and positive.

He glanced up at her, a hint of surprise in his voice. "What are you doing?"

"I'm waiting to speak to you. To apologize to you."

Well that is certainly a step in the right direction," he said, pushing his sunglasses up over his forehead into the dark richness of his hair.

She breathed in the fresh morning air as her eyes met his. Fighting the flood of warmth rushing through her body, she looked him over carefully. His casual pants hung flawlessly over his narrow hips. His dark hair held a slick dampness from the shower. Mr. Gorgeous was a perfect male specimen—no doubt about it.

"Would you like a cup of coffee?"

He gave her a quizzical look. "Are you offering?"

"Yes. I wanted to talk to you, to explain my behavior last night."

He shrugged. "Okay, then. Cream. No sugar. Do you want me to come up?"

Temptation floated on the air. Sitting across the breakfast table from Sam would be a visual feast... But she needed to stay focused on talking to him, which meant it would be better done somewhere less cozy, less intimate.

"Have it all ready. I'll bring it down."

A few minutes later she carried two coffees over to where Sam stood on the front lawn.

"What a view. I never grow tired of it," she said as she passed a cup to him. A familiar knot formed in her chest as her eyes followed the fence from the road up along the property line. "I remember one time when your uncle and I watched a deer and her fawn cross the field in the early twilight."

"That would have been a beautiful sight," Sam said, taking a sip of his coffee. "When I was a little kid, I thought this place was great. Mum loved it so much that she insisted that I spend part of my summer vacation here." He took another sip, and nodded to her appreciatively.

"Good coffee."

"Thanks. I'm glad you like it." Sam's happy reminiscences were the perfect opportunity for her to discuss the farm and her ideas about how they could keep it safe.

Because she hadn't found a new will, she needed to find out what Sam planned and that meant she had no choice but to come to some sort of truce with this man.

"Your uncle would stand here every morning and

gaze out over the field. He used to say this view needed to be sipped like a fine wine," she said, a familiar lump rising in her throat.

"But things change..."

Forcing a smile to her lips she said, "I'm really sorry about last night. I didn't mean to surprise you. I had planned to go over earlier, but went jogging and then...a friend of mine arrived wanting me to go to the show with her," she said, hoping he didn't inquire any further about what she was actually looking for in the office—or about the file she'd found.

"Did you look in the filing cabinet? And what was that file you took with you?" He gave her a sidelong glance. Her heart sank.

"I...I... Your uncle's filing is not really that great, but I did try. As for the file I took with me, just something I needed to look into..." She glanced at him to gauge his response, but his expression gave nothing away. "To be honest I'm really concerned about the farm and what will happen to it. There will have to be changes, I suppose," she said as she walked over to a narrow bench beside the house.

Sam joined her on the bench, his cologne playing havoc with her thoughts. "There is so much I need to think about, and yes, change will be necessary if I am to do my job as executor."

She had no idea what an executor had to do, but she was willing to listen if it meant she could solve the mystery of the missing will.

"I know what you mean about things changing. When I came here, I thought this place was just like any other place, except for your uncle. He taught me how important our relationship is with the land..."

They sipped their coffees in companionable silence, accompanied only by the whirring of the soft breeze through the line of tall pines that stood alongside of the house. The dew, trapped in the rays of early light, made a silvery pattern over the long expanse of grass leading to the road.

"If you worked with my uncle you must know he owes a lot of money, beginning with a very substantial mortgage on this property," Sam explained.

"No," she said, running over her conversations with Herbert and finding nothing that would indicate he had financial difficulties. "Herbert never talked about money to me. He did say he had a plan to pay some things off but I assumed he was okay financially."

"Why did you think he was okay?"

"I guess because he seemed to be able to afford whatever he wanted."

"Do you know if he'd had unexpected expenses with the farm? Like maybe a new roof, new barn renovations?"

"No. I do know from talking with him that he spent a lot of money looking after your aunt while she was ill. Your uncle didn't want her taken to the hospital. I imagine that all the extra nursing care to help him keep her comfortable must have been expensive."

"I should have been here for him, and I'm sorry. But the few times I called him, he only mentioned that she wasn't feeling well... I should have realized that there was more..." He gave her a sad look, so sad that she wished she dared put her arms around him.

"I'm sorry too. I really am." She waited for him to continue.

He gave a deep sigh and glanced at her, a slight smile curving along his lips. "I'm also sorry for something else."

"What's that?"

"I misread you. I should have realized that the L. O'Neill on the mail box was you."

"It is. I'm Lisa," she said, waiting for him to recognize her name, to remember she'd asked him out on a date years before. She held her breath.

He squinted at her but said nothing.

He hadn't even recognized her name. How was that possible? For a few seconds she was angry, but quickly relief set in. He might be willing to include her in what he saw as the future of Harmony Farm without the distraction of going back over past events.

She focused on his face, the smooth shaven cheeks, the razor nick and the perfect symmetry of his eyes. "I came to live here because your uncle offered me a place to stay while I did work for the bird observation program. I came here for the job, but when I got to know Herbert, I came to love this place almost as much as he did."

"How long have you been here?"

"A little over a year."

"And what will you do when this job is over?"

"I...I don't know." He clearly had no idea of her role here, of Herbert's plans. That meant he likely didn't have Herbert's final will.

Sam sighed as he scuffed his penny loafers over the dewy grass before directing his gaze at her, his expression open and assessing. "I feel as if I know you from somewhere."

Did he really not remember her? And yet if he didn't it might be easier...

She shifted uncomfortably and sipped her cooling coffee. She shrugged and a sudden stab of loneliness shot through her, making her feel sad. "We might have met in Middleborough...sometime. I went to school there."

A hammering noise shattered the morning stillness.

They both looked in the direction of the sound. At the end of the driveway, a woman stood pounding a "For Sale" sign into the earth.

"What!" Lisa gasped. Surprise rushed her, followed quickly by dismay. While she'd been busy trying to find a way to work with him, he had been busy doing what she'd feared the most.

Would she ever learn to stop trying to rescue people, and stick to saving animals? What mental deficiency on her part had led her to believe that he was anything other than what she'd first seen? He may not have remembered her a few minutes ago, but when she was through with him, he'd find it hard to forget her.

"You've already made arrangements to sell?" She pointed at the woman pounding away at the sign.

"I have to—"

She rounded on him, her anger running hot and free. "Of all the miserable, sneaky things to do. You didn't even give me a chance."

Sam's glance slid past her to the woman vigorously pounding the signpost into the ground.

Let the Trust make an offer, indeed...

Incensed by his deviousness, she gritted her teeth. "Well, I hope your precious money makes you happy."

She saw what might have passed for anguish in his eyes, and didn't really give a damn.

Guilt rocked Sam's stomach as he watched the hurt and fury run its course across Lisa's face. An unexpected need to comfort her ran through him, but the cold disdain on her face stopped him short. He tried to think of something soothing to say as he fidgeted with the coffee cup in his hands. "Lisa, I know this is upsetting for you."

"Really?" Her eyes were slits. "Just how upset do you think I am?" Lisa moved toward him, her coffee cup lurching dangerously close to the front of his shirt.

Remembering his shoes and the tree-planting incident, Sam kept his eye on her cup as he moved back a little. "I have to sell the farm as soon as possible. I've got to get back to my job."

"Well, I'm not surprised." Lisa's words were punctuated by the hammering at the end of the driveway. "Never let it be said that the great sky jock left his cockpit for long. And certainly never to do the right thing." She beat a tattoo on his shirt with her finger.

Lisa's words stung. *Did she really think he was such a cad?* "I told you my Uncle Herbert left a large mortgage on the farm. To pay it, I have to sell for a good price."

"Money, money, money." She waved her hand in the air like a conductor at the Philharmonic. "Do you ever think of anything else but your bulging bank account?"

Lisa lowered her hands, allowing him a sneak peek at the bottom of her coffee cup. *Empty.* He breathed a sigh of relief. She couldn't douse him with cold coffee if the urge struck her. In fact, the lady had no hold over him of any kind. Nor did she control what he did with the farm. And he had less than two weeks to finish what he came to do—with or without the help of the fire-breathing witch standing too close to him.

Just as he was ready to answer her in kind, his eyes met hers and his libido lurched into gear. Warmth oozed through his loins and as she spewed vitriol, the ruby ripeness of her lips...like crimson magnets made him want to kiss her to silence.

Kissing her would be so nice... *What was happening to him?*

It must be all the fresh country air. He gathered his scattered wits and plunged forward.

"Speaking of money, I assume you were paying rent for the apartment. I'd like to see a receipt for payment."

Lisa's cheeks glowed white while a cluster of freckles stood out in stark relief, highlighted by the early morning light. "What do you mean? A receipt?" She stepped away from him and eyed the real estate lady with fierce concentration.

"Just what I said. I need to know what you paid and when."

"Why? I will be leaving when you sell the farm." Lisa brushed a stray curl from her forehead as she continued to frown toward the end of the driveway.

"I can't figure out which bank deposits include your rental payments."

Lisa turned to him as she ground her fists into her hips and planted her feet wide apart.

"And why does it matter?"

"As executor, I have to look after my Uncle Herbert's interests. I want to be sure you paid your rent. Besides, the new owners may want to rent the place. An apartment bringing in a steady cash flow each month would be a selling point."

Lisa stood toe to toe with him, her curly red crown bobbing in indignation. "Well, Mr. Scrooge—" She pushed her fingers into his chest yet again.

"Now, don't get carried away," he said, moving out of her reach. As he did so, his heel caught on the soft edge of a flowerbed, tilting him backward. Unable to move his foot into position to stop his fall, his body started a slow slide toward the ground. He reached out, locking his hands on the only thing within reach—Lisa's outstretched hand.

"Oh no you don't!" A second too late, Lisa wrenched her hand away.

They fell together into the flowerbed, her body landing on his, with her pelvis touching down on his half-mast erection. His body quickened to full alert at the forced contact with her warmth and softness.

He stared up at her and saw the flash of awareness on her face. The gray-green of her eyes flared with fire; her breath was hot against his cheek. The mix of raw earth and wild roses intoxicated his senses. He smiled up at her and saw the tremor on her lips. He slid his arms over her shoulders, his hands edging toward the back of her neck.

He waited for her to push off from him, or worse, to poke him in his most vulnerable spot. Instead they lay together, breathing in unison, their bodies snug together. Needing to taste her lips, he lifted his head and brought his mouth to hers. His fingers nestled in her hair as he pulled her to him. She tasted sweet, inviting. He held her closer, wedging her lips apart with his own...

The kiss exploded, searing hot, sending his pulse into overdrive. His hips rose to meet hers. She melted against him like butter over a baked potato.

He held her head gently and deepened the kiss.

Suddenly she wrenched her lips from his, and shook her head. "What do you think you're doing?" she gasped against his throat.

"Kissing you to get you to be quiet." He sighed as his fingers found their way down her back.

"No." Lisa pushed off him, dropping her knee to his groin as she did so.

Sam groaned at the pain. He gulped for much-needed air, and wiped his lips with the back of his hand, hoping to remove the taste of her.

Stumbling to her feet, Lisa rescued the two coffee cups from the ground where they had fallen. Her glance never once came close to meeting his as she rubbed her lips and sniffed. "Don't get any crazy ideas. I'll never be one of your conquests."

Sam couldn't help admiring her feistiness. And he now knew that under that stern exterior lived a very compelling and passionate woman. He stood up and assessed the damage. He was intact except for the dirt on his pant leg and the dull ache in his groin.

Lisa squared her shoulders. "I had hoped that you and I could come to an agreement: one that would allow the Nature Trust to bid on the property. I had hoped you might want this beautiful place to be kept for the enjoyment of everyone, and not just sold to satisfy your money interests and those of people like you."

She swiped a cluster of curls off her cheek as she looked toward the end of the driveway where the realtor had just finished putting her things back in the car. "I was wrong."

Sam saw the sadness in her eyes and his sharp retort remained unspoken on his lips. Here was a woman willing to fight to stop him from selling the farm to someone who didn't share her passion. "I wish I could do what you want. I really do."

Her shoulders slumped as she turned to go. "No. You don't, or you wouldn't let that woman"—Lisa pointed at the car making its slow trek up the long driveway—"sell your uncle's dream to the highest bidder."

As she walked away something deep inside Sam urged him to call her back, to make amends. He'd never experienced this feeling of remorse, of wanting to ease a situation, where a woman was concerned. He didn't understand why, and he couldn't let himself care. After all, she meant nothing to him and she never would.

She was not his kind of woman.

CHAPTER FOUR

Anything is possible. Anything.

The next afternoon when she thought about Sam's kiss, something akin to the sound of Beethoven's 5th Symphony soared through her, filling her heart and flooding her with joy. Never in her wildest dreams had she ever imagined she'd hear music just because Sam kissed her. And yet it had happened. Lisa could still feel his lips on hers, despite spending hours trying to think of anything but him.

To ease her heated thoughts she watched the gathering of people who waited for the local news channel to set up by the brook.

The appearance of the "For Sale" sign at the end of the driveway had mobilized Lisa. Several phone calls yesterday had brought members of the Naturalist Club and concerned citizens to Harmony Farm today, some of them probably more out of curiosity than anything else, but Lisa didn't care. It was the effect that counted.

Sam Jackson had to be exposed for the callous, money-hugger he was.

The huge oaks behind her stood in elegant silence as the crowd milled about.

Reverend Anderson was in his element. He'd been more than willing to act as the group spokesman when Lisa called him to support the press conference. That suited her just fine. All she wanted was to have the media get the message out there that a treasure was about to be destroyed by a fat-cat lumber company. After the way Sam had led her on, let her think that she had a chance to secure the farm for the Trust, she no longer believed what he said about anything, and that included that Herbert was in debt.

Anyway, Sam was away—probably in town with his real estate agent. She stared across the field toward the farmhouse. She'd love to be a fly on his wall when he watched that evening's news.

With a satisfied smile on his lips, Reverend Anderson hitched his pants up and trudged over the slope toward her. "It's a great day, isn't it?"

"It certainly is."

The reverend tugged his stringy ponytail in place and adjusted his peace symbol. "The reporters are ready to start. Are you sure you don't want to be the spokesperson? After all, you're the one Herbert depended on, and confided in."

Lisa pulled her "Mug a Hunter" sweatshirt over her hips and gave him a reassuring smile. "You know as much about this whole thing as I do. Even more. You and Herbert were friends."

Willie rubbed his jaw in thought. "Yeah... I was just thinking that his nephew, Mr. Jackson, might not like what we're doing... I wonder if we shouldn't wait until Sam returns."

Lisa frowned. "And give him an opportunity to stop us? Anyway, he doesn't own Harmony Farm yet. It belonged to his uncle."

"And now who's the owner? Rumor has it that everything was left to Sam Jackson."

She scuffed the soft earth with her sneaker, and remembered another spot of soft earth where a tree had been planted only the day before—and that had nearly been her undoing.

"As far as I can see, he's as much a trespasser as we are."

Lisa knew her words sounded tough and sure, but her stomach quaked at the thought. What if Sam did come back angry and ready to do battle? Would she be able to stand up to him after the way he'd kissed her? She clenched her fists against the memory of Sam's lips devouring hers.

Reverend Anderson touched her arm. "Yeah, the nephew seems to have taken over, but let's have a little faith. Herbert didn't want the farm going to a lumber company. We can make a difference just by being here. At the very least, this should slow down the process until we can come up with a better plan."

"I'm counting on it," Lisa said with conviction.

He glanced at her, his double chin keeping time with his words. "What we're doing is right and just." He smoothed his hand over his peace symbol.

She went back to chewing her nail full time as she waited for the interview to start.

"Reverend Anderson," the interviewer began, "you claim that Harmony Farm, the land we're standing on now, was meant to go to the Nature Trust. Can you explain your reasons?"

Lisa gawked in surprise as the reverend launched into a lengthy tirade on the terrible fate about to be visited upon the helpless forest behind him. How it was God's will that the oak forest be saved from the marauding capitalists who sought to destroy the forest for profit. Lisa glanced around the group to see how his sermon was being received. Every eye was on him, but then again, he was preaching to the converted. The entire Naturalists Club wanted the oak forest saved. The longer the reverend talked, the more animated he became, his hands whipping the air, his Santa tummy jiggling.

Lisa walked along the edge of the group to get a

better view of the proceedings. She hugged herself with suppressed glee. The great Sam Jackson would not be too quick to sell to the lumber company after his callous financial motivation was revealed.

She tipped her head back, tossing a web of curls off her forehead. Sam Jackson would rue the day he tangled with Lisa O'Neill. Everything was going to work out just fine. Sam Jackson would be gone, drummed out of town by his own greed. She turned at the soft rustle of someone coming up behind her; maybe someone wanting to congratulate her on her brilliant idea.

His familiar male scent reached her first. Her body froze.

Oh no...

With the reverend's sermon singing in her ears, she turned. There he stood decked out in hunter-green from head to foot, including Herbert's rubber boots.

"Hi, Sam," she said, giving him a finger-wiggling wave. "I see you decided to change your foot gear this time."

"My uncle had more pairs of rubber boots than he had shoes."

"That should tell you something about him."

"It does. But nothing that will help me settle his estate." Sam scowled at the crowd listening intently to Willie. "What's going on here?"

"We've decided to take our case public. You know... About selling the farm to a lumber company." Her stomach lodged in her throat as she peeked at him.

Danger glinted in his eyes; a muscle twitched in his jaw. "So, while I was away you decided to play."

Tension leaped the gap between them and crackled down her spine. "I told you this is serious. I can't let you sell the farm out fr—"

In one easy movement he spun her around and stared down at her. "This is *my* business. I'll handle it *my* way." He glanced over her head, at the people eagerly huddled around the Reverend, and back at her. "I hope your friends know what they've done."

Despite what she'd hoped to accomplish there, Lisa had a wild urge to melt into his arms—and she hated herself for it. Obviously Sam was accustomed to getting what he wanted and the farm was no exception. "You don't care what happens here, but these people do. We're taking the only action left open to us."

"And damn the consequences, is that it? You have no right to interfere in my business," he said, his voice hard.

"I see we have been blessed with the arrival of Mr. Sam Jackson," Reverend Anderson roared. "Let's see what he has to say for himself."

The camera crew started toward Sam, angling their equipment through the crowd as they approached. The reverend pointed an accusing finger at Sam. "This is the man who is intent upon bringing this scourge down upon this heavenly place."

Lisa watched in alarm as the crowd, fueled by Willie's words, flooded toward Sam, their faces stern, and accusing.

"What do you have to say for yourself, young man?" Reverend Anderson pulled himself up as tall as his portly physique would allow.

Sam glanced from one hostile face to another. "I'm the executor of my Uncle Herbert's estate. I'm following my uncle's instructions as stated in his will."

"To sell this beautiful farm." Reverend Anderson skipped a glance across the faces of the people standing near him.

"Yes. As my uncle instructed."

"Without giving the Nature Trust a chance to buy it." The reverend rubbed his hands together slowly.

"The Nature Trust can bid on the property if they

like."

"But you'll take the highest bid which will likely come from a logging company." The reverend leaned toward Sam.

The camera blinked, ready to record Sam's comments.

Why didn't Sam mention the mortgage? These people would understand a problem like that. If it were true, it was his best defense. She grimaced, thinking that was probably his only defense.

Should she remind him?

Sam was a big boy and could look after himself. She curbed the impulse and watched.

"Sell it to the highest bidder is what you plan to do, isn't it?" Reverend Anderson asked.

Sam's grim expression singed Lisa as his eyes focused on her. "There seems to be this mistaken idea that my uncle left Harmony Farm to the Nature Trust. Nothing could be further from the truth. Uncle Herbert made no such request."

"Well, it's not too late to change that. *If* you wanted to." The reverend moved closer.

"I believe it is," Sam said, his voice dripping with finality.

Willie pointed a pudgy finger at Sam's chest. "Then, it's true. You really don't care what happens to this wonderful place as long as you get your money and can return to your big city life."

She watched Sam's expression tighten. She suddenly felt badly about what she'd done.

She hadn't intended to embarrass him this way. She only wanted him to understand that he was doing irreparable damage to a beautiful place if he sold the property to the lumber company.

But what she'd done had put him in a difficult position, one he didn't seem to know how to get out of.

Maybe he didn't want people to know his uncle owed money...

She had to defuse the situation as quickly as possible. She glanced from one person to the other along the edge of the crowd. "We all know what we want to see happen. We want the farm saved from the loggers. Isn't that right?" she asked.

There was a general shuffling and nodding.

"Well, let's see if something can be worked out?" She glanced at Willie for support. "Maybe we could all sit down—"

"We have to stop him from destroying the forest. This protest was your idea, Lisa. Have you changed your mind?" Willie asked.

Sam stiffened as he glared at her. "So this is what you meant about finding a way to stop me?" His voice was low, cold, and snaked through Lisa like ice water over rocks.

The press conference had seemed like such a good idea at the time, and the only way to stop Sam from doing what was morally wrong.

"I wanted—"

Now it seemed wrong to attack a man who was only trying to look after his uncle's business... *Had she gone too far?* "This was a mistake. I'm sorry," she whispered to Sam. "I'm going to fix it. You'll see."

"You won't get the chance." His eyes were dark, foreboding. "You are finished at Harmony Farm."

Sam could feel the blood pounding in his temples as he stared at the woman standing so close to him. Lisa made him angrier than any person he'd ever known.

He was mildly aware of the group's curiosity as he faced down the meddling female. Under normal circumstances he would have preferred a private conversation away from prying eyes and ears. But this situation was a long way from normal. "You have stuck your nose where it doesn't belong for the last time."

"I tried to reason with you. I tried to get you to see how important protecting this land, this farm, was to your uncle." Lisa's eyes were shrouded in uncertainty her voice was soft, almost too soft to be heard.

"Important to you. Not my uncle. He wanted the farm sold to pay the mortgage and you knew that."

"He wanted the farm left to the Nature Trust." She emphasized her words as if he didn't have the mental capacity to understand her. *Where did she get off treating him as if he were a small boy who'd misbehaved?*

"I want you to keep your nose out of my business." Never had a woman irritated him like Lisa had in the past few days, and those few days were beginning to feel like a life sentence. He had to get his business finished as quickly as possible and get back to the sanity of his life. What he wouldn't give to be in the cockpit of a jet, flying anywhere as long as it was far away from here and the woman whose pouty red lips compelled him, against reason, to...

Ignoring the siren call of her perfect cupid's bow, he dug his rubber boots into the soft ground and made his escape toward the house by crossing the open field.

"Wait. Please wait." Lisa ran up to him, her curly locks scattered over her head, her face pale.

He stopped. His anger receded a little as he watched her slide to a stop beside him; her eyes shimmering with unshed tears.

Awareness rushed through him as her gaze met his. Her eyes glowed with a passionate inner fire. He couldn't just walk away from her unscathed. This woman who irritated him and intrigued him seemed destined to tweak his heart. Forcing his feelings aside, he asked,

"What do you want now?"

"I want to apologize to you."

"What for, this time?"

"For allowing that to get out of hand." She squinted in the general direction of the brook.

He wasn't going to let her off that easy. She owed him an explanation. "Allowing what to get out of hand?"

"The way Willie treated you."

"Does the apology include the promise you'll stop meddling in my affairs?"

She lowered her eyes and stared at her hands. "I need you to realize what will happen if you sell to the logging company."

"Will you give it a rest?" He gritted his teeth in exasperation. "Did anyone ever tell you that you're a nosy woman who needs—"

"Who needs what?" Challenge added a hard shine to her eyes and a daring smile turned up the corners of her mouth, making his heart stir in his chest. Searching for some place, any place, to put his hands he ran his fingers through his hair. "You're a woman who needs—"

"Go on," she said, her voice laced with honeyed sweetness with a hard edge.

The scent of warm spring, dark earth and something floral hung in the air around them where they stood. He couldn't let himself be involved with this woman. She was earth and fire. His life was cool detachment.

Emotion and logic didn't mix. His relationships with women were all about staying in control, keeping one eye on the exit when things got too touchy-feely. Better to cut his losses and make a reasoned decision. "Never mind," he said and started up the hill.

She caught up with him and grabbed his arm. "Never mind what?"

His skin hummed beneath her touch. Despite all that had happened that morning, he had the foolish urge to take her in his arms and kiss the worried expression from her face. But in the long term that wasn't going to work: He had to put her out of his mind. Morgan Lumber was going to call later that afternoon. They wanted to walk the land and find out how much lumber was available for cutting. If all went well, he'd be able to strike a deal for more than the asking price. He'd received other calls from lumber companies, and that gave him leverage.

In the meantime, he needed to settle with the woman standing so close to him and distance himself from the havoc she threatened to create in his life.

"I've had enough." He ground the words out as he nodded in the general direction of the forest and the brook. "You went behind my back, trespassed on my uncle's property, and made unfounded accusations against me—"

Her eyes spewed green sparks. "Don't let your imagination run away with you. Yes, part of what you say is true. I did make a mistake, and I want to make amends. We could talk about this like rational people if you'll agree to consider my position."

His temper fraying, he glared at her. "Why should I? Your position is irrelevant in this. I made myself clear, but you seem set on undermining my authority and my ability to do my job."

He banked the fire threatening to burn out of control in his chest, and spoke his thoughts as quickly as possible. "If this continues, you'll leave me no choice but to evict you."

"You can't do that! Herbert said the apartment—"

"My uncle's dead," he shot back.

She stood perfectly still; her eyelashes flickered. "I'm sorry I offered to apologize to the likes of you. You're not like your uncle at all."

"This coming from a woman who didn't tell me her

name when we met. *Who does that?*"

"Well you know it now, and a fat good that did."

He raised his hand to fend her off. "You need to learn a few manners. Didn't your mother teach you anything?" *Why was he trading barbs with this impossible woman?* Wanting to escape her closeness, he stormed off ahead of her, his breath coming in deep gulps.

"My mother didn't stick around long enough to teach me much of anything," she muttered to herself, but he heard what she said.

Guilt about his senseless remark rippled through him. Sam hadn't meant to hurt her, but at the same time, he didn't want to know about her past. He wanted to return to his life and the enjoyment waiting there—with no emotional strings attached.

Yet, knowing the hurt his words must have caused her, he stopped and waited for her to catch up. He rubbed his forehead as he searched for the right thing to say. "I'm sorry about your mother."

"Don't be. My dad and I managed very well without her." Lisa's eyes were dry, despite the loneliness seeping around her words.

Sam wanted to comfort her, to reach out and smooth a red curl from her forehead. Feel her skin under his fingers. Exactly what he shouldn't do…

He shoved his hands into his pockets and said, "Your mother missed so much."

"You think so?" Her expression was proud, defiant.

And he liked her for it. Unfamiliar sensations flooded him. He loved the way she fought for what she believed and the determination that exuded from every pore of her body. He grabbed a lungful of air and fought for self-control.

Being involved with her romantically was out of the question, yet he couldn't ignore the way she made him feel—warm and alive…

And the kiss, well what was there to say?
"I think so," he confirmed.

CHAPTER FIVE

Skating on thin ice can be...difficult.

Half awake, Lisa paced the living room of her apartment. She had spent the entire night tangled in a kaleidoscope of dreams about Sam. Sam kissing her. Sam holding her. Sam making love to her. After each dream, she fought her way awake, only to fall back to sleep and dream of him again.

After he'd walked away from her yesterday her mind filled with images of him, and with them came the wild desire for romantic abandonment clashing with her need for self-control each time he looked at her. Even his angry words couldn't ease the thrill when he focused his attention on her.

She'd truly messed up yesterday. In anger she'd made impulsive decisions that were wrong. She wanted to tell him how she'd do things differently from now on. But after the press conference and the unpleasant tone of it all, she was pretty certain he would move ahead to sell the farm and put her out of the apartment. *And who could blame him, really?*

She'd handled the situation badly yesterday.

Should she go back to Sam and tell him that the apartment had been a partial payment for her help with the nesting Bald Eagles along the tree-lined ridge at the back of the farm?

She assumed Sam had found paperwork on that, but

perhaps he really didn't know. After all, who would have told him? She knew he hadn't been in touch with his uncle recently because he hadn't even known she was staying at the apartment.

And if he did evict her, where would she go? She had no money to pay the rent for another apartment. She cradled her half-filled coffee mug against her chest as she paced the apartment searching for a solution to her problem.

Over the past hours Lisa had come to one conclusion. After what she'd done yesterday she didn't stand a chance of convincing Sam to sell the farm to the Nature Trust because he didn't trust her. She had to come up with an acceptable alternative...

She glanced around the place she'd called home for the past year—at the narrow kitchen that shared a half wall with the living room, the wicker furniture she'd scrounged from the attic of the farmhouse, and the huge rubber tree that leaned protectively over the two mismatched chairs in the corner. The ancient refrigerator that groaned as it rumbled to life. She loved it all, in equal measure.

Living in this apartment, surrounded by so much natural beauty had made her happy. But Sam Jackson didn't know her well enough to care about her happiness and he wasn't the sort to appreciate the farm the way she and Herbert did.

Maybe she could talk to Sam and tell him about her work on the farm, her need to be here to carry out her observations. Yesterday she'd been emotional and might not have made a lot of sense, she had to admit. But today she was ready to talk to Sam in a reasoned way to see if they might find a way to let her remain here for as long as possible.

She pursed her lips in thought as she stood near the windows. Down below she spotted Sam and another man as they started across the lawn toward the garage. *What was going on? And who was the gnome in the pin-striped suit carrying the briefcase? Did Sam really in-tend to carry through with his plan to evict her?* Lisa rushed to the door and down the stairs.

The doorbell rang just as she grabbed the knob. She stopped dead in her tracks. *What if they wanted to go upstairs? What if Sam discovered that Barney was still in residence?*

He'd asked her to get rid of the animal... She glanced back up the stairs. The little raccoon was loose in the apartment somewhere. It would be her luck that it would do his food-washing routine in the flush the way he had the other day. She grimaced at the thought. Any evidence of Barney would only add fuel to Sam's evic-tion crusade. She let out her pent-up breath. Too late to remove Barney now.

She pasted a wide smile on her face and yanked open the door.

"Oh, hi!" She gave the two glowering males a wob-bly smile. "What can I do for you gentlemen today?"

She glanced Sam's way. Cool detachment clung to him, dripped from the Ralph Lauren plaid shirt with knotted tie, all the way down to his soft leather loafers.

Don't panic. Lisa tucked her unruly curls behind her ears and smoothed her hands over her snug-fitting blue jeans. She didn't like the grave expression on Sam's face.

"How can I help you?"

"Karl Lott, Herbert's attorney, and I are here to talk with you." Sam's words landed like an anvil in the space separating them.

Why did he need a lawyer to tell her anything? Couldn't he simply have come over and told her to leave without bringing a lawyer? Anxiety welled up in her throat. They couldn't just toss her out like this. They couldn't. She had nowhere to go and had to think of some way to stop them. Lisa stood blocking the door as she considered what to say.

She focused on the lawyer as she tried to bring a smile to her lips. "I understand that Mr. Jackson wants me to leave, but his uncle—"

"We'll talk about that later," Sam interjected.

The lawyer offered a cool smile. "This isn't about you vacating the apartment. Although I understand that Mr. Jackson wants us to discuss that with you as well. It's about your behavior yesterday."

Lisa glanced from one man to the other as her stomach flipped over and tied itself in a knot. *What was he talking about?*

"My behavior yesterday was hardly a criminal offense."

Karl Lott lifted his briefcase. "We'd like to talk to you."

"I'm on my way out. Can we do this later?"

The two men exchanged glances. The lawyer's lips thinned to a hard line. "This is important. May we come up?"

"No. You may not," Lisa said with more certainty than she felt. She couldn't stop them if they insisted. Clutching the first idea that came to mind, she said, "I've just washed all the linoleum floors and they aren't dry. We can talk over at the house, can't we?" She stepped out and pulled the door closed behind her before they had a chance to question her.

"If that works for you," Sam said, his voice suspended in midair as he turned and led the way to the house.

Seated across the kitchen table from the two of them, Lisa wondered what it was they were going to accuse her of. She hadn't been rude with anyone, though she'd admit to being a little snappish with Sam—maybe. Reverend Anderson had been the one whose behavior had been a little over the top. She pressed her lips together with worry, her heart tripping in her chest as she tried to keep her voice steady. "Would anyone care to tell me what's going on?"

"Lisa, I spoke to Morgan Lumber yesterday. They've withdrawn their offer," Sam said.

"That's good news." She didn't try to disguise her happiness. She wanted to leap up and do a little dance of joy, but Sam's expression made her sit still and wait for the rest of the story. "And?"

"I'm advising my client that he has a legal right to sue you for the loss of the sales contract." The lawyer whipped the words at her with knifelike precision.

Cold, heart-numbing fear surged through Lisa as she faced the two men who sat across from her, prepared to ruin everything. She searched her mind for a snappy retort, but drew a blank.

CHAPTER SIX

Some days are worse than others.

Karl Lott's tough stance may have been just a little too tough by the look on Lisa's face. Sam wanted to put his hands over Lisa's and ease the trembling of her fingers, but one look at his lawyer brought him back to his senses and the business at hand.

"Surely, you understand Mr. Jackson's position. He has a right to sell his property to whomever he wishes. Your media event influenced the buyer in a negative way. Without your interference, the deal would have gone through," the lawyer said in a stern tone. "It is our position that you acted to stop the sale because you want the land to go to the Nature Trust."

"I'm sure Sam can find another buyer..." Lisa's face held the sheen of pale porcelain, with two spots of color high on her cheeks. She gave Sam a questioning glance.

His heart gave an urgent tug in his chest as his eyes met hers. Again the urge to touch her swept through him.

"Lisa, you have to see that I can't wait around for your nature group while they try to come up with the money. And I've already explained to you that Herbert made no provision in his will for the Nature Trust."

"That can't be true. I saw a file. Herbert said—"

"Where is your proof? I've been Herbert's lawyer for years, and I certainly didn't do up a new will," the lawyer said. "Is there such a file, Sam?"

Caught off guard, Sam said, "Lisa, you had a file with you that day, didn't you? What was in it?"

She glanced from Mr. Lott to Sam. "I believe Herbert made a new will," she said stubbornly.

"Whatever you may think you have, papers of intention don't weigh in against a completed and signed will. One recorded with the courts," the lawyer said, his narrow lips pulled across his teeth in a thin pink line.

Sam knew he had to be firm with Lisa, to make sure she understood the harm caused by what she'd done. Whether or not he could or would collect any money was a whole other issue. "I asked you for a receipt or proof that you paid rent. You didn't provide one." Aware of his smug tone, he smiled at Lisa, whose alarmed expression made him doubt that this was the best way to deal with her.

Should he change his plan, call a truce?

What if he tried to talk to her about his concerns, and about why she was so convinced there was a newer will? He'd check for the file and see what that was about. In the meantime, he had never met a woman he couldn't charm, and Lisa was every inch a woman. She was just a bigger challenge than most. A little more time, and a more delicate approach might be needed to do the trick.

The more he thought about changing his approach, the more convinced he became that it could work. But first he had to remove the source of Lisa's irritation. Bringing a lawyer here hadn't been a great idea.

"Karl, I think I can handle it from here." He gave Karl a sideways glance and weathered the open disapproval in his lawyer's eyes. He shrugged mentally. The lawyer would be paid when the property was sold, and it was up to Sam to convince Morgan Lumber to return to the bargaining table. But for now he needed to have a reasonable conversation with Lisa.

"Really. I'll call you later," Sam said as he stood up, prepared to see Karl to the door.

"Whatever you say, but I think you'd be better off if I stayed."

"I hear you"—Sam lowered his voice—"but let me try something first." He clapped Karl on the back. "I'll call you tomorrow."

The lawyer mumbled to himself on his way out, but Sam ignored him. Rubbing his hands together, he walked back to the table and sat down across from her. "Now, let's get to work. I need to discuss a couple of things with you, not the least being the scene you created with the media."

"I told you. I was shocked to see the 'For Sale' sign go up. I reacted without thinking it through. I didn't mean for it to go that far." Lisa's eyes were dark, anxious, and for a few moments Sam wanted to lighten things and forget the problems between them.

"Lisa, you have to understand that I need to sell this farm in order to clear my uncle's debts. The mortgage has to be paid. Believe me, if I had the money I would pay it out myself. But I don't. The continued costs of maintaining the property have to be paid as well. And each day I don't find a way to pay the mortgage puts it closer to going into default. And then if the bank decides they have to have their money, with no income here and no one to pay the bills…"

"I want to save this place from harm, but I need time," she said.

"And you must see, from what I said, I don't have time."

"Is there any possible way you'd be able to wait until we see if we can raise the money?"

"As I said, I don't have the money to support the costs of this farm. And if I wait and you continue to interfere in my talks with potential buyers, that's hardly fair."

"If you'd talked to me before you put the farm up for sale, I would have explained everything to you then—how important all of this is to the community and to me." Lisa chewed her lip and looked away.

"So what do we do and where do we start?" he asked.

Lisa raised her head, a challenging look on her face. "Why do you want to do something so destructive as to sell the farm to Morgan Lumber? Do you realize how long your uncle held out against those people?" she asked, her gaze trapping him in its grip.

She did have the most beautiful gray-green eyes... "He never talked about it... Not to me," he said.

"I don't think he talked to you about anything important," she said, her eyes showing her disappointment. "I wish you'd rethink your decision." She spoke so softly he hardly heard her.

The slope of her shoulders, her vulnerable gaze, held him in its thrall. The now-familiar urge to protect her rose up in his chest, making him want to end this discussion and let her stay. "Lisa, all I'm asking is that you stay out of my business. Let me finish up with Uncle Herbert's estate," he said inhaling the fragrance of her hair. As his focus changed he wished he could run his fingers through the curls cascading around her face.

She glanced at him, her chin raised. "We have to talk about this, we really do. You don't seem to understand what's at stake."

Sam was tired of the whole thing: the farm, Lisa's determination, and the mixed up feelings she stirred in him. One minute, he wanted to yell at her, and the next he wanted to kiss her soft lips. But he had to get back to his air-freight business, a business that urgently needed him.

Staying here could jeopardize his personal financial

situation. He needed to get back to where he belonged and to do that he needed to work out a compromise as quickly as possible. "I think I might have a solution."

"And that would be?" she asked, her eyes wide with interest.

"If we talk this through like adults we might be able to find a way to settle things."

She gaped at him. "You're the only one not acting like an adult here."

Why did she have to be so bitchy? What if her misbehavior made Sam reconsider trying to compromise?

The sound of a dripping tap echoed between Sam and Lisa, the minutes edging past as Lisa waited. She shifted her glance to him: the deep pools of his eyes, the wide set of his shoulders, perfect shoulders for cuddling against. She gave her head an impatient shake. She couldn't let him know how attracted she was to him.

"I'm being pretty flexible here and I think you should meet me halfway," he said.

Determined to find a way to reach Sam, to have him understand how wrong he was in what he was doing, she said, "I haven't been paying rent. Herbert wanted me to be here to continue the work the Nature Trust is doing related to the eagles that live on the property. Allowing me to live here was his contribution to the Nature Trust's drive to protect the birds."

Sam's expression softened. "That sounds like my uncle. Why didn't you tell me sooner?"

"Because you came into town with all your big plans, and I believed that if I told you the truth you'd put me out."

Sam gave her that smile of his, the one that made her weak-kneed. "We have gotten off to a bad start. So what do you believe we should do?"

"The Nature Trust would care for this farm, and protect this beautiful place. You need to give them a chance to buy it," Lisa said.

Sam rubbed his jaw in thought and Lisa dared to hope that he would consider her idea.

Sam shook his head. "Here's the problem as I see it. I have a responsibility to the estate, and an obligation to the people my uncle owes money to. Selling the farm can't be delayed or the bank could call the loan and the property would go through foreclosure, then sold just to cover the mortgage. At the moment the lumber companies are offering more money than the bank might get from a foreclosure. It doesn't make financial sense to let anyone or any organization buy this place for less than it's worth."

"Is this only about money?" she asked, her heart sinking into the back of her chest.

"Yes. Under the circumstances it has to be about money."

"The Nature Trust cannot raise that amount of money so fast. It doesn't have the resources." Lisa could see no way out, as her mind whirled around and around the problem, like a dog worrying a bone. "I don't know what to say," she said, as she stared at him in defeat.

Sam shrugged his shoulders. "Look Lisa, I need to work something out fast. There's a lot of money owing on the property. Your Nature Trust has not even contacted me about their interest in buying the farm. How do I know they're really interested?"

Lisa's face, a shocking white mask sprinkled with cinnamon freckles. "They *are* interested."

"Look, you've got to understand what's at stake," he

muttered, as anger blossomed in him—anger at himself, and the situation. But coming back from town to face an onslaught of strangers and the press yesterday, not to mention the calls he received from Morgan Lumber in the aftermath of the press conference, hadn't been easy.

"Lisa, I have to do what I came here to do. Neither you nor I can change the fact that my uncle's dead, but we can find a way to make the best of it."

"And selling the farm to a lumber company is how you see making the best of it... Can you imagine what this place will be like when they're finished clear cutting? The eagles have been nesting in those beautiful trees for decades." She shifted in her chair, her hands working restlessly along the shiny edge of the maple table. Then she nervously ran her tongue over her lips.

As he watched her movements Sam wondered what it would be like to have such a friend as Lisa in his corner, a friend with such loyalty and passion. He had never met anyone like her. All the women in his life—and there had been a few—held their feelings in check. He couldn't remember even one of them caring enough about anything to take a stand. Except to debate which restaurant he could take them to...

Yet, Lisa's passionate belief could ruin his chances to sell, and he couldn't let that happen, no matter how pretty and vulnerable she was at the moment.

"I don't know of any reason why you have to stay here now that the decision has been made to sell, unless of course you want to be the custodian until the new owners take possession."

"Did you not hear what I said? I have to continue to do my job. There are the Bald Eagles at the back of the farm to think about." She stood up, re-tucked her blue shirt into her jeans, ran her fingers through her red curls, and began to pace. "I worked with your uncle. We were collecting observation data on the eagles, their nesting habits, the flight patterns, anything we could gather that might help increase their numbers. This project was Herbert and the Nature Trust working together. He spent years on it."

"But where you live doesn't affect that project, does it? And when I do sell—"

"The buyer you're talking about will remove the trees the eagles are using for their nests without a second thought."

"Come on, Lisa, I don't believe that. They have an obligation in all of this. I can make the sale conditional on them not touching the back part of the farm."

She sighed as she turned back to face him. "Have you asked your lawyer about that?"

"No."

"Then I think you should check and I'm betting he will tell you that you can't put that sort of stipulation into a sales agreement."

Lisa knew she was losing. Sam would never understand what the farm meant, except in terms of the money it would bring. What had ever made her think she could convince him anything without a price tag was important, especially protecting the Bald Eagles?

"Why did you suggest we try to talk this out, when all you've done is make your case for selling the farm?"

"Is that how you see this?"

Clearly he did not see the problem. It would be his way or else, and she was tired of fighting with him. She would pack up and get out of there. She had no idea where she'd go, but she was pretty certain Annie would give her a place to stay, at least for now.

Knowing this was probably her last chance to look at him, she took her time. His athletic frame was just what any woman would wish for; his black hair edged his ears in the most endearing way. His blue eyes watched her, much as a cat would watch a mouse, only *his* pounce would see her bounced right out of her home.

"Lisa, I think asking the lumber company to leave the trees at the back of the property *will* matter. You have a very jaundiced view of the lumber companies."

Without warning she felt tears burning behind her lids, a strange pain arcing through her chest. "I miss your uncle. I wish he were here to explain to you the damage you're about to do."

"I'm sorry," he murmured as he left his chair and came around the table.

She looked into his darkened eyes, and saw genuine concern for her, and it touched her deeply, even as it spelled out that she'd lost. Yet there was no point in fighting with him, at least for the time being. She needed to talk to someone who really cared about the farm, and Sam wasn't that person.

Sam rubbed his hands slowly over her shoulders. "I shouldn't have been so hard on you."

CHAPTER SEVEN

It's always more exciting when cupid pays a visit.

Feelings of concern and disbelief poured through Sam as he stood in front of her, massaging her shoulders. He liked this feisty woman, and although he didn't agree with her, he admired her.

"Look, I realize you and I don't see eye to eye, but I had hoped we could find a compromise you'd accept."

She glanced at her hands and back at him. "I know this may sound strange but your uncle was like a father to me."

"That's a really nice thing to say. I'm sure my uncle felt the same way toward you, and because of that please stay in the apartment until the property changes hands—and longer if that suits the new owners when they take over. You may find they want you to continue your work. I know you don't believe that." He shrugged.

"Well, at least it gives me a chance to talk with them," she said.

Any time before, a woman tearing up would have made him wonder what she wanted. But Lisa was different. Pleasing her gave him a warm feeling in the pit of his stomach.

She gazed up into his eyes. "I will do everything in my power to convince whoever buys the farm to behave in a responsible way toward this wonderful place. I only wish you would be part of seeing to it...could make sure they did the right thing," she said, leaning so close to him that he felt the heat of her body.

Hot, urgent need poured like oil into every part of him. His arms went around her and he pulled her close. Her body fit his like a glove. She didn't say anything, but her eyes widened, their liquid green coaxing him closer. Wanting more, he touched the red curls clinging to her cheek. "I believe you will do everything you can to protect this place," he breathed over the words.

She looked him over from his forehead to his chin, and he loved the feelings her close scrutiny gave him. "Sam, I know we've had our difficulties, but that's because we're coming at this whole thing from two different perspectives. Why don't we start over? I'd like you to understand how your uncle Herbert felt about this place."

He was powerless to resist the sweetness of her expression. "Yes, I'd like that." Talk was so much safer than the arousal he'd felt when he touched her. "Why don't we sit down?"

Wanting to hold her, and knowing he shouldn't, he edged her away from him. When he resumed his seat opposite her he took her hands and held them across the table. "You know what? After all we've been through, I don't know anything about you. Where did you live before you came here?" he asked.

Her fingers fluttered in his, like a bird about to take flight, but he wanted to keep the contact, so he held fast.

"I've always lived in Middleborough," she said, her eyes fixed on the surface of the table.

"I spent my summers here for a couple of years in high school, but I don't remember meeting you. And I would have remembered your red hair." His eyes roved over her face. "And those eyes of yours…"

She met his gaze head on, sending a cascade of excitement through him. "What do you remember about your time here besides being here on the farm?" she asked, her eyes holding his, her gaze so direct he suddenly wanted to glance away.

"For a couple of years I came here after school got out, worked with my uncle, and went into town sometimes. Made a couple of friends, but we've gone our separate ways over the years. Why do you ask?"

"Just wondered what you remember about your time here," she repeated, but there was a distinct unsettled edge in her voice, and her gaze flitted around the room.

She was uneasy. *What was going on here?* Before he could ask her, she got up and started pacing around the dining room, past the huge collection of beer steins on the window ledge.

The lady had something on her mind.

"Why did you ask what I did here?" he asked. Sam looked at her as she paced. The soft blueness of her cotton shirt struck a sharp contrast with her red hair, much better than her usual purple or magenta. Her movements were laced with tension and she continued to pace.

"I...just wondered... That's all." She gave a nervous laugh.

"Look, if I've done something to upset you. Well, I know I've upset you over the farm, but is there something more?"

She gave him a quick sidelong glance, just long enough for him to see she was anxious.

Sam tapped the table in thought. Looking back, Lisa had been more than just annoyed with him since he came here. "Is this about the other day when we were talking and the real estate agent put the sign up?"

She shook her head vigorously. "No. Although that was a pretty awful thing to happen just when I thought we were getting to understand each other a little bit."

"I did too, to be honest."

"Well, we agree on that much," she said, still pacing around the room.

"While we're talking about things, I don't understand why you're so sure my uncle wrote a new will."

"Because he told me he was going to, that he wanted to leave the farm to the Nature Trust and put me in charge of overseeing the farm."

"Are you saying he named you as beneficiary in a new will?" Sam asked, realizing that Lisa might have a lot more at stake here than he had first assumed.

"I believed he did, in the interim," Lisa said.

"Is that what you were doing up in the office the night I caught you in here? Looking for a new will?"

"I was looking for a file. I told you that."

"Okay. Let's settle this once and for all. Come on," he said, getting up from the table and coming around to stand next to her. "We're going upstairs."

"There's no point. I took the file back to the apartment with me. I mean the file that contained Herbert's notes on a new will. I can get it if you like."

"I would like that very much," he said.

With that, Lisa got up and went to find the file.

When she got back she spread the contents out in front of him. "Have a look," she said. "This is what I found that night you discovered me in his office."

Sam took the file and scanned the first couple of loose pages. "These are notes on his plan... He talks about..." Sam turned the file sideways reading along the edge of a page. "My uncle's writing is a little difficult to read but it does look as though he was considering a change to his will," Sam said with a hint of uncertainty.

"See. I told you. He may have chosen a different lawyer to draft the new one." She glanced over Sam's shoulder to get a closer look at Herbert's familiar scribble. Suddenly she was back to that day when Herbert had told her he wanted her to protect his legacy and her throat tightened.

"It doesn't say anything about a new lawyer. No names scribbled here."

"Let me look at that." Lisa read through the pages and couldn't find any mention of a new lawyer or whether or not Herbert had taken these notes to anyone. "Would you help me find out if Herbert made a new will?" she asked, holding her breath.

Sam shook his head. "Lisa, face facts. If my uncle had written a new will and had it properly processed we would have found it, or the lawyer acting on his behalf would have been in touch with the beneficiaries after Herbert's death."

But she couldn't accept the logic of what Sam said until she was certain. "I can't believe that Herbert wouldn't have followed through on this. He said he would."

"But he didn't. And if he had, you and the Nature Trust would have inherited a property wallowing in debt."

Clutching the file, Lisa turned to him. "I want to read through these notes one more time, to see if there is even the smallest indication that a new will was drawn up. If there wasn't, then I have no choice but to accept that you have to sell this farm. If the lumber company is taking over I have a lot to do. I haven't been keeping up with my scheduled work since your uncle died," she said, giving him one last glance.

With that she walked out the door with the file before he could see her tears.

CHAPTER EIGHT

You can tell a good man by the way he smiles.

Lisa hadn't slept in the past two days. Reading Herbert's notes made her miss Herbert even more. Despite Sam's position that a new will had not been formally drawn up she couldn't give up hope just yet. She'd called Annie for her advice and they'd agreed to meet and talk over what they could do.

"I'm convinced that Herbert has a new will. I just can't find it," Lisa said as she and Annie watched the boys playing in the McDonald's Play Place. Their delighted giggles were in sharp contrast to the dark state of Lisa's mind and heart. Tommy Junior and Jeffrey were two of the sweetest little boys Lisa had ever met. She was their godmother and proud to be so.

"Where do you think it is?" Annie turned from watching the boys and looked at Lisa with concern in her eyes.

"Maybe it's with another attorney."

Annie squirreled her eyebrows together. "Why would he switch lawyers at his age? What do you think you can do about it?"

"I'm going to call every law firm in town and ask if Herbert was a client."

"They can't release the name of a client simply because you ask."

Lisa shrugged her disappointment. "Am I crazy to

think that somewhere there is another will?"

"I think maybe you are—crazy, I mean. You're also hoping to hang on to Sam a little longer. What I really believe is going on here is that you're still wanting Sam to notice you, to say he remembers you." Annie gave her a sad little smile. "Lisa, face it. If he hasn't remembered you by now, he's not going to."

"Trust me. I am well over that idea. He made it clear to me when we were talking about Herbert that he didn't have a clue who I was."

"So you're willing to admit that it was silly on your part?" Annie asked, her eyes searching the play area for her boys.

She couldn't tell her best friend that she still felt something for Sam—something far beyond her high school crush—regardless of how things ended up between them. She couldn't say anything because she knew how absurd it would sound to her friend. "May I remind you that you married your high school sweetheart?"

Annie nodded, her gaze searching Lisa's face. "But Sam hasn't recognized you. That dance you invited him to didn't leave an impression on him. But if he does remember you, what difference will it make? You and he aren't getting along. Him remembering you under different circumstances won't change that."

"You're right. I think the whole thing was a severe case of teenage infatuation on my part."

"Almost certainly."

"You think I'm still a pushover where he's concerned because of how I felt years ago?"

"I know you are."

"That's not true. I changed my mind about wanting him to recognize me. That part of my life is completely over, " she said, remembering Sam's touch, his closeness as they stood in the kitchen earlier today.

Annie spoke gently. "Lisa, I want you to be careful where Sam is concerned. He had a reputation when he spent the summers here. Tommy used to tell me some of the stories, until I told him I didn't want to hear any more."

"Not to worry." Lisa was so thankful she hadn't told Annie about hearing the music, Beethoven's 5th, when Sam kissed her—or even that the kiss happened. Hearing about the kiss and the music would be the final proof she was still infatuated, or certifiable.

"I want your word that you will forget all about him. The Sam Jacksons of this world do not make good husbands." Annie glanced over at her boys playing in the huge, net-covered box of colored balls.

"How did we jump from a date gone wrong to marriage?" Lisa countered.

"Remember me? I'm the one who was there through all of it."

"You were. But as you say, Sam will be gone soon, and I will probably have to find other employment."

As she smiled at her dear friend Lisa realized that despite her bravado, she still had a silly crush on Sam. Having him around made her aware of how much she wanted him to see her for the woman she'd become. A woman still hoping that the man she'd dreamed of all those years ago might be available to her. "Do not worry about me," she said to reassure herself, as much as her friend.

Two days later bright sunlight warmed the morning air as Lisa settled back on the step at the entrance to the apartment, thankful that she'd made the decision to see as little of Sam as possible until he left. She had been sunning herself, thanking her lucky stars that Sam had gone into town and she had a chance to sit outside and enjoy the day.

Avoiding Sam had been easy because he'd been very busy, if the number of times he'd hopped in this dazzling red sports car and driven off was any indication. Willie Anderson had called her to say he'd heard the lumber company was back and willing to resume negotiations. Sam must be rubbing his hands together with glee.

Despite everything that had happened, and her assurance to Annie that she was over Sam, Lisa yearned to spend time with him, like iron filings wanting to be drawn by a magnet. Yet, all she and Sam seemed to do was argue with each other. They were as different as earth and sky, and equally determined to have their own way. The whole Sam thing was a pointless exercise, and deep down Lisa knew that. So why couldn't she give up on such a silly, childish dream where the man was concerned?

Lisa watched Barney as he made his way under the tall pine tree next to the garage. She had to let him go. He'd become a house pet, something she hadn't wanted to happen, but he would soon adjust to his life in the wild. She sincerely hoped he hadn't developed a taste for the garbage cans at Harmony Farm. She could just imagine the raised eyebrows, Sam's disgusted glance, if he found his garbage cans ravaged.

The throaty roar of Sam's Corvette had her scrambling off the step and inside. A conversation with him was not on her wish list. She took the steps two at a time. Ducking into the apartment, she peered out the kitchen window and was surprised to see old Max McGarrity's half ton pulling into the yard behind the sports car. Lisa looked again.

The bed of Max's half ton held four yipping dogs...

Herbert's dogs. How could she have forgotten about

them? Chocolate, Peanuts, Scotch and Soda. Chocolate was a chocolate Lab with big soft gray eyes and a sweet personality; Peanuts was a high-energy Jack Russell that barked at anyone coming near the farm; Scotch was an elegant, but aging Gordon Setter with long black ears and a graying muzzle, while Soda was a Bassett hound that bayed at the moon whenever the opportunity arose.

Lisa loved them all dearly and under other circumstances she would have rushed down to greet them, but the scene unfolding below kept her nose pressed to the window. Sam was sitting in his car with the most peculiar look on his face. Intrigued by what was happening in the yard below, Lisa eased open the kitchen window and climbed up on the sink to get a better view.

The dogs set up a loud discordant howling as Max shut off the engine. The old pickup kicked and sputtered before finally sighing into silence. In unison, four tails wagged as four canine faces waited and watched for him to open the door of the cab. As he did so, the four leaped over the tailgate of the truck with Soda needing a little help from Chocolate. Leaping and bounding, their tails thrashing, the four dogs made for Sam who was just getting out of his sports car.

Lisa chuckled and pushed the window open farther. *This was going to be better than any movie.* A dog lover Sam wasn't; anyone could see that. And Herbert's four were incorrigible. Inching forward on her perch, Lisa waited for Sam to make it past the dogs to the other side of the car.

"Good morning," Max boomed, his hand extended across the rush of dogs to shake Sam's hand.

Sam looked kind of cute as he tried to fend off the leaping dogs and extend his hand in greeting. "Good morning," Sam said as he waded though the dogs. "I'm Sam Jackson. What can I do for you?"

"Max McGarrity. Friend of Herbert's." He pumped

Sam's hand.

The expanse of dogs parted long enough for Lisa to get a glimpse of the clumps of dog hair clinging to Sam's smooth black chinos. Lisa grinned from ear to ear as she watched him let go of Max's hand and start picking the dog hair off his clothes.

"Down! You bunch of unruly bastards," Max yelled. "I can tell you, they've been a handful."

"I can imagine," Sam said, plucking away at his pant leg. "Do they always shed like this?"

"Well, you're about to find out." Max lowered the tailgate on the truck and started wrestling with a huge bag of dog food. "I'm returning them to ya," he said, hefting the bag on his shoulders and starting toward the back door of the farmhouse.

"Wait. Where are you going with that?"

Max kept right on walking. "I'm taking it to the house. That's the least I could do for you under the circumstances."

"What do you mean? Whose dogs are these?"

Max stopped so suddenly the bag slipped off his shoulders and he caught it just before it hit the ground.

"You don't know?"

"No, I don't."

Lisa smiled at the look of disbelief on Sam's face. What was he going to do? An urbanite like Sam wouldn't have the first clue about looking after the dogs. And Lisa trusted Max not to waste any time letting Sam know his thoughts. Lisa hitched closer to the window and waited for things to unfold.

"Well, I'll be darned. You're Herbert's nephew, aren't ya?"

"Yes." Sam struggled across the yard, his legs entangled in the four dogs determined to give him a rousing welcome.

"Well, these four..." Max eyed the romping dogs.

"These guys belonged to your uncle. Didn't anybody tell ya?"

Sam glanced up at the apartment and Lisa ducked behind the curtain. "No. No one said a word."

"Well, that's too bad. I had the four of them at my house as a favor to your uncle. He was busy with the Eagles and he didn't want the dogs around. Then when he died, I thought you'd appreciate me keeping the pooches until you had things straightened away."

"I appreciate your help, I really do," Sam said as he slipped past Chocolate and stood with his back braced against the back door of the farmhouse.

"Well, that's not all I came here for. I was wondering if you'd had time to think about a headstone for Herbert. I know he was cremated." Max made a sign of the cross on his chest.

"A headstone?" Sam's fingers covered the doorknob, and a smile broke out on his face, the first Lisa had seen since Max's arrival.

"Yeah, I sell them. Real nice they are, too." He pulled a shiny pamphlet out of his jacket pocket and held it out to Sam. "I have a special on this month. Take a look. It's a real beauty. It's real marble, and has a special place for perennial flowers."

"He means plastic flowers," Lisa whispered to Sam even though he couldn't hear her.

"I don't think I'm interested," Sam said, turning the knob of the back door while keeping one eye on the romping canines.

"What do you mean? You're going to make a fortune off your uncle's farm and you're too cheap to put up a headstone in his memory? What kind of nephew are ya?"

"Not the kind you expected, obviously. I have no plans for a headstone for my uncle. He didn't include that in his funeral plans."

"The old bastard," muttered Max. Max glared at Sam, his beady eyes narrowed in thought. "I suppose he didn't happen to mention my bill for services rendered?"

Sam opened his mouth, closed it again, and gave Max a rueful smile. "No, he didn't. In fact he didn't mention you or the dogs in his will at all."

"Well, this is a sorry mess. What are you prepared to do about it?"

"Nothing, I suppose. I didn't know about the dogs, but I imagine I'll be able to find homes for each of them...or give them to the SPCA." His voice trailed off as he glanced at the tongue-lolling pack sitting in a semi-circle in front of him.

"Well, in the meantime, you owe me kennel services for the past two months. Four dogs, food, grooming, exercising—"

"What do you mean?"

"Well, I had hoped to sell a headstone to you. I'm a business man, you understand, doing a favor for another business man." Max scratched up under his peaked cap, and adjusted it over his eyes in a very businesslike manner.

"Oh, I get it. If I'm not buying a headstone, I'm buying pet care services."

"Tell Max to take a flying leap," Lisa growled as she glared out the window.

"How much do I owe you?" Sam asked, resigned to the situation.

"Well, I'd have to go home and do you up an invoice. In the meantime, I'll leave the dogs here with you."

"No, please. I'm not prepared to look after them. I'd like you to keep them until I can find suitable homes for them."

"Not gonna happen, pal," Max said as he chomped on a toothpick. "My deal with your uncle has ended.

Look after your own dogs." With that, Max packed his lanky frame into the cab of his truck, started the engine, and called out over the engine's thunderous roar: "I'll be in touch."

Lisa noted the helpless expression on Sam's face. It seemed that Sam wasn't very happy.

An idea formed in Lisa's mind. If Sam were rescued from his dilemma by the kindness of his neighbor, wouldn't the neighbor gain a few brownie points? Maybe Sam would be willing to talk about the future of the farm with the right incentive.

Hope rising, Lisa climbed off the sink and raced to the bathroom. Giving her hair a good finger combing, she dabbed on a little lipstick. She glanced at the effect in the mirror.

"Girl, you're looking good." She grinned at herself in the mirror, tossed her lipstick on the counter and made for the door.

⌁

Sam stood stock still as he peered from one furry body to another. What was he going to do with four dogs he hadn't the faintest clue how to care for? His Uncle Herbert hadn't mentioned them and Sam couldn't remember them being around the last time he'd visited. Bracing his shoulder against the door, he turned the knob and was about to push it open when the dogs turned in unison and ran barking toward the garage.

"Whoa! What a sight you boys are. I've missed you, all of you." Lisa held out her arms and all four dogs leaped into the space. She rubbed chins, backs and assorted other dog parts.

"You might have told me about them," Sam said, and cringed at the near-whining tone in his voice.

"I thought you knew."

"No. I didn't," he said as he pushed open the door and moved inside.

"Well, you know now."

"Where did they come from? The last time I visited my uncle, he had one dog..." Sam glanced at the four of them, and pointed. "I think the black, long-eared one."

She eyed him in disbelief. "You mean Scotch? It's pretty clear you haven't seen your uncle in a long time. I don't know where they came from, but they're not new to Harmony Farm."

"Well, they're new to me." Sam rubbed his jaw as he considered his options. "I don't have the time to look after them with all the other things I have to worry about. But I'm going to have to do something with them..."

"Sit," she commanded, and all four dogs sat down and looked up at her expectantly. "And what would that be?" she asked as she stood surrounded by the pack.

Sam couldn't help but notice how the sun turned her hair a golden auburn color and the way her stretchy black tights accentuated the curving muscles of her legs. His glance moved upward to meet the black spandex top that covered every curve of her breasts.

He pulled his thoughts away from her curves, and back to the matter at hand. "I'm going to call the animal shelter and have them come and get the dogs."

Lisa placed her hands on her hips, and glanced at him quizzically. "Why would you do that? These four wouldn't harm a flea."

Sam didn't want to hear a discussion of fleas, any more than he wanted to admit he didn't know the first thing about dogs. "I can't keep them, and besides, the man who brought them here is billing me for his services. It seems Mr. McGarrity thought he'd get a headstone sale out of my uncle."

Lisa sighed as she walked toward him. Not one of

the dogs moved. "That's old Max for you. He still has the original penny he earned. And don't make the mistake of hiring him to look after them, he'll charge for things you've never heard of."

"Thanks for the advice." Sam stared past her at the quiet grouping of dogs. "How did you do that?"

"Do what?"

He pointed. "The dogs are all sitting quietly. How did you do that?"

She shrugged and tipped her eyebrows. "It's called obedience training and it's something every conscientious dog owner learns. Want to see some of the skills your young nephews have acquired?"

"They're not my nephews," he said quickly, his eyes on the dogs.

She gave him a wry smile and flicked a wrist at him. "Just in a manner of speaking. Watch this."

She gave a whistle and the four dogs pranced over and sat down in front of her, each with one paw raised. "Good boys," she cooed, and they put their paws down. "Lie down," she commanded and all four dogs lay on their tummies with their chins between their front paws.

Lisa did it with such ease. There was very little doubt that she was comfortable around the beasts. "That's part of their training, I assume. Do they always obey you like that?"

She chuckled. "Mostly, unless a rabbit or a squirrel has the audacity to cross their paths. Then it's every dog for himself."

Sam liked the happy smile on her face, and the smooth way she handled the dogs. "You really like this troop, don't you?" he asked, glancing at the perfectly behaved dogs.

"Yeah, we're buddies," she said as she patted each of them.

"Do you think you could show me how to do that?"

he asked before he'd even thought about it. What good would it do for him to learn about a bunch of dogs he had no intention of keeping? But he had to admit to himself it would be a different experience, and one he might enjoy; especially with Lisa as his teacher.

She moved closer to him, and again he could smell the fresh scent of strawberries. "I could, but it would take time, and you'll be gone in under two weeks, right?"

Her gray-green eyes held a hint of amusement—at his expense, he assumed—but he must look a little weird pressed against the door the way he was. He stepped back out into the yard, standing close enough to her to enjoy her scent. "I need your help with these dogs. I can't make them obey me, and they are clearly devoted to you." He looked at the four of them, their eight eyes watching Lisa.

"So." She pushed a clump of curls off her forehead and gave him a cheeky grin. "What kind of deal are we talking? You don't want me to take them up to the apartment, do you? You're against animals in the apartment."

"Naturally. Who wouldn't be?"

She gave him a speculative look. "You'll be pleased to know that Barney's gone back to the wild."

He had to think for a minute. "*Barney?* Oh, yeah, the raccoon you had as a house guest."

"One and the same."

"That's good. But no, I don't think it would be reasonable if we let the dogs into the apartment. Maybe a dog house..."

"A four-dog dog house. I don't think so."

"Then, where do they normally sleep?"

"They lived in the house with Herbert. Sometimes, he had to boot them off his favorite chair so he could watch the evening news."

Then a thought struck him. "Why don't you help me

take them to the animal shelter?"

She stared at him as if he'd just admitted to a crime. "The animal shelter? Have you ever been there?"

"No, but I'm sure—"

She shook her head. Her mass of curls swung across her forehead. "Oh, no you don't. That place is not fit for these four. They'd die of loneliness in no time. Besides, no one would take Scotch. He's an old dog. See his muzzle?" She whistled to Scotch and he strolled over. His big-dog smile and easy loping ways made Sam wish he liked dogs.

"He's a nice old fella."

Sam reached toward the dog. Scotch immediately sidled up to him and held up a paw. Sam gave Scotch a tentative pat on the head and took the outstretched paw.

"I think you're bonding," she said.

"It's that easy?"

"With Scotch it is." She pointed at Sam's pants. "I'd watch him though, Scotch is a champion shedder."

Sam looked down and was surprised to see a fuzzy fur line along the leg of his pants. He caught her amused glance when he looked up.

"Just call me fuzzy-wuzzy," he said, suddenly feeling amused and happy.

"As a bear, right?" she countered. "You're being a real good sport about this. Why don't you and I make a deal? I'll help you take care of the dogs as long as I'm staying at the apartment." She gave him a wide grin. "I'll even teach you the basics of obedience training."

Unable to stop himself, he smiled at her—a smile that felt so good, so uplifting he wanted to take her in his arms. Lisa had spoken his thoughts exactly, minus the obedience stuff, but what difference did it make? He would enjoy spending time with this woman who continued to intrigue him.

"Consider yourself hired," he said and saw approval

in her eyes. Finally, he'd done something she liked.

CHAPTER NINE

Some moments in life are to be savored.

L isa didn't know whether to shout or sing. Sam had agreed to them working together to look after the dogs, in addition to letting her keep the apartment. Lady luck was definitely smiling down on her today.

Did this mean there was a kinder side to him? She bit her lip in determination. *Did it matter?* With a little time Sam might come to like the dogs and to appreciate the lifestyle his uncle had enjoyed on Harmony Farm. And today that smile of his had made her head spin as dangerously as it had once long ago. Though she knew how this would end, she didn't want to let go of the moment, the excitement of being with Sam.

"I have an idea. Why don't we go inside and toast our new partnership?" she asked.

Sam glanced anxiously in the direction of the dogs.

"Don't worry, I'll manage the dogs."

"Iced tea?"

"Sounds great," Lisa said as she led the dogs into the house behind Sam. "There boys, you know where you belong. Don't give your Uncle Sam a hard time."

She pointed to the mat in front of the sliding glass doors that looked out on the open expanse of field along the side of the house. Pangs of loneliness for her old friend made her throat go dry. *How many times had she come into this house with the dogs in tow, to discuss the eagles project?*

She turned away, and came eye-to-eye with Sam's questioning glance. "I used to spend a lot of time with your uncle here."

Even across the room, Sam's gaze was warm, understanding and took Lisa completely by surprise. He held up his hands. "I didn't mean to pry. I know you miss him. Uncle Herbert was lucky to have a friend like you."

He shoved his hands in the pockets of his chinos, and Lisa heard the distinct rattling of change. *Was Sam nervous?* It couldn't be.

She looked him up and down, her heart doing a thundering beat in her chest. A man willing to give Herbert's dogs a chance deserved an explanation. "No, I was the lucky one. I came home from university without a job, and my dad gone. I had nowhere to go. Your Uncle Herbert gave me the apartment over the garage and told me to raid the furniture in the attic—" Hot tears stung her eyes.

Sam pointed to the fridge. "Maybe a cool drink of iced tea will help. Care to join me?"

"Sure." She gulped over the tightness in her throat.

Sliding into the chair across from him, Lisa clutched the glass in her hand. Her feelings of loss were all mixed up with the sheer maleness of the man sitting across from her. The warm awareness in his eyes fed the rising excitement pouring through her. She loved the way he looked at her, the way he seemed to be looking at her as if he wanted to paint her portrait...or kiss her again. She straightened her shoulders and tried not to superimpose her desire on Sam.

She reminded herself: Sam was not interested in her, and never had been. She blinked and looked away, seeking respite in the large framed print of two men fishing from a canoe. She sat up straighter again, rearranging her thoughts.

"My housekeeping skills aren't great," he said as he wiped up the drops of iced tea that had dripped onto the table.

"Join the club." Lisa met his gaze. His eyes locked with hers, the power of his gaze holding her captive, making her unable to break eye contact with the man.

"To us," he whispered against the rim of his glass.

"To us." Lisa waited, hoping he'd say something to cool the super charged air swirling between them. When he didn't, she launched her own attempt to ease the situation. "Would you like to discuss—"

"Yes, we need to discuss how we're going to look after them." He cleared his throat, and looked over at the mat full of dogs. "They need to be exercised, right?"

Though he had changed the subject, his blue eyes hinted at banked emotions she could only speculate about because she knew so little about the tall, handsome man who, for the moment, was back in her life. Even more perplexing was the fact that the stranger with an air of authority had begun to change into the boy next door, and that rekindled the attraction she'd felt for him as a younger man—and set her senses on fire. *Could she trust what was happening? That it was real? Had Sam truly changed, or had she simply become more in tune with him and what he was like?*

He took a sip, and his lips seemed to caress the glass, making her remember how it felt when he'd kissed her. And the music...it hummed in the air all around them. A warm spot glowed in her stomach and spread through her.

She had to stop this fantasy she was creating. Though it seemed to be gathering momentum, it was going nowhere. Men like Sam kept a fat little black book. There couldn't be more than a passing flirtation with someone like Sam.

"Yes… The dogs... We'll have to walk them at least once a day," she told him.

"Why don't we start now?" he offered.

"You think you're ready to take your first lesson?"

"Positive. Lead on." He stood up and reached for her hand.

She placed hers in his, and experienced a sense of closeness that threatened to swamp her. Eager to be near him, she stood up, bringing her face close to his broad chest. His deeply male scent slid over her, sending beads of tension and lethargy darting through her.

"Shall we kiss to seal the deal?" he asked, his fingers sliding under her chin and lifting her face to his.

He was so close, so enticing, so male... She edged closer, her heart in her throat, her lips remembering every nuance of his last kiss. Her hands started a slow ascent up his arms, toward his neck.

"Kiss?" she whispered, her breath mingling with his.

"Like this," he whispered back.

Sam slid his fingers over the smooth spandex of her top, and across her back as he held her tighter. She returned his kiss willingly, sinking into his arms. Tender endearments flooded his brain, words he couldn't say, had never said to a woman. Words that would bind him to her if spoken.

"Please." There was a steady, impassioned plea in her eyes as she shifted in his arms, fitting her body to his.

Her luminous green eyes, and the pleading in her voice left him unable to resist. "Anything you want," he offered as his body rocked to his aching need.

Her breath came in short gasps; there was a blush of

color on her soft lips as she moved against his arms.

"I can't do this. We can't. I mean, we don't have—" Her gaze skirted his and came to rest on his shirt front. Slowly, she tucked her hands against his chest and pushed him away.

"What do you think we're doing, other than exchanging a kiss?" Sam asked. He needed to think clearly to avoid complicating things even more…but he loved the closeness of her, the way she fit so neatly in his arms. "Did anyone ever tell you how nice your smile is?"

She swallowed and looked away. "I think we should get back to the job at hand. Remember the dogs?"

"How could I forget," he asked as he released her. Lisa was clearly enjoying the moment. Knowing he was giving her pleasure made it even more enjoyable for him. "How long will it take to train me in dog care?"

"Let me think…" She tapped her forehead and smiled up at him.

"Don't take too long," he said, searching for somewhere to put his hands other than around her shoulders.

"You're sure you're ready to be covered in dog hair at least daily?" There was lightness in her words, mingled with her husky whisper.

He wanted her…

But as good as she had felt in his arms he couldn't let himself become involved with this woman. He had a life he needed to get back to, and a business that was struggling. He glanced around the room, trying to find something to concentrate on that would ease the desire running rampant through him. Searching his mind for a neutral topic, he said, "Maybe we should take the dogs—"

"Super. Great. Let's do that," Lisa answered quickly as she turned and strode away from him, her tight-fitting pants highlighting the well-muscled body beneath.

An urge to drag her off to bed and damn the consequences nearly blocked his ability to reason. Every time he was with Lisa, he wanted more of her. *Was there no limit to his attraction to her? Did he want there to be?* He followed her to the back door and watched as she put a leash on each dog.

"Here." She held out two leashes attached to Peanuts and Soda and showed him how to put leashes on Scotch's and Chocolate's collars. As she led the way with all four dogs rustling around her legs, she smiled encouragingly at him. "I'll take the two bigger dogs."

"This isn't right," he said, glancing from the two pint-sized dogs he had to the two big ones she had. "I'll take the two big ones. After all—"

"After all, you're bigger and stronger than little ol' me." Her eyebrows danced upward. "You're chauvinism's showing."

"No, it's common sense. The Labrador and the setter are big dogs. I can handle them easier than you can."

"Okay, Hercules. Show your stuff." She switched leashes, bowed, and waved him ahead of her.

With just a ghost of a second thought, he hesitated.

Her gaze met his, as they stood on the step. "Or are we abiding by the ladies first rule?" she asked.

"I'm ready when you are." Ignoring the sense of a calamity in the making, Sam worked his hands into the loops on the leashes and pulled the dogs forward. "Here boys. Let's go."

They headed down the path leading away from the house. "They're pretty good about walking along beside you. Now, all you have to do is hold them steady," she cautioned starting across the field to Willow Brook.

Sam gripped a leash in each hand, waiting for the dogs to pull away from him. Instead, they sauntered along on either side of him as if they'd done it a thousand times. "This is nice," he said as he glanced over at Lisa.

"I had hoped you'd like it. Having a dog as a pet can be very rewarding, especially when they learn to trust you. And dogs are very trusting. Once you get the hang of this, we'll go without the leashes."

A feeling of contentment, fueled by her smile, slid through him. "Having one dog would be great, I'm sure. What I can't figure out was why Uncle Herbert had four."

"I have no idea, but knowing him, they were dogs that needed a home. Your uncle was a very open, caring person."

"I wish I'd spent more time with him. I used to be here a lot when my mother was alive. She loved spending time with Herbert on the farm..."

They strolled along the path leading to the brook, the heat of the morning gathering around them in sultry waves. "I didn't know what to expect, but this is not bad," he said.

"The next time we do this, I'll show you how to get them to sit for you." Lisa moved behind him as the path narrowed near a large pine.

Sam felt the yank of the leash as Scotch, the Gordon Setter, pulled over and cocked his leg.

"Pit stop," Lisa offered. "That's one of the major reasons for walking a dog."

He lifted one eyebrow at her. "Give me a little credit."

Scotch gave the ground a good digging, sending dirt and assorted pieces of pine and broken cones cruising through the air in Sam's direction.

"I'd give Scotch a little space if I were you. His nickname's Digger."

"Sure," Sam said, stepping closer to the pine and out of range of the flying dirt.

Sam waited and watched as Scotch made suspicious snuffling noises in the underbrush beneath the pine.

Chocolate paced back and forth, entangling the leashes as fast as Sam separated them.

"I hope they haven't found anything," Lisa said with just a hint of concern in her voice.

"What do you mean, found something?" Sam asked, dancing the two-step as he tried to keep the leashes straight.

Lisa tightened her grip on Peanut and Soda's leashes. "There might be—"

Suddenly Chocolate filled the air with the most unearthly howling sound. Scotch, his head up, tail pointed heavenward, and his right paw held forward, sniffed the wind.

Lisa reached for Sam as his leash struggles brought him within reach. "It might—"

Sam stumbled, propelled by Scotch and Chocolate. "Wait up, you guys!" Sam yelled as he tugged on the leashes.

"Hang on," Lisa shouted.

Holding on was all Sam could do as the two dogs yanked him forward and in line behind them as they raced ahead on the path. The dogs, their noses tucked close to the ground, vacuumed the earth ahead of them as they pulled Sam along behind them.

"A rabbit! It might be a rabbit!" Lisa's cry of alarm was lost on Sam as he scrambled to keep his feet under him.

Sam couldn't see the rabbit, but he remembered Lisa's warning and dug his heels into the soft earth. "Oh, no!" he whooped, skating along behind the dogs. Desperately attempting to regain control of the dogs, now clearly in hot pursuit of the rabbit, Sam yelled and pulled and stumbled along.

"Wait up!" he called out as they hit a mound of earth. The abruptness of the bump nearly dumped him on his knees. Lisa yelled something, but her voice was just a distant blur as Sam rocketed over the field, straight for a clump of cedars. He leaped over a rock, swung out around another mound of earth and barreled on with only scattered remnants of organized thought whistling through his mind. Glancing up, he saw the tree with its beckoning branches hurtling toward him. He crouched.

He smelled it first, the soft spicy scent of the cedar, as he barreled over the rough ground. Seconds later he slammed his feet into the earth and pitched forward, landing hard on a branch, his face buried as the long wavy green branches surrounded him.

The dogs growled, grunted, and paced as Sam sucked in air.

"Are you all right?" Lisa called from somewhere beyond the tree.

Sam's cheeks stung, his left ankle hummed with pain, and his wrists were chafed raw.

"I'm fine, just fine," he muttered.

"Wow, I'm glad to hear that. You certainly made good time coming over the hill."

He swore he could hear a chuckle in her voice. "Track and field was my favorite sport in school."

"The hundred-yard dash was your best event, I presume."

He ignored her this time and instead concentrated on picking the cedar bits off his face, a tough assignment with his hands bound together by the leashes.

"Are you coming out any time soon?" she asked.

"I can't come out without the dogs," he said as he tried to pull his body out of its half crouch.

Lisa gave a low whistle and suddenly Sam was being propelled back the way he'd come.

"Whoa, wait a minute," he called as he cleared the tree right behind the dogs.

"Well, aren't you just about the cutest thing ever to come out of a cedar hedge," Lisa said, her voice studded with humor.

He stopped, nearly falling forward when the leashes tightened around his legs. He worked his face into a scowl. "If I ever get untangled from this mess, I'll show you a whole new meaning for the word 'cute.' "

Her whole body rocked with laughter.

He struggled to hold his scowl in place.

Meeting her gaze was his undoing. He burst out laughing.

CHAPTER TEN

Just when you think life couldn't get more complicated...

L isa nervously tucked two twisted curls behind her ears as she remembered the events of yesterday. It had been a long time since she had spent such a pleasant time as when they walked the dogs. And Sam had been such a good sport about being dragged into the cedar hedge. It took every bit of self-control not to follow him into the house when they got back yesterday.

Thankfully she remembered Annie's warning and made her way to the apartment where she spent the rest of the day staring out the window hoping for a glimpse of Sam. When he sped off in his car she reluctantly focused on her unfinished paperwork.

Sam had called her this morning to come and walk the dogs with him this afternoon. She had to go, if only to ensure that Sam learned why the farm was so important. A nice long walk along the bank of the brook, followed by a stroll along the lane leading through the oak trees should convince him of the pleasures of country life and the beauty of the oak forest.

It would also mean that she'd have to once again face her attraction for him.

If anything did happen between them...

She crossed the yard and went to the back door. Knocking softly, she waited. Not a sound, not even the dogs. *Where was Sam? And where were the dogs?* There must be something keeping their attention. They couldn't all be asleep. She tapped again and when she still didn't hear anything, she opened the door a crack.

There was a grunting sound followed by a thump, followed by a padding sound. Curious, Lisa tiptoed into the hall leading into the den, and the sounds grew louder. She peeked around the doorframe and saw Sam, his shoulders flexed, muscles bulging as he raised a barbell with weights at either end, over his shoulders. The dogs were lined up along the paneled wall of the den watching the performance, their heads uniformly tilted to one side as if waiting for something.

Lisa watched, mesmerized by the wealth of muscled male displayed before her. Tiny rivulets of sweat shone on his brow, his face was flushed a rosy hue, and his black tank top clung to him in all the right places.

Lisa sucked in her breath and repeated her reasons for avoiding the all-male hunk working up a sweat within easy reach of her eager hands.

He liked the high life, not the country life...

But his shoulders were so broad, so touchable.

He didn't care about the farm and what it meant to her...

But his abs, in all their muscled glory, coaxed her forward. A delicious sigh slid from her.

She crinkled her brow in thought. He was such a chauvinist, and fancied himself a lady killer... She wetted her lips at the sight of the drops of sweat meandering down through the black hair on his chest.

You only had to look at him to know he had women stashed everywhere...

Oh, those thighs, and the way they met his hips, rising to his tight buns. Lisa nearly groaned out loud.

Out of here, girl, now. She backed away as silently as possible.

"Taking in the view?" he asked.

Stopped cold in her tracks, Lisa turned. "The last living chauvinist speaks."

She heard the breathlessness in her words, and cursed herself: A schoolgirl; that's what she sounded like. A silly, infatuated schoolgirl.

Sam gently dropped the barbell to the floor, while the dogs rushed to Lisa. Much as she wanted to disappear through a hole in the floor, she had no choice but to stay and greet the dogs.

"Hi, guys." She rubbed each bobbing head in turn as they gave her wide dog smiles and pranced around her.

Sam rubbed a towel over his sweat-dampened face as he watched her. "Anytime you want to come and watch me work out, you only have to ask."

"The door was open. You didn't answer when I knocked."

She must sound like a petulant child, but at least annoyance was much better than the heated thoughts of a few moments ago. She peeked at him over the dogs' writhing bodies. She could tell by the look in his eyes that he was well aware of his impact on her. She straightened.

"Tell me. How did you get all this…"—she swung her glance around the jumble of weight-lifting gear scattered around the room—"and all your clothes in that tiny little car of yours?"

"Easy. I rented this stuff in town. If you'd like to use any of it, feel free."

She could see it all now. She'd be sweating and huffing while he sat and watched. And knowing him, he'd be telling her what she was doing wrong. A picture of his hands on hers as he showed her how to lift a barbell popped into her head, sending a flush of heat through her. She muffled a groan. "Thanks, but no thanks."

He continued to wipe sweat from various parts of his anatomy, and Lisa continued to stare at the wall. *Would he ever be done wiping all those body parts she'd love to touch?*

Sam slipped the towel around his neck, and walked over to her. "I'm going upstairs for a quick shower. See you in a few minutes."

The smell of male sweat mixed with the remnants of a heady cologne emanated from him, making her pulse bounce. "The dogs and I will be waiting in the yard," she said with as much self-assurance as she could muster.

"I'm looking forward to our walk today. I really mean that." He lifted her chin and smiled, his eyes shining with sincerity, his lips so close...

As she watched him move toward the stairs leading to the bedrooms, she fought for control of her trembling limbs. *What had gotten into her these past few days?* Sam was everything she didn't want in her life. Everything.

This had to end before something serious happened, something she'd be powerless to stop if she didn't soon get a grip on herself. "Come on, you guys," she muttered to the dogs as she led the way to the back door.

Later as they crossed the field and followed the pebbled path to the brook, Sam noted that Lisa hadn't uttered a word. They had walked in an easy silence that kept a careful distance between them, but he'd seen the outright lust in her eyes as she watched him work out. He had to admit that he'd enjoyed every minute of it. A couple of times it had been difficult not to let her see that he knew she was standing there.

He whistled tunelessly as he walked beside her. The

four dogs roamed ahead: Peanuts, the Jack Russell in the lead and Soda, the Bassett hound bringing up the rear.

It looked like he and the redhead had a future—at least a couple of weeks' worth, while he finished up his uncle's business. The real estate agent had told him that as well as Morgan Lumber a second lumber company had shown an interest. While the bidding pot boiled, he'd have a chance to woo the perky redhead walking beside him with her head held high and a delightful pout on her full pink lips.

Yes, the day had possibilities.

"Where are we headed?" he asked.

"I thought we'd go over to the oak trees on the other side of the brook. I want to show you what it is about this place that made your uncle want to protect it."

"And you want a chance to show me what I've been missing." He glanced at her, thinking about what he didn't plan to miss. The dark forest green of her golf shirt deepened the red of her hair. Her cheeks glowed with healthy vigor. "I could stand to get more fresh air."

She ignored his remark as she started across the narrow stream, stepping from one tipsy rock to another. "Follow me."

"I'm right behind you."

To be ready for whatever footwork was required, Sam had borrowed a pair of his uncle's rubber boots. They were hot and smelly in the heat of the day, but he'd vowed to never again sacrifice another pair of shoes to the fields of Harmony Farm.

He hadn't counted on the stones being quite so slippery or for the movement of the water to make him so tipsy. He swung his arms for balance, making wide windmill movements that attracted Chocolate who was standing on the other side watching him. As he cursed at nearly slipping off the rock, the big Labrador came bounding back down the bank and soared into Sam, sending him backward into the brook. He stuck his hands into the cool water behind him, barely managing to keep his butt high and dry.

"That's enough, Chocolate," Lisa scolded, as she came back across the rocks and held her hand out to Sam. "Two things you should remember about rubber boots. They don't work well on wet rocks, and with rubber boots you can wade the brook, you don't have to perch on a rock." She smiled down at him with just the tiniest hint of superiority and humor in her gaze.

"Thanks for telling me," he said as he juggled his weight on his arms, looking for a graceful way to get back up without landing his butt in the water.

"Here, don't be shy. Take my hand."

"I'll pull you in."

She sighed and rolled her eyes. "Highly unlikely."

He wanted her didn't he? What better way for that to happen than wet beside him in a brook? They would have to get out of their wet clothes. And they could do that together.

Shifting his weight to his left hand, he grabbed for her hand and pulled. He held his breath as he felt her start to fall toward him.

"Oh, no you don't!" She yelped in dismay as she saw the glint of mischief in his eyes. She gave him a push back and he landed in the water and onto a barely concealed pointed rock.

It found its mark in Sam's left butt cheek. "Ouch," he howled and scrambled to get up, his hands slipping on the rocks. "Thanks a lot."

"Any time," Lisa said as she dusted off her hands. "You had it coming."

He grabbed for her, but she raced up the bank toward the woods. His pants dripping water, and his left butt cheek flaming, he chased after her, his rubber boots clunking along the rough ground. "You're going to regret what you just did."

She reached the woods and stood waiting for him as the dogs raced around, barking and leaping. She giggled as she pointed at his mud-spattered pants, and the large wet area between his legs. "I think you should give up flying until you learn to walk and run."

Knowing he looked ridiculous made him reckless. "You come here," he said through gritted teeth.

"Like I said, catch me."

With her call to action, he closed the gap between them, yanked her into his arms, and kissed her hard on the lips. His body warmed instantly as his hands spread over her back. Without lifting his mouth from hers, he scooped her into his arms and laid her on the soft earth under a tree. He drank from her lips like a man dying of thirst. Overhead the branches murmured, and the dogs whined, but Sam ignored everything except the woman lying under him.

She laced her fingers around his neck and pulled him closer. "*Hmm.* This is pleasant."

"Is that all?"

Her gaze caught on his and he saw the laughter in her eyes. "Let's try this," he said as he sucked her lower lip, drawing the soft skin into his mouth. She moaned and opened her lips in invitation.

As he deepened the kiss, he slipped his fingers under her shirt and worked the fabric free of her jeans. His hands sought the firm ripeness of her warm breasts as his tongue probed her mouth. Her body rose under him, urging him on, but some part of him balked. This would be so easy for him. He would have what he wanted from her with no regrets. She would be just like all the rest...

But she wasn't like the other women he'd known.

He eased his lips from hers and looked into the dark pools of her eyes. For the first time in his life, he wanted more from a woman. And especially from this woman who had somehow, in a matter of days, come to mean so much to him. He met her gaze, and saw the uncertainty in her eyes as well.

"I'm a bit of a cad, aren't I?" he said.

"I'm not sure what you mean," she whispered, her gaze fixed on his lips.

"I don't want you to feel you have to—"

"Have to what?" She looked up at him and her vulnerability hit him in the gut.

He wouldn't do anything to hurt her. "You and I, we need time."

She wiggled away from him and sat up. She studiously picked pieces of dried leaves out of her hair as she spoke. "You're right, of course."

Not knowing what to say next, he sat down beside her and glanced around. The canopy of trees protected them from the heat of the sun as they sat shoulder to shoulder on the soft earth. In the distance, a single-engine Cessna hummed along the horizon.

"Do you like to fly?"

She shrugged. "I've only flown a couple of times, and I liked it."

"I love to fly."

"I imagine you do." She slid her gaze toward his, her green-gray eyes warm and aware.

"I wanted to be a pilot for as long as I can remember," he said and felt a self-conscious tug. He was sharing something with her that was very important to him. Was it the surroundings, or the woman that made him willing to talk to her so freely?

"It must be a nice feeling to know what you want. I've never been sure of what I wanted until my time in Africa with the Jane Goodall Institute."

"You're serious?"

"Yes. Being there, working with the organization, with people so committed to the chimps and the environment was life changing for me. I came home inspired to continue being involved with the environment. I met your uncle who wanted to do just as I did... The eagles here are beautiful, majestic birds. They deserve our protection." With one hand she lifted a stray curl off her face; with the other she picked up a stick and drew circles in the soft earth.

A funny ache filled Sam. "I wish I had known him the way you did."

"I was one of the lucky ones."

"I always took him for granted; somehow I just assumed he'd always be here."

"I know what you mean. I felt the same way about my father, and when I lost him..."

He sensed her body tighten, and turned to look at her. There was a tension around her mouth, and her eyes glistened.

"I didn't mean to make you sad."

She leaned closer, making him feel ridiculously good about himself. "Thanks, Sam."

He put his arm around her shoulders, his heart thrashing in his chest as unexpected desire for intimacy roamed through him. "What are friends for?" he asked, his voice falling to a whisper. Holding her, he glanced around the space where they sat huddled together. The four dogs had taken up positions just at the edge of the clearing.

"Did you know these trees have stood here for over a century?" she said.

"I had no idea," he said, kissing the top of her head, feeling her body lean into his. He hadn't experienced this before: the simple act of holding Lisa close, of being together while he breathed in the scent of grass and other green things Sam couldn't identify.

He spotted a patch of small yellow and white blooms nestled near the roots of the tree. On impulse, he picked the flowers with his free hand, and added a few of the shiny green leaves to the impromptu bouquet.

"For you." He passed her the bouquet.

She took it in her hands, before throwing it on the ground. "Sam, you picked a bouquet of poison ivy."

CHAPTER ELEVEN

Being right can sometimes be a pain in the butt.

"Can't you make this car go any faster?" Lisa asked as she scratched the palms of her hands. "We need to get to the pharmacy."

"There are such things as speed limits, you know," Sam said, rubbing his palms on the steering wheel of the Corvette as he roared around the bend in the narrow country road.

"Live a little, I say." Lisa leaned forward and scratched the back of her waist. "To think we were actually lying in a patch of poison ivy. I can't believe how dumb we were."

Sam glanced at her, his aviator sunglasses flashing her image back at her. "Speak for yourself. You should have known better. As for me, I'm pleading ignorance."

"Really?" She scratched her nose, knowing it would only make it redder, but she had to scratch that itch.

"Yes. I'm the city slicker, remember?"

Lisa hated to be reminded of her own words where Sam was concerned, but it was true. He wouldn't know poison ivy from cattails.

"You're right. I just don't know how I could have been so stupid."

He pushed his glasses down his nose and stared at her, his eyes brimming with challenge.

"I don't think it was stupidity."

"No? Then what?"

"I think the heat of passion dulled your brain." He tipped his glasses back up on his nose and gave her a smile that bordered on a leer.

She fought down the blush on her cheeks, and glared at the mirrored images of herself in his glasses. How she wished he'd take those glasses off so she could see his eyes. "Hardly. I just didn't look where I was going."

"That's one way of putting it. As I recall, I put you there, and you didn't even whisper a complaint."

Lisa could tell by his cocky grin that Sam was enjoying himself at her expense, and she was tempted to put him in his place. But why bother? She was enjoying herself too in spite of the persistent itch of the poison ivy. Being in Sam's arms had been worth it.

"Well, then you can share in the blame. Oh, and by the way, the next time you want to give a girl flowers, be a little more discerning, will you?"

"From here on it will be flower-shop flowers," Sam said as he took the turn so fast the tires squealed.

"I must admit, I didn't expect you to go all sentimental on me."

"Why?"

"You don't strike me as the type."

"There you go. The things we men do to please our women."

"Since when am I your woman?"

"Slip of the tongue, I guess."

His gaze met hers, and a ball of heat formed in her chest. "That's not the only slip of the tongue you've made..."

He gave her a startled glance and then a knowing laugh. "Care to name another?"

"Forget I said that," Lisa muttered, thankful that her sunglasses covered her eyes.

"Much as I'd like to pursue the topic, I'll respect the lady's wishes," Sam said with humor sliding like silk through his words.

They drove in silence past a tall white church, its elegant spire reaching toward the sky and its lawn sloping away from the building like a billowing skirt.

Lisa liked speeding along the narrow country road with the sun-warmed wind whipping past her shoulders and the heated rays beating down on her. She could have enjoyed this so much better if her skin hadn't been so itchy. But a bottle of calamine lotion would fix that.

Sam sped up over the hill and along the winding road leading over the railway tracks. "You're going to need help getting the lotion on."

"You think so?" she asked.

"Sure you are. Just like suntan lotion. Someone has to smooth it over the affected areas."

"And you're volunteering."

"If you ask me in a nice, ladylike way."

"And if I don't?"

Sam geared down as he approached the outskirts of town. "You'll have to suffer it out by yourself, I suppose."

His smug grin deserved an answer. "And you think I can't put lotion on myself without the help of a man like you?"

"A bit testy, are we?" he asked over the sudden whine of a siren.

They turned in unison and glanced back. A police cruiser with its lights flashing was coming up fast behind them.

"I think you're about to get yours," she said, sucking in her cheeks to keep from grinning. "It looks like Jimmy Babcock's going to have his way with you."

Sam shrugged in resignation. "I should have known," he said as he pulled out his wallet.

The officer swaggered toward the car, his hands on his hips. "Sir, can I see your driver's license and registration?"

"Hi, Jimmy," Lisa said. "How're you doing?"

"Well, hello there." Jimmy's voice flooded with welcome, as he stuck out his chest and smiled.

"One of your old boyfriends?" Sam muttered as he passed the paperwork to the officer.

"None of your business," she said.

"Mr. Jackson, you were speeding."

"I know, officer. I was in a hurry."

"Aren't we all these days..." Jimmy gave an exaggerated sigh as he scanned Sam's license and registration.

"Jimmy, Sam was rushing on my account. You see, I got into a patch of poison ivy, and I need to get to the drugstore."

"I don't believe it for a minute. You're too smart for that..." He looked suspiciously from Lisa to Sam.

"It's true." She scratched her hand for emphasis. "I fell down, sort of."

"And I was just giving her a lift into town to get what she needed."

Jimmy peered at Sam. "What's that red area on your hands?"

Sam tucked his hands under the wheel. "Hard work, I guess. I'm trying to learn to manage my uncle's farm."

Jimmy squinted at the driver's license. "So, you're the Sam Jackson everyone's been talking about."

"Really?" Sam scratched his palm, and smiled benignly at the officer.

Jimmy rubbed his jaw. "Folks are saying you're going to sell out to one of those lumber companies."

Sam's neck stiffened. "And what else do folks say?" Sam asked, his voice low, controlled.

"Not much, except you aren't from around these

parts." Jimmy shrugged. "None of my business, any-way."

"I'd have to agree with you there, officer," Sam said as he glanced in Lisa's direction, a scowl clouding his handsome face.

"Don't glare at me like that." Lisa propped her sun-glasses farther up on her nose and stared off.

"Why not? Your little public relations stunt is reap-ing rewards." He chewed the words out between gritted teeth.

"More likely the gossip mill," she muttered back at him. This wasn't getting them anywhere, and by the tone in Sam's voice there could be trouble brewing.

Maybe if she appealed to Jimmy's better nature she could save Sam any further embarrassment. And saving Sam was in her best interests at the moment. She glanced up at Jimmy. She had known Jimmy since grade school, and she liked him. Beneath his puffed up exterior there was a heart of gold. She offered up a pleading smile. "Look, I know we shouldn't have been speeding, and it was my fault, Jimmy. But if you let us go this time, I promise we won't do it again. Deal?"

Jimmy gave her a stern glance as he considered the problem. Then he winked. "For old times sake," he said.

"Thanks, Jimmy," she said, relieved.

"Don't mention it to anyone. It wouldn't be good if word got around that I gave you special treatment." He glanced back at his cruiser.

"You can count on us," Lisa said settling back into the soft leather of the seat.

Jimmy gave her a quick salute. "Get going before I change my mind."

"What was that all about?" Sam asked as they watched the officer get into his cruiser and drive away.

"Jimmy Babcock owes me a favor."

"Really?" Sam pulled off his glasses and stared intently into her eyes. "Care to tell me why?"

She hadn't known Sam long enough to confide such things in him. Besides, he seemed far too suspicious of her. "I would, if it were any of your business."

On the way back from town yesterday Lisa had been in a very quiet mood, Sam thought to himself. She'd taken the dogs out by herself in the evening without saying much of anything to him. He'd grown accustomed to her high spirits and good humor, and to see her in a funk had him worried. And feeling worried about a woman wasn't something Sam was used to.

As he stood by the kitchen window, staring out across the yard, he wondered what he could do to get the old Lisa back. Not wanting to leave the house until he'd heard from her, he let the dogs out for their morning run in the yard. Even their noisy barking and friendly growling hadn't brought her out of her apartment.

He'd have to go and check on her if she didn't come out pretty soon.

Indecision gnawed at him as he went out into the yard with the dogs bounding around his legs, but for a change he hardly noticed them. He glanced across the carpet of green to where the lawn swing squeaked in the gentle breeze and imagined he and Lisa spending a few moments there.

He felt just a little foolish, standing outside like some lovesick Romeo waiting for a woman he hadn't even known a few weeks ago. And the jealousy he'd experienced when she talked to the police officer yesterday...

"Get a grip," he muttered to himself. Star-crossed lovers they weren't. At times like this she annoyed the hell out of him. The women he dated wanted to be around him, to spend time with him. He was usually the one trying to peel them off him.

Not Lisa. She didn't have a clingy bone in her body...

What was he saying? He wasn't dating Lisa, and if this morning was any indication they weren't even on friendly terms.

Annoyed with himself and his jealous thoughts, he paced back and forth across the yard with the four dogs trailing along behind him. He couldn't really be jealous. Jealousy implied something more than what they had between them.

He walked over to the garage and stood just beneath her bedroom window, trying to decide what to do. On a whim, he tossed a pebble against it, and waited for some sign of activity. Growing impatient, he tossed another.

"What are you doing?" Lisa asked from the corner of the garage nearest the rose arbor.

Sam jumped in surprise. "I thought you were upstairs, sick or something." Embarrassment had him picking imaginary flecks of lint off the arm of his Calvin Klein sweater.

She strode over to him, her eyes brimming with fun. "You could have knocked," she said as she quickly crossed the space between them and looked up into his face.

There was something so attractive about her, so intriguing. He couldn't describe it, but he wanted more. Right this minute, he wanted to wrap his arms around her, but instead he settled for shoving his hands in his pockets. "I was worried about you. When you didn't show up this morning..."

Her expression softened. "That's sweet of you. I was just out in the rose garden puttering. I didn't sleep very well last night and I needed to clear my head. Working in the earth helps me think."

"Was it something I said?"

She dusted her gardening gloves off and tucked them into the pocket of her jeans. "No. What happened yesterday brought back old memories, that's all."

"Pleasant ones?"

She frowned. "Things have a strange way of happening."

He watched her, the way she swiped at the dampness on her forehead, the way she twisted a curl back behind her ear, little rituals he'd come to associate with her.

"Can I help?"

"You think I was angry with you yesterday, do you?"

He did, but he didn't want her to know. "I think you were upset when I asked about your friend, Jimmy."

She turned and walked toward the rose arbor. "Let's sit down for a minute."

The scent of earth and roses flooded his senses as he followed her into the rose-encircled space. "I haven't been in here for years," he said, amazed at how perfect the setting was.

"I love it here," she said, sliding onto the old wooden bench. "Your Uncle Herbert started this garden for a woman he once loved. Did you know that?"

"No, I didn't." Sam glanced around the shrub-enclosed space. Long tendrils of climbing roses flowed down over a trellis. Luxuriant bushes with shiny leaves stood proudly holding tiny pink rose buds. Everywhere he looked there was evidence of careful attention on someone's part. "Have you taken over the care of this?"

"Yes. After your uncle told me the story, I couldn't resist trying to bring the rose garden back to its original glory. It must have been beautiful." There was a hint of wistfulness in her sigh.

"It's a perfect lover's hideaway," he said, meeting

her gaze and feeling his heart beat just a little harder from the impact of her liquid green eyes.

"I know what you mean. It's as if it's haunted by love. I wish I knew the story. Herbert wouldn't tell me very much. He didn't want me coming here when I first moved in over the garage. But after a while I convinced him to let me work on the rose garden."

"Having been exposed to your persuasive techniques, I can see why my uncle gave in." Sam saw the guarded glance she gave him. *Had she invited him in here to explain more about her relationship with his uncle?* Up until now, she'd said very little.

Curious, he slid onto the bench beside her, his whole body aware of hers. Had his uncle had the same feelings? "What did you want to tell me?"

"I was in university when Jimmy Babcock's sister, Emily, got pregnant. Her family, except for Jimmy, was angry and wanted her to have an abortion. When she wouldn't, they disowned her. She came to live with me in my apartment at university while she waited for the baby to be born. Jimmy gave his sister money for her expenses."

Sam felt foolish and relieved at the same time. "You helped his sister because Jimmy was your friend. So that's the favor he owed you... You and he must be close."

"We were. Jimmy and I played baseball together when we were kids."

"So, you were a bat-swinging terror in your youth?"

A mischievous look danced in her eyes. "Remember that the next time you decide to argue with me."

"You bet." He sobered. "So, how did the story end? Did Emily put the baby up for adoption?"

"Yes. She didn't have much choice. Her parents didn't support her, and she was a high school student." Lisa pushed the curls off her forehead.

"And you were caught in the middle?"

"Yes. My Aunt Clara wasn't very happy about it all. She thought I shouldn't have been involved in Emily's problem. It was a misunderstanding that we eventually resolved, but it was painful."

Lisa's concern for a friend went much farther than he'd experienced among his own friends. They might offer to help, but not to open their apartment to someone they weren't close to. *Were they shallow, or had he just assumed that everyone behaved the way his friends did?* "You and Jimmy have shared a lot more than most friends would—"

"What do you mean?"

"I was just wondering if you and Jimmy…"

She whirled on him, her eyes snapping. "You think Jimmy and I have a thing going, don't you?" She turned away, and Sam felt as if the sun had gone behind a cloud.

"No, I don't." He felt the lie to the bottom of his toes. He was suddenly aware that he didn't want anyone to have a relationship with her but him.

"What is it with you? First, you're convinced I'm having an affair with your uncle, and now you think I did a favor for a friend because I had designs on him."

CHAPTER TWELVE

Sometimes it's better to say nothing at all.

Lisa was angry at Sam's suggestion that she had an affair with her friend. If he assumed that, and taking that further, did he think he could have a casual affair with her? She had taken every opportunity she could to get close to Sam, which might have led him to think she was easy. The good news was that she had yet to succumb to his charms: not that she hadn't wanted to practically every time she saw him. "You have no right to say anything about my friends, or my life."

"Wait a minute—"

Lisa got up off the bench and grabbed up the trowel she'd been working with. Kneeling down, she jabbed it into the soft earth. She'd been wrong about Sam Jackson. He really was a chauvinist, and despite that she had to admit she liked him all over again.

She'd been led astray by her romantic notions about this man, not the reality of who he was. A male chauvinist couldn't change his stripes even if he wanted to— which Sam didn't. *Why was she wasting her time? And why in heaven's name did she care?* She was furious with herself for wanting him more with each passing day. She poured her fury into the trowel, sending wide arcs of dirt flying in every direction while letting her anger seep slowly away from her. The quiet of the rose garden helped to soothe her erratic feelings. Once she calmed down she turned back to face him.

He was gone. Her heart dipped in her chest.

She returned to scattering fresh earth to ease her hurt feelings.

Thankful for the chance to work out her disappointment, she gathered the rose fertilizer and bone meal and placed some of each in the hole she'd dug. At least she could make a rose happy. She arranged the roots of the rose in the hole and packed the earth around it. Working in the soil soothed her, gave her a sense of contentment, and helped her put things in perspective.

And getting a perspective on Sam was essential if she had to convince him not to sell to the lumber company. She'd talked to Ed Chambers, the president of the Nature Trust, and he said he'd try to see if they could find a way to finance the purchase of Harmony Farm, but their prospects didn't look good.

She smoothed the earth, and gently watered the newly planted shrub, glancing around as she did so. The space was so beautiful. And being angry with Sam was hardly worth ruining her day. As much as she liked him, he wasn't the kind of man she wanted in her life for the long haul. And why had she expected anything different from a jet jockey with designer clothes and fancy cologne?

It was moments like this that made Lisa wish with all her heart that she had a mother who cared about her, her life, and her problems. "Dream on," she muttered.

"Sorry?" Sam's voice sent a jolt through her.

"You're back," she said to cover her surprise.

"I'm here with a peace offering," Sam said as he squeezed past the hanging rose.

Lisa's heart did a backward flip, landing in her throat, but she didn't turn around. Despite her earlier intentions to forget about him all she wanted to do was run into his arms. She glanced around to see him standing there, looking more handsome and appealing than any man had the right to look. "I must be hearing things. Did you say you have something for me?"

"I do," Sam said, kneeling down beside her and reaching for her hand. "Come with me."

Caught up in surprise and propelled by delight, Lisa took his outstretched hand. "Where are we going?"

"Ever since I arrived here the day of the funeral, I've wanted to try out the old lawn swing by the apple tree. Come on."

Feeling like a newly minted fairy-tale princess, Lisa followed him out to the grassy knoll where the old swing moved gently on its sliders. On the seat was a thermos as well as two cups, a plate of butter, a jar of jam and a basket covered with a honey-yellow cloth.

"Don't tell me... Lunch?"

"Call it a snack," he said as they sat down together and the swing began to move ever so slowly back and forth.

She peeked under the cloth. "Scones?"

"Yeah, cooking's one of my hobbies." He scratched his palm and grinned at her.

His endearing smile and the way he tilted his chin at her, made her head spin again. *Would she ever get control of herself around this handsome rogue?* "What's the occasion?"

"I want us to kiss and make up."

"After what you said, kissing's out of the question."

He smoothed his hands over the thighs of the skin-tight jeans he wore. "Would you consider an apology?"

"Possibly."

"I didn't intend it to sound as if I suspected you and Jimmy of anything." He pointed to the tray. "I'm sorry and I hope this will make up for the misunderstanding."

She wanted to leap into his arms, and forget every little nasty thought she'd had about him, but surrendering to Sam wasn't a good idea. He was too tempting... "So you figure the fastest way back into my life is through my stomach?"

"Am I right?"

She eyed the food, smelled the coffee, and nodded. "I can't cook. My can opener keeps quitting on me; so yes, you're right." She gave him a wry smile and was incredibly happy they were together.

"Then dig in," he said as he poured two coffees and spread a napkin on her lap.

Lisa couldn't believe how good the scones tasted. "Do you cook like this all the time?" she asked through a mouth-watering morsel.

"Mostly. I make bread too. Something my mother taught me."

"You're kidding!"

"Lots of men cook."

"You just don't seem the type..."

"You, stereotyping? Life's full of little surprises, isn't it?"

She blushed to admit he'd been right. Life was full of surprises all right, and none more surprising than the man sitting next to her. With the swing swaying easily and this man giving her a look that would melt icebergs, Lisa reconsidered her position. It wasn't that she disliked him. She actually liked a lot of things about him, but even that change in her thinking didn't matter if he'd be gone as soon as the farm sold. And he hadn't recognized her yet, which at first she'd been upset about but now she felt was a good thing. No messy explanations needed. As Annie said, that was a long time ago. "You're right; life's full of surprises," she said, smiling.

Sam's glance shifted from her face to somewhere behind her. "Speaking of surprises, here comes one now."

"Well, hello there folks." Max McGarrity nodded.

"Lisa, good to see ya."

He turned to Sam and stuck out an envelope. "Thought I'd deliver this personally."

"Your bill," Sam said as he took the envelope and put it in his pocket.

"Well, aren't you going to open it?"

"No. I won't be able to pay it until the farm is sold. I'll look at it then."

"How long before that happens?" Max picked at a fingernail, and gave Sam a sidelong stare.

Sam shrugged and glanced at Lisa. "I'm not sure. I'm waiting for word from my real estate agent."

"Well, it had better be soon, as far as I'm concerned. I need the money."

"Don't we all," Sam said, his gaze never leaving Lisa's face.

"I can't see how you can say that. You're a pilot for one of them big airlines. Herbert left this farm to you, lock, stock, and barrel."

"Along with the debt," Sam said, his eyes pleading with Lisa to understand.

Sam still clung to the excuse of the debt that Herbert had left, but that didn't make sense. Herbert never mentioned money problems to anyone, or that he was worried. And if he had been, why would he tell her he was going to offer the farm to the Nature Trust, knowing that they couldn't possibly expect to get it, not with a large debt to be settled first?

Lisa shifted in her seat, and placed her cup carefully on the tray. "Max doesn't mean to make an issue of this, do you Max?"

"Well, I'll tell ya, I'll wait a couple of weeks, but that's all."

Annoyance glinted in Sam's eyes. "You may wait longer than that. I have no way of knowing how soon the farm will sell."

Max gave a disgruntled snort and headed for his battered pickup.

"Did you mean to be so unfriendly with him?" Lisa asked.

"No, but he has to understand. There's no money until the farm sells."

"That bad?"

"That bad. Uncle Herbert mortgaged this place to the limit, and now I'm getting credit card statements that need to be paid, and his income won't cover the installment payments."

"I had no idea..."

"I gather no one did, except maybe his bank. That's why I have to get as much money as I can for this place." Sam glanced all around, and Lisa saw the first real glimmer of uncertainty in his eyes.

"I wish there was some way to sell the farm to someone who could pay the price and not take the trees, or destroy the eagle habitat," Lisa said as a sense of hopelessness slid through her.

Sam tossed his napkin on the tray. "I don't know what else I can do, other than sell to the lumber company."

"How long will the bank wait?"

"I have no idea. But I have an appointment with Herbert's bank manager. I'm going to talk with him and see if there is anything they can do to manage the debt. I doubt there is, but I can always try, I suppose."

"Sam, why don't we sit down together and see if we can come up with a solution? I realize that you and I have not been getting along well enough to work on a real answer to this problem, but maybe now..."

"There's not much point. I have only a few days left before I have to get back to work. The longer I wait to sell the farm, the more the debt will increase. And you insist that I wait for the Nature Trust to make an offer, when I have no idea when that will happen or what the offer will be."

If she could convince Sam to postpone the sale, at least until Ed Chambers had time to approach the local businesses for more money, they might come up with a plan to present a reasonable offer. "Surely we can work something out."

"What's your idea?"

"I...I don't know for sure. But I would like to talk to the Nature Trust and see what we can do."

"But you're leaving me to make a decision, and to consider what you'd like to see happen without giving me any reason to think your organization can make a bid that will cover what is owed," he said.

She sighed, pushing back the curls from her cheeks. "That's true at the moment. But if we are to make an offer we need to raise more money than we have at the moment. Would you let us know when the lumber company makes another offer?"

"And you won't go to the press with your story?" he asked, his eyes assessing her.

"I promise no press conference," she said, her voice thick with emotion and resignation.

CHAPTER THIRTEEN

Learn to expect the unexpected.

The next morning Sam rubbed the sleep from his eyes as he plodded into the kitchen. The rising sun spread long panels of light across the hall floor and into the kitchen. The dogs were cross-piled on one another, soaking in the early morning warmth pouring through the sliding glass doors.

The kitchen was so peaceful, offering a contrast to the long sleepless night during which thoughts of Lisa had filled his muddled mind, sending sleep packing like an unwelcome intruder.

Her offer to work with him was as unexpected as it was pleasant. He suspected that working with her would be a whirlwind experience, given what he'd seen of her and her enthusiasm for any project she believed in. More and more he found himself wanting to have things work out between them. She was so unlike his usual type and so appealing. She was bright, articulate, with a killer sense of humor, but none of the brittle veneer of most of the women he spent time with.

Besides he had to face the fact that Lisa couldn't be a permanent part of his life. He would be going back to New York and his job. A world he knew she'd have no interest in. Yet, he would miss her more than he cared to admit.

Deep in his heart he accepted that wanting Lisa

made no sense at all. She wasn't his type. He loved the fast-paced life he led, the rush of adrenaline each time he entered the cockpit of a jet, bound for wherever. He'd spent time in most major cities in North America and Europe, an opportunity that had taught him to see the world as a wonderful adventure.

He put the coffee on to perk, and beat eggs for an omelet. Scotch, the Gordon Setter ambled over and rested his chin on the table. His sad eyes warmed at the sight of a loaf of bread on the cutting board.

"Hey, old fella," Sam greeted the dog, rubbing his hand over the dog's back. He'd become more attached to Scotch than the others. He liked Scotch's quiet ways, his elegant stance and knowing eyes. Sam sliced fresh bread and put it in the toaster. He added the eggs to the bubbling butter in the bottom of the frying pan. The egg mixture sizzled, throwing off the warming scent of Sam's favorite breakfast. He buttered toast and absently threw a corner crust to Scotch who caught it in mid air.

The other dogs rushed to him, their heads up, their tongues lolling. "Okay, get in line," he said as he popped another four slices in the toaster, and poured himself a cup of coffee. "One slice each and that's all. I'll fill your bowls, and then I'm having my breakfast in peace. Got it?" He glanced at the four dogs, their tails wagging eagerly.

What was he doing, talking to these four as if they were human? And enjoying it to boot. Had this happened to his uncle? It would explain how he came to have four dogs when one would have done for most.

Sam filled the dogs' bowls, buttered their toast, and passed the slices out to satisfied gulping and lip-smacking sounds. He folded his omelet onto a heated plate, and was about to sit down when a large van lumbered past the kitchen window and came to a gravel-scattering stop near the old swing. The dogs set up a chorus of barking that set Sam's nerves on edge.

He went to the window and watched in disbelief as the van disgorged an assortment of men and women dressed in a mix of jeans, overalls, jackets and hats— each with a pair of binoculars strung around their neck.

"What's going on out there?" Sam asked the dog-filled room as he surveyed the group. The back of the van opened and a mound of scopes and other paraphernalia were deposited on the ground outside the van. Sam had never seen such a strange group, or such strange cargo.

The tripods they handled looked like surveying equipment, but no one had requested the opportunity to survey. Morgan Lumber would be the only company with reason to do so, but Sam was certain that Morgan Lumber company employees wouldn't be wearing vests with flowers and birds emblazoned on them.

Sam was about to go out and see what was happening when suddenly everyone in the group raised their binoculars in unison and pointed them skyward. As if under the direction of a concert conductor, each binocular-covered face turned toward the brook.

"What are they doing?" he muttered to himself.

An urgent knocking at the door sent the dogs into a new chorus of barking. "Quiet down you guys," Sam yelled as he yanked the door open.

Lisa spilled into the room, her face flushed, her eyes shining. "You're not going to believe this," she huffed. "I spotted a Western Tanager this morning when I was out at the eagle site. We're going to have birders from all over the eastern seaboard here at Harmony Farm before nightfall."

Bewildered by the muted babbling outside, and Lisa's breathless chatter inside, Sam eased the door closed behind her. Taking Lisa by the shoulders, he spoke as calmly as he could.

"Now, from the beginning, would you? What are all these people doing in my uncle's backyard, and why is it a good thing that I should expect more people to arrive before nightfall?"

Lisa took a deep breath, rolled her eyes and rubbed her nose. "The Western Tanager is seldom seen in this area of the country. It's native to California. Don't you understand? It's off course by thousands of miles?"

He didn't see at all. "What's so special about a bird getting lost?"

"No, silly. It's not about it getting lost. It's about it being here for us to see. For most people, they'll never get another opportunity to see this bird unless they go to California to bird watch."

Sam didn't see why it was such a big deal. "So, what's next? Do you try to catch it or something?"

"No, of course not!" Lisa peered at him as if he were ill. "We just want to watch it for as long as it stays around the area. I've put the word out on the bird alert line, so it won't be long." She glanced around. "Why don't you get your uncle's binoculars and come out and join us?"

"I would, if I knew where they were."

"On the shelf over the window." She eyed the four dogs. "They'll have to stay in the house for the time being. They might disturb the bird."

"Not to mention the odd assortment of people standing around the yard," Sam offered.

"Yeah, you're right." She fluttered her hands. "Come on, grab those binoculars and follow me."

Sam didn't know whether to follow Lisa or close the door on her. She looked so excited—why he didn't know. All birds were alike to Sam, wings, feathers, beaks, and in some cases extremely dangerous to jet engines. "And if I do go with you?"

She gave him a sidelong glance. Her eyebrows knitted together and she radiated impatience. "You just might learn something worth knowing about Harmony Farm."

"In my underwear?"

Lisa grinned as her gaze touched down on his chest and skirted over the rest of his torso to his long legs. "Now, there's a thought. We all might learn something entirely removed from the subject of birds."

"Give me a minute," Sam said, his body warming to her not-so-casual survey of his body. "I'll be right back."

Lisa couldn't believe her good luck. If Sam showed even the remotest interest in the birds, he might also see firsthand, what would be lost by his plan to sell to the lumber company.

"You see," she said to Sam as he followed her into the back yard a few minutes later. "I was out at Sander's Ridge, down where it meets the marsh, and I was watching the nesting pair of Bald Eagles feeding their two hatchlings when I spotted the Western Tanager."

"So why would a bird fly all the way across the continent?"

"To shop at Dillards Department Store?"

A faint twinkle lightened the depths of his dark eyes. "Maybe I can give it a lift home when I go back to work? A free flight."

"Very funny," Lisa said as she struggled to sound stern while leading the way into the enthusiastic group of naturalists scanning the branches of a tree near the bank of the brook. "Can you see him?" she asked Willie Anderson.

Willie hitched up his jeans and pushed his binoculars against the fold of flesh between his eyes. "I think so..."

"How do you know it's a him?" Sam asked, his voice hushed, his body invitingly close to hers.

"Because only the male of the species has a red head."

"So there's chauvinism in the bird world, is there?"

"It would take a chauvinist to see that," Lisa quipped as she raised her binoculars to her face and checked to see that the Tanager was still in the tree.

Squinting, Sam put the binoculars up to his eyes, and stared. "I don't see anything. It's all a blur," he muttered to Lisa.

"Here, let me take a look," she said as she reached for the binoculars.

Sam took them off his neck, and passed them over. Lisa couldn't see anything either, and knew the reason. She passed them back. "Here's what you have to do. It's a lot like sighting a gun."

Sam glanced at her, a look of surprise on his face.

"Not really; but there are similarities. Let me show you." She gave him the instructions that would allow him to see clearly through the binoculars. "Now, find that tree." She pointed to the one near the brook. "Near the top, you'll see a bird shape, and you should be able to see the bright yellow body and the red head."

"I see it," squealed Mr. Heatherton who happened to be standing at Lisa's elbow.

"I don't," said Sam.

"Do you see the tree?" Lisa leaned closer and was immediately surrounded by the pure male scent of Sam. She reveled in the sensations sparking through her. She wanted to slip into the circle of his arms created by his hands raised to look through the binoculars, but resisted the urge. Too many people would see, and gossip would flow like cool summer wine on a hot day. She didn't want anyone to think that she chased men like her mother had.

"Yes, I do..." Sam moved the binoculars upward. "Oh, yes, I see something."

"Now, adjust the dial." She pointed to the tiny wheel on the bridge of the binoculars.

Sam fumbled for a minute as he steadied his hands. "Yes, I see it." He adjusted the binoculars. "The colors are so bright. It looks like someone poured red paint over his head. What's he doing in the top of an oak tree?"

"He's searching for food. Like a lot of birds, they like the trees for shelter and for food. And this bird has flown thousands of miles out of his way so everyone here could get a look at him."

"Planes do it every day." He glanced at her. "Just kidding. I'm impressed. I've never in my entire life looked at a bird this closely except in *National Geographic*, maybe."

"Can you see that it might be important to keep these trees? And appreciate how they contribute to the habitat essential for birds and other creatures?"

Sam let the binoculars dangle at his neck as he looked around the crowd. "I'm beginning to see... How many more people do you expect to show up here?"

"I don't know, but there will be quite a number, especially if the bird is still here tomorrow. The longer the bird stays, the more people will try to get here."

"I don't understand it."

"You don't have to; just accept it. This is a major find for anyone interested in adding to their life list."

"Life list?"

"The number of birds you see and record during your lifetime," said Ed Chambers as he moved to stand next to Sam. "I'm Ed Chambers," he said to Sam as he held out his hand.

Sam smiled and shook hands. "Didn't I see your picture in the *Middleborough Courier* the other day?"

"That you did. I'm involved in the Chamber of Commerce. We're always promoting the area and its attractions."

Ed smiled at Sam and glanced across at Lisa. "Lisa and I have been working on finding a way to buy this lovely property for the Nature Trust." He rubbed his jaw and frowned. "But so far we've come up short."

Lisa listened to Ed's explanation of what they had talked about, but said nothing. Sam seemed to be listening intently and that pleased her.

Ed grew more animated in his description of some of the activities carried on by the Nature Trust. Ed Chambers was a very persuasive man, and he seemed to be making points with Sam. If there was only a way to let them continue the discussion there might be a way of getting Sam to see the need to reconsider his decision to sell to the highest bidder. And a delay might give them enough time to find another big donor to the Nature Trust.

Lisa bit her lower lip in concentration. They needed a social event, something with a relaxed atmosphere. She knew exactly what she'd do. She waited for a break in the conversation, and then made her pitch. "Why don't we hold a barbecue here, this evening? It would be fun, give everyone a chance to get to know one another better. I'd be willing to get the food."

"I can line up another barbecue and we could get a couple of the women to make salads," Ed said, his smile spreading to include Sam. "What do you think?"

Sam shrugged and toyed with the edge of his binoculars. "Sure. Might be fun." He glanced at Lisa and she saw the ambivalence in his eyes. "...I guess if we had everything set up."

This chance could make all the difference in the world to the success or failure of saving Harmony Farm. She'd work the rest of the day if she had to. "Don't worry about a thing. I'll look after everything, and you'll see. We'll have a great time."

"Did I hear someone mention a great time?" said a woman standing behind Lisa, her voice, sweet and sensual, with its all-too-familiar southern drawl.

Samantha Mitchell was the girl Sam had taken to the dance while she stayed home and played sick.

Lisa considered moving away but saw Annie striding toward them with a dangerous look in her eyes. The look on Annie's face said that whatever had her rushing over was something Annie was passionate about—Annie had strong feelings on a lot of things, starting with the importance of home and family, going all the way to an abhorrence of nuclear weapons.

"I remember you," Sam said to the woman he obviously *did remember* from high school. His voice was filled with welcome and his eyes locked on the willowy blonde in the safari jacket and matching pants.

"How are you, Sam?" Samantha asked, her hand touching his arm in a very intimate way.

Feeling trapped between the two towering centerpieces of a clothing marketer's dream Lisa edged out of the way.

"I'm good," Sam said.

"Me too...." Samantha breathed the words out through perfectly red lips, as she raised her long, slender manicured fingers to lift an errant strand of blonde perfection off her cheek.

Lisa was going to be sick.

"I can see I'm here in the nick of time," Annie whispered in her ear as the two Sams cooed at each other.

"No, you're about one twitter too late. Our favorite beauty queen has just opened for business." Lisa knew she was being nasty, but who was there to notice except Annie?

Samantha wedged herself between Lisa and Sam, miraculously maintaining eye contact with Sam the whole time.

"Did I hear correctly? Are you hosting a party here this evening? If so, I'd like to offer to help you host the gathering..."

"You would?" Sam preened like a peacock, and Lisa wanted to whack him. Jealousy reared its head and batted its lashes in a most annoying way.

Time with Sam was short and she realized she wanted his exclusive attention, not to have him focus on this bimbo. *But what could she do about it?* Lisa couldn't hold a candle to Samantha. Never had during their school years together. Samantha was the swan and Lisa the ugly duckling. But this wasn't a movie set and there was no likelihood of a magical transformation...

Annie physically parted the two as she approached the group. "Who said anything about a party? Anyway, any party at Harmony Farm should be hosted by Lisa and Sam, don't you think? They both live here on the farm." Annie reminded them, gently slipping one arm into Sam's and pulling him to the side with her, a smile of appreciation on her face. Sam looked from Annie to Samantha before hugging Annie's arm in his.

Lisa watched in amazement. Annie knew how to handle any situation, even hopeless ones like this one.

"Lisa, do you need help getting things organized? I'm sure Sam would be more than willing to help, wouldn't you Sam?" Annie smiled up at Sam and winked at Lisa.

"I want to help too. It would be so much fun," cooed Samantha.

"Do you have any experience, Samantha? At setting up parties, I mean," Annie said as she pulled Lisa closer to her and Sam.

Now as she listened to Sam and Samantha talk

about the party Lisa wished she hadn't mentioned the idea. The site of Sam nose to nose with Samantha, like a bear around a honey pot, took all the excitement out of her idea.

"I'll get the burgers organized for the party," Lisa muttered and moved off.

An hour later Lisa and Annie drove into town to get some more supplies for the party, giving them a good opportunity to talk.

"Can you believe that woman? She was like that in high school, but I thought she might have changed." Annie spat out the words.

"Not likely. She has no reason to change. Her daddy gives her whatever she wants, and she thinks all men will do the same."

"Samantha thinks that just because she won several beauty pageants she's entitled to special privileges from the entire world," Annie chimed in.

"Did something new happen to make you so pissed at her?" Lisa asked, half afraid of the answer.

"A couple of years ago she tried to put the make on Tommy. And she had the nerve to try it in front of me."

"You're kidding!"

"I wish I were. We were at a party given by Tommy's boss. Samantha's father is a partner in the business, so I guess Samantha got to come on Daddy's arm. I don't know who was angrier, me or Tommy, when she sidled up to him doing her usual little-girl-lost routine."

"Too bad Sam didn't have Tommy's common sense."

"If you ask me Sam's not interested in her. He never went out with her again after the dance. I heard afterward that Sam made an excuse and left the party early.

Too bad you hadn't been there to see that part," Annie muttered. "And now you're ducking away when you should stand your ground for what you want."

"Who says I want him?"

"I do. I told you before. I see it in your eyes. And Sam would have to be completely blind not to know how you feel."

Lisa's face reddened. "I'm that transparent?"

"You're as much in love with him as you ever were. But you still think you're the ugly duckling, not worthy of a man like Sam. And that's not true. You think you're to blame for your mother running off... You're mother's leaving had nothing to do with you, and it doesn't mean that other people will leave you."

Lisa wanted to deny what Annie said, but it was too close to the truth. When Lisa's mother left her father for a man in Chicago, Lisa had been devastated. In her anger, she'd vowed never to be anything like her mother. She had her mother's signature red hair to deal with and that was enough. As far as Lisa was concerned her mother's lying and deceit, and then her leaving the marriage, had hastened the heart attack that killed her dad.

Maybe she should have stayed with Sam instead of leaving them to chat without her. Samantha was the interloper, not her. Maybe she *had* inherited her mother's tendency to cut and run. Lisa desperately needed her friend's advice about what to do. "Do you think I should have stayed?"

"Maybe so. Sam didn't have a chance once Samantha started batting her eyes. And if she bats those eyes again tonight..." Annie scowled as she drove her Jetta around a sharp turn in the road, making her tires squeal on the inside of the tight curve.

Lisa leaned her elbow on the window and gazed unhappily at the passing scenery. "He could have put up more of a struggle, that's all. It's not like he doesn't have experience with women."

"Lisa, face it. Sam will always behave like this. As long as there are women to flirt with, Sam will take up the challenge. It's who he is."

Annie was right. Sam had proven it today. When he could have politely declined Samantha's advances, he chose to encourage her. The whole thing made her very sad. Deep down she'd hoped that Sam had changed, and she'd been part of why he had.

How silly and lovesick was that?

CHAPTER FOURTEEN

Just when things couldn't get any worse....

Later that day Sam stood at the sliding glass doors watching Lisa as she strolled across the field with the four dogs ambling along behind her. Her easy stride showed off her lean legs and her curved waist to full advantage, as her hair fell in easy waves of red around her face. He enjoyed the sight of her more every time he saw her. In fact he liked the whole package from her porcelain complexion to the passion she showed for the things she cared about.

What would it feel like if her passion for life were directed toward someone she loved? Lisa was one hell of an attractive woman, and probably had a long list of lovers to prove it. The thought made him feel disgruntled and out of sorts. He shoved his hands into his jean pockets as he waited for her to reach the house. The dogs would stay in the house during the party, an unpopular decision from the dogs' point of view, but necessary. Otherwise, half the hamburgers would go missing.

He slid the door open as Lisa approached. "You looked like you were having a wonderful time out there."

She shot him a look clouded with indecision. "I like walking the boys," she said, sweeping past him with the dogs in her wake. She filled the dog bowls, tidied the leashes—anything but look at him—and it stung. He wanted to ask her what was wrong, but the closed expression on her face didn't invite inquiry.

Making her way across the room to the door leading to the yard and the garage, she scooped up the ears of corn she'd brought with her. "I'd better get going. The burgers should be arriving any minute and I promised Ed I'd help him set up."

"I can help you," Sam offered.

She looked him up and down, her hair shading her eyes. "No thanks. I'm sure you'll want to greet your guests when they arrive." Something was definitely off with her.

"Hey, it's your party, not mine. I don't mind helping you, and then we can both greet the guests."

"I don't think so," she said, as she studiously polished the doorknob with her fingers. "I'm sure you'll have lots to keep you busy when the guests arrive." She was out the door before he could respond.

Had he said something that put her off? He rubbed his chin, his fingers catching on the late-day stubble. The man who could figure women out was a hell of a lot smarter than he was. He wondered if such a man existed. He shook his head in resignation. He'd shave and join the bustle outside whether Lisa liked it or not.

Later as Sam reached the cluster of people in the backyard, he noticed a peculiar off-putting odor coming from the general direction of the barbecue grill. He'd have to ask Lisa about it when he caught up with her.

Sam wanted to enjoy himself that evening. He'd done little else but work and worry since he'd arrived at Harmony Farm, and it was time to relax a little. A bar had been set up over near the rose garden and someone was tuning a fiddle. Sam wasn't crazy about fiddle music, but for one night...

"Hi, Sam, I hope you have a good time this evening," Ed Chambers said as he approached.

"I'm sure I will." Sam scanned the gathering crowd. "Have you seen Lisa?"

"She's here someplace. I saw her a little while ago. She's put together quite a spread, don't you think?" Ed glanced around at the Chinese lanterns strung between the tree and the back of the house, and the picnic table loaded with salads and rolls. "The Naturalist Club members love a reason to get together, and there are some great cooks among them." Ed eyed a tray of sweets being moved into position at the corner of the picnic table.

"I see her now," Sam said as he caught a glimpse of Lisa near the barbecue.

Ed glanced his way, a slight frown on his face. "I'll catch you later and we can finish our discussion from this morning."

Sam was inclined to follow Ed and get a beer, but first he needed to talk to Lisa. Her earlier coolness rankled. He'd hoped to spend the evening with her, but his prospects didn't look too good at the moment. Lisa was deep in an animated conversation with Kenny Appleby, the expression on her face a mixture of excitement and irritation.

"Well, what have we here?" Sam asked by way of introduction.

"Not much." Kenny scratched his jaw and pushed his glasses up on his nose. "I'm going to get a veggie burger." He gave Lisa's arm a squeeze. "I'll catch you later."

"Veggie burger?"

"Yeah. Have you ever had one?"

He welcomed Lisa's closeness, her scent made his heart lurch in his chest. "Good old-fashioned American beef will do."

Lisa's glance was cool, assessing. "You can have a chicken burger but most of the group eat veggie burgers."

"Including you?"

Her eyes gleamed as she tilted her chin in defiance and leaned closer. "Including me."

Sam slid one arm over her shoulders, and waited for her to draw away. "So what are they made of?"

Mischief mixed with awareness shone in her eyes. "Vegetables of course."

Sam fought the image forming in his head of a large head of cauliflower and a couple of carrots sticking out of a bun. "You mean—"

"I mean, soy, bean sprouts, things like that."

Sam didn't know much about soy, but he'd seen sprouts in the grocery store. "And you eat these things?"

"Sure, they're so much healthier for you than fat-soaked hamburgers." Lisa moved to the barbecue table and picked up one of the burgers Willie had just put to-gether. "Here, try this."

Sam stared in disbelief at what looked like an emp-ty bun. "Where's the patty?"

She pointed at a thin dark line separating the two halves of the bun. "Right there."

Sam leaned closer. "*That's it?* I'd need a magnifying glass to see it. No ketchup or mustard?"

Lisa pulled the two halves apart and painted them with Sam's choice of condiments. "There you go," she said and passed it back to him.

He stared down at the insipid burger. His stomach did a warning flip as he eyed the strange concoction. He didn't want to put his pearly whites anywhere near the veggie burger, but if it would improve his rating with the woman watching him, he was willing to try.

"Down the hatch," he offered as he took a tiny bite. The mealy dryness mixed with ketchup and mustard was as unappetizing as anything he'd ever eaten.

"What do you think?" Lisa inquired as she took a bite of her own burger.

What could he say? Say he loved it and stuff it in his pants pocket? "It's all right, I guess. Maybe an acquired taste? Do you always eat this stuff?"

A smile twinkled at the corners of her mouth, making Sam wish he could kiss her full red lips. "Lots of times," she said as she eyed him from behind her burger.

Sam wanted to wrap his arms around her, and drag her off to some quiet spot where they could make love until dawn. Instead, he settled for light banter. "Have you been a member of the nuts-and-berries crowd for long?"

"Most people involved in protecting the environment adhere to some level of vegetarianism or veganism. It's healthier and gentler on the environment."

He eased closer. "You didn't answer my question."

She let out a tiny sigh as she gazed up into his eyes. "I prefer a diet high in vegetables rather than a high in fat." She caught her lower lip in her teeth as she held his gaze, her eyes lighting up.

This amazing redhead standing next to him was driving him crazy. "Well, don't let me interfere in your pursuit of veggie heaven," he said, wrapping the remainder of his burger in a napkin and placing it in his pocket.

"What do you plan to do with that?" She pointed at his pocket.

"Give it to the dogs?"

"They won't like it."

"I think that says it all. If the dogs won't eat it, why should I? Where are those chicken burgers you mentioned?" But he really wasn't hungry for a chicken burger at all.

"Have it your way," Lisa said as she nibbled her way around the edge of hers, watching him with a knowing smile on her face.

Sam couldn't be this close to her much longer without something happening. He sighed in resignation.

"What about a beer?"

She shrugged. "We have ginseng tea, kefir, kombucha, all natural fruit drinks, cranberry cocktail..."

He should have known. Sam smothered his disgust at the drink choices and instead concentrated on the possibility of cranberry juice. The vodka in his uncle's liquor cabinet would go well with it. He'd tiptoe into the house and make his own health drink. Vodka came from grain, didn't it? "I'm going to have a cranberry juice. Can I get anything for you."

She shook her head, the look in her eyes unfathomable.

Sam hesitated. If veggie burgers and ginseng tea were all he had to look forward to this evening, he might as well go for broke. "You were pretty distant with me earlier. Lisa, have I done something?"

"No, not at all." The abrupt tilt of her jaw belied her words.

He touched her arm. "Come on, there's something eating away at you."

She leaned away from him. "Really? Like what?"

"You tell me."

She looked into his face, her lips tight. "I don't know why you're worried about what I think when you have someone like her"—Lisa peeked around him—"willing to look after your every wish."

"Someone like *who*?"

Lisa lifted one eyebrow, and gave him a don't-pretend-with-me smile. "You know who I'm talking about. Samantha Mitchell is on her way over here right this minute. I'm sure you'll not want to miss one moment of her titillating repartee."

"If you don't mind, I'll pick my own women. Samantha's undoubtedly wonderful, but I'm not in the market." *Where did that come from?* He certainly *was* in the market. Always had been.

"You'd better rethink that decision. Samantha's like a heat-seeking missile, and in her eyes, you're the hottest thing to hit town in a while." Lisa peeked around Sam again, and glanced up at him. "If I were you, I'd batten down the hatches. Samantha Mitchell always gets her man. You should know."

Lisa turned away and disappeared among the people milling about the barbecue, leaving Sam to his thoughts. *What had she meant when she said he should know?*

If he were honest, he hadn't liked Samantha since the day she invited him to the last high school dance of the school year when he came to visit his uncle during his senior year... And figuring out the layers of this didn't matter because he'd be out of here soon anyway. Not wanting to seem impolite and with his thoughts circling his conversation with Lisa he offered Samantha a noncommittal smile...

Lisa fumed and fussed as she made her way across the yard to her apartment. All her old feelings of being left out and not being interesting enough to men washed over her, making her walk faster. Anything to get away from what was happening behind her.

All the pep talk from Annie hadn't made a dent in her insecurities where handsome men were concerned—especially Sam. She remembered that summer day when she had bleached her red curls blonde, straightened her hair and set her sights on Sam Jackson. The student council had organized a dance for the end of the school year, and she'd invited Sam, the coolest guy ever to hit Middleborough. She'd spent her entire savings on an outfit that she thought he'd love. Then the humiliating few moments in the locker room at school when she overheard Samantha Mitchell tell one of her friends that she and Sam were interested in each other.

Lisa could still hear her talking about how he'd been invited by someone he hardly knew, but didn't feel he could break the date. She remembered the day before the dance when, embarrassed about putting him in such an awkward situation, she'd called Sam and told him she was too ill to go.

That embarrassing experience had left her wishing she could get over her insecurity where men were concerned. But when someone as pretty and sophisticated as Samantha hooked up with someone like Sam there was no point in Lisa thinking she might have a chance.

It had been that way as long as Lisa could remember. Really attractive men liked Lisa when they wanted a good game of tennis or squash, or a friend to share their women troubles with. But when it came to romance, they looked right past her.

She had put all that behind her, or so she believed until Sam kissed her. After that moment everything had become so intense. She'd begun to believe she had a chance with a totally unsuitable man. Silly woman, she was—and likely doomed to be an old maid, if she didn't smarten up.

She changed direction and headed for the house. Everything at the gathering was under control so she'd just take the dogs for a walk before it got too dark. A walk might cool the strange mix of feelings roiling through her.

Then it came to her. And she knew how she would spend the rest of the evening. She wasn't proud of what she was about to do, but she couldn't seem to stay away from Sam, even if it meant a covert operation. She'd hang out on her counter in front of the kitchen sink as the party wound down.

Meanwhile at the barbeque Sam had successfully fended off Samantha Mitchell, and now he sat wondering why he'd done it. The old Sam would have delighted in the chase, the flirtation, followed by the conquest he knew he could win. Samantha had made her intentions clear, and all he needed to do was follow her lead. Women were naturally drawn to him, and he accepted this gift as his right, without considering what exactly he wanted from it, other than the gratification of knowing he was attractive to women.

Now, he stood watching a bunch of tofu-chewing, ginseng-swilling birders and wished he could be more like them. He shook his head in dismay. *What was happening to him?* Loneliness settled around him like an unwanted draft of cold air.

"Hi there." Ed Chambers slapped Sam's back in a show of camaraderie. "How's it going? Are you enjoying yourself?"

"Yeah," Sam said, wishing he felt more upbeat.

"You've met most of the people here, I guess."

Sam glanced around. He'd met as many of them as he wanted to. "Yes, I've met most of them." Not wanting to be left by himself and his thoughts of a few moments ago, he offered Ed a warm smile. "Quite a group."

"You got it." Ed glanced around, pride showing on his face. "They're a very dedicated group of people, and we have your Uncle Herbert to thank for most of it. When he got involved, his enthusiasm inspired a lot of people to get into all sorts of nature projects. Herbert would even go into the schools and talk to students about nature and our connection to it." Ed looked appraisingly at Sam. "Your uncle was the heart of this community."

"I know that," Sam said, wondering what people would remember him for. "So many people have told me stories about what my uncle did..."

"He will be missed for a long time."

Would Sam ever be missed? Maybe by his flight crew that changed frequently—the only family he had. Suddenly feeling the loss of his uncle like a physical blow he moved off toward the edge of the party, to find a place where he could grapple with the rush of emotions that had taken hold.

After a few minutes several of the people he recognized formed a group not far from him. Thinking about joining them for a few moments he took a couple of steps toward them, stopping suddenly when he realized they were talking about him.

"Willie, have you talked to Sam Jackson? The one that is making all the decisions where the farm is concerned?" a tall, lanky man with glasses said as he stood only a few feet from Sam with a glass of a yellow liquid in his hand.

"There's no point talking to him. He's already made up his mind. He's going to sell Herbert's farm. Lisa said so and I believe her," Willie said.

"So what happens next?" the man with the glasses asked as several in the group leaned in closer.

"I don't know. Lisa is convinced there was a new will. She's been trying to find out from other lawyers in town if they did a new will for Herbert. We've all tried to convince her it's a pointless exercise, but she doesn't believe that Herbert left the property to Sam Jackson."

"Really?" two of the people in the group said in unison.

"Yeah. She's sure Herbert left the property to the Nature Trust with her in charge of managing the farm. I think she's right but she has no proof without the new will. Herbert never made any secret about how much he admired Lisa and appreciated her help. What surprised me the most when she first came to the farm was that

Herbert let her have the apartment. Seemed a little strange at the time… Don't know for sure when Herbert made her the offer to manage the farm, and no one else seems to know anything about it. But you know Lisa, when she sets her mind on something, she can be pretty determined."

Even though he knew he was eavesdropping he couldn't help listening to the conversation. His mind went over what he was hearing. She'd led him to believe she'd accepted what he'd said and had stopped looking for a new will. Willie, someone who knew Lisa well, seemed to think she was still searching and then his remarks about Lisa and the apartment... Well it was obvious there was more going on that he knew nothing about. Had he been a fool? So easily fooled? Had he made himself vulnerable, an easy mark? Was she planning to take advantage of him now that he'd come to trust her? Were they all laughing at him? Watching her play him…?

Lisa had already organized one effective protest against what he was planning to do with the farm. *What other devious behavior might she be involved in or planning?*

From the discussion he overheard, it seemed obvious Lisa O'Neill was working to delay the sale of the property and wangling a position to make some sort of claim against the estate. He didn't know if it were possible, but with everything else she'd done, from kissing him to lying to him, he was no longer certain what was the truth or what she was capable of. She had a key to his uncle's house. Any time he'd asked her directly about her involvement with his uncle, she'd given him a whole lot of attitude but not a direct answer.

In turmoil, he moved quietly away from the group. He didn't want to hear any more about Lisa and her deviousness. It was clear he no longer could trust her.

When he'd come to the farm Lisa was simply someone who was trying to stop him from doing what he'd come to do. As their relationship grew he had come to admire and like her. He had started to trust her when she'd been so passionate about Herbert's wishes, but now he questioned why, whether her passion for the farm had driven her need to deceive him.

Feeling alone and confused he walked away from the party. The truth was he wanted to trust Lisa, believe in her and everything she stood for. He wanted her to believe in him too.

CHAPTER FIFTEEN

For every up, there's a down.

Early the next morning Lisa ran up over the knoll and along the dirt track leading from the back of the farm to the stand of oak trees and the fields beyond. She was in the mood to leap tall buildings, run fifty miles, or, heaven forbid, clean a closet.

The day was perfect and her spirits were high. All because she'd seen Samantha Mitchell leave the party last night long before it ended. Samantha Mitchell was exactly the kind of woman to turn Sam's head: tall, blonde, skinny and sophisticated. And she'd left without Sam Jackson by her side. He had the golden opportunity and had walked away from the former beauty queen.

Lisa shook her head in delight. "There may still be hope." She huffed the words out into the cool air as she pounded along the path leading along the knoll.

Lisa glanced over her shoulder. Even the dogs seemed happier this morning. They ran along behind her, their eyes intent on the path and their tongues hanging out. Soda, the Bassett hound, had opted for the comfort of the back step as he always did when Lisa went for a run. But the other dogs loved the long, loping run that took them through the open fields and out to the back of the property.

She returned her thoughts to the pleasant topic of Samantha's failed conquest. *Had all Lisa's worry been for nothing?* It would seem so. Lisa chuckled. She'd seen Samantha give the old eyelashes a good workout, and for a while it looked like her smile would electrify the cosmos. But from what she could see from her window perch last evening Sam seemed impervious to the woman's charms.

Lisa reined in her smugness as she gave her sweaty curls a flip. It had to be the first time in recorded history that Samantha hadn't landed the man she set her sights on.

Maybe Sam had changed, just the tiniest bit. She'd seen a different look in his eyes, especially in the last few days. And the way he'd been with her over breakfast on the old swing... *Could it be possible that he cared for her? Was it more than just friendship?* He'd certainly kissed her as if it were.

"Come on you guys; let's get a move on," Lisa called out to the dogs as she raced forward, anxious to get back to her apartment and get cleaned up. With Samantha out of the way, Lisa could concentrate on Sam and begin working out some kind of compromise on the sale of the farm. She couldn't wait to spend time with him. Knowing that they would be working so closely made her heart skip in her chest.

Lisa sucked in the early morning air, and admired the red ball of sun as it cleared the horizon, bathing the fields and brook in a pale iridescent light. Early morning was easily the best time of the day with its freshness, its crisp air and the promise of another new day. And today held more promise than most. With Sam willing to work with her, and the feelings she had for him, Lisa began to believe that they might have a chance to drop their old animosities and start anew.

She leaped the brook, nearly falling backward into the stream, but she didn't care. Getting wet couldn't dampen her pleasure, not one little bit. She'd left a coffee cake cooling on the counter and planned to invite Sam to have breakfast on the swing. He loved that old swing. And what better way to get started on their planning than to have a delicious breakfast in the fresh morning air?

As she neared the house, she saw Sam open the back door and walk toward her. Her optimism rose when the saw how his pearl gray shirt draped his body, hinting at the muscled chest beneath. His dark hair glistened in the sunlight.

He had never looked handsomer, more appealing, more gorgeous.

Something shifted inside Lisa, revealing a need for Sam she could no longer deny. Being near Sam was all she wanted out of the day—being near him and being part of his world. Sam may not have been the most likely person for her to love, but her heart had overcome the most important of her objections.

Lisa grinned in greeting as she raced across the lawn with the dogs in hot pursuit, their bark of welcome bouncing off the solid walls of the garage.

"Good morning," Lisa said, waving to him as she drew in a deep breath of early morning air—the sheer pleasure of the day lifting her spirits. "I tapped on your door this morning to see if you wanted to run, but there was no answer. I assumed you were still asleep."

She strode toward him. "Early bird gets the worm, you know." Very aware of her sweat-soaked skin so much in contrast to Sam's scrubbed perfection, she tucked back a strand of hair off her face, and wiped her forehead with the back of her hand. "You would have loved it out there this morning. It's so beautiful, so invigorating."

Sam, his brows drawn together in a stiff frown, stared past her toward the brook. "I have to go into town. There's some business I have to attend to right away." He jangled his car keys, deep in the pockets of his navy pants.

Her early morning happiness clouded over, and in its place was a deep, unsettling feeling that Sam was annoyed. "Oh, I thought you'd like a bite of breakfast before you head out."

"No. I don't have time." He glanced at his watch, and scowled at the dogs. "Would you mind putting the dogs in the house for me?"

Cold dread sandwiched by disappointment formed a lump in her throat. "Certainly." She swallowed to clear the anxious sensation threatening to block her words. "I'd be more than willing to help any way I can."

"That's not necessary. I'll be back in about an hour," he said, his mouth forming a grim line. "Oh, and by the way, I want you to contact the authorities about these dogs. I can't keep them much longer, and I think it's only fair they each have a decent home."

Dismay crackled through Lisa. How dare he even think of doing such a thing to these innocent dogs? "What's going on with you?" she asked, straight up.

"Nothing. Nothing at all. Other than the fact that I have a lot to do in the next few days."

"Right," Lisa said quietly, but she was seething. *What had gotten into him now?* He was behaving in the same cold way he'd been when he'd first come to Harmony Farm. Had something happened, or was he just reverting to his real self?

She whipped an exaggerated salute his way. "Any other orders, chief?"

Sam glared at her, but didn't answer. Not one word of explanation offered for his curt behavior either. Not one word of banter to break a difficult moment.

Lisa searched his face for some hint of warmth. His expression was one of calm detachment, accentuated by a touch of impatience tightening his mouth. "Fine. I'll look after the dogs, and I'll be waiting. Just give me a call when you're ready to talk about—"

"There's been a change of plans." He stepped away from her, his tasseled, charcoal loafers shining in the sunlight as he did so. "I won't be needing your help."

He turned and strode toward the car, his wide shoulders blocking her out as effectively as his words. She watched him walk away, fighting the urge not to race after him.

Where was the warm, flirtatious man who had tried to eat a veggie burger to please her only a few hours ago, and who had passed up Barbie Doll Mitchell? She couldn't let him go without finding our what had gone wrong. Hurrying toward the car, she called out to him.

"Sam, wait, please!"

Sam stopped, but he didn't turn around. "I'm in a hurry. What is it?"

"I was wondering—"

He turned to face her, his cold expression drowning her unspoken words.

She cleared her throat and started again. "You seem upset. I don't understand. Did I do something?"

"What do you think?"

"What do I think? I don't understand what you're talking about. Yesterday, you and I were going to work together to find a buyer for Harmony Farm. I thought you had a good time last evening." Her heart filled with fear as she tried to control the trembling of her limbs by rubbing her sweaty palms down the sides of her running pants. "Today, you can hardly bring yourself to speak to me. You owe me an explanation."

He grabbed the car door and yanked it open. "I don't owe you anything. Nor does my uncle's estate. You have no claim against the estate."

"What are you talking about?" she asked, her face ashen.

"I'm talking about your reasons for trying to delay

the sale until you find a new will."

"What?"

"And your unhealthy interest in what I am doing with the farm. I think that maybe your interest in the farm comes from something you think my uncle owed you rather than your concern for the environment."

"How dare you!"

"Then why did you keep pushing to find a new will when there wasn't one?"

"Because I believed what Herbert told me—and that was early on before we talked about all this."

"Or you believed that a new will would give you control of his estate." His eyes sparked with danger. "I've been open and honest with you from the beginning. You've done everything you could think of to stop me from doing what needs to be done. I've had enough."

The brake lights on Sam's Corvette blinked once at the end of the driveway as he roared onto the road leading into town.

How could he think she'd been having a relationship with Herbert and that she wanted her share of the estate? Where did he get that idea? She'd explained to him... *Or had she?*

She'd been angry with him about his callous behavior toward his uncle, and maybe she'd come across as more than protective, more caring than a regular friend might be.

A few days ago, it wouldn't have mattered that much. Sam was a big-city man with little or no interest in the country life she loved, but for a few precious days she'd fantasized about something more. Much more.

Her dream of perfect happiness with someone to love, a home, and children she would cherish in a way her mother never had, dominated her feelings. The memory of the day she watched in terror and disbelief as her mother loaded her suitcases into the small, red sports car and left for the last time still burned in Lisa's mind. She had clung to the hope that all the unhappiness and insecurity brought on by her mother would disappear when she met the man of her dreams. Her dream was the antidote to the pain she disguised with such determination.

She always believed her dream would come true, and when Sam didn't show much interest in Samantha, she believed her dream had a chance.

Now, Sam's words had brought her dream crashing to the ground in lifeless pieces.

Half-blinded by tears, she made her way up the stairs to the apartment. As much as she cared about Sam, if his impression of her and the way he treated her could change on a dime like it had this morning, a fantasy was probably all that was left of her relationship with him. *Was that what old maids lived on? Fantasies about handsome men they could never have?* And she'd be an old maid soon, if she didn't watch it. Lisa pealed off her sweaty clothes and climbed into the shower.

Spikes of hot water pounded her skin as she tried to figure out why Sam had changed his mind about her. For her own peace of mind, she needed to find out what was going on with him. When she finished she shut off the water and climbed out of the shower. She'd seen him talking to Ed Chambers, and after that he seemed to be just drifting around the groups of people, talking to a few of them, but other than that...nothing.

With her hair dripping tiny rivulets of water all over the counter, Lisa dialed Ed's number. Her fingers shook as she waited for him to answer. *What would she say? How would she phrase her question?*

"Hello." Ed's voice was at once reassuring and authoritative.

Lisa took a deep, cleansing breath. "Hi, Ed. It's me, Lisa. I'm calling to see if you know where Sam is."

There was a long sigh on the other end of the line. "Lisa, I know how much you want to save Harmony Farm, but your efforts may have been in vain. Sam was in town this morning and came to my office. He said he's selling to Morgan Lumber and that he'll be going back to New York on the weekend. He didn't explain any further, but I assume that it had to do with you."

"*With me?* Did he say that?"

"He didn't spell it out in so many words. He did ask me how long you'd been living in the apartment at the farm. I suppose he's getting things ready for the purchaser."

Lisa's heart pounded in her chest, her mouth felt as dry as tissue paper. *What had changed his mind about her?* "I've got to convince Sam to give us more time."

"Lisa, I don't think that will do much good. Although I've found a few new donors, it isn't going to mean we can make a bid. I'm running out of people to approach for the money we need. I think our best hope is to try to convince Sam to put a clause in about the eagle area. That way, we might be able to protect the eagles' nesting places."

"Ed, I can't let this go. We have to find a way to convince Sam that he's making a mistake."

"Lisa, it was pretty hopeless from the beginning. If Herbert Stackhouse had made a provision in his will we could have had a chance, but as it stands, there's little we can do."

"But it seems so unfair..."

"Look, I'll see if I can find Sam. I imagine he's at the real estate office by now. If I can get him to postpone signing the sales agreement, even for a couple of days, it might give us a little wiggle room. You know the one person I didn't approach was Tom Mitchell. He's been out of town."

"You mean Samantha's father?"

"Yeah, he doesn't usually contribute to any of our causes, but anything's worth a try."

The air eased from Lisa's lungs. If Samantha's father would help out... "If only we could make this work."

"Don't get your hopes up," Ed cautioned. "Like I said, it's a last-ditch thing. Tom Mitchell likes bigger, flashier projects than ours, but the least we can do is try."

"Thanks Ed," she murmured, and meant it with all her heart. Ed Chambers had done everything he could to help, unlike her who'd recklessly set up the ill-begotten media disaster, and had let her history with Sam interfere with opportunities for open and candid discussion. "Is there anything else I can do?"

Ed's voice was warm but emphatic. "I suggest you stay well out of Sam's way, or with the mood he's in, he might just evict you."

"He's all ready threatened that," she said.

"Well, he might proceed with it this time."

After saying good-bye to Ed, Lisa started pacing the tiny apartment. *What could she do to stop Sam from selling? Was there anyone who would change his mind?* Willie Anderson had made Sam angry when he acted as group spokesman at the press conference. And Ed was already doing everything he could to help.

If Sam arrived back with the sales agreement all signed, there was nothing left for her to do but apologize and leave. Feelings of loss bubbled up in her throat.

She wanted Sam more than she'd ever thought possible. Despite differences between them, she really cared for him. And his unfair impression of her hurt so much. She admitted she had done a stupid thing in setting up the press conference, but for the best of causes, and she would find a way to make amends to the Trust, whatever the cost. If there were any way of saving Harmony Farm, even if it meant losing Sam, she'd do it.

CHAPTER SIXTEEN

Which red wine goes well with eating crow?

S am geared down and roared up the driveway to Harmony Farm. His visit with the real estate agent had gone extremely well, a fact that helped to ease his exasperation over Lisa.

He parked the car on the curved drive in front of the house and climbed out. From the corner of his eye, he noticed Lisa on the swing surrounded by the four dogs.

For a few minutes he debated what to do about her. He had a long list of things he wanted to get done before he called his supervisor and returned to work earlier than planned. After all, there wasn't any reason for him to stay a moment longer, given what the realtor had told him about the lumber company offer.

But he'd found himself having difficulty focusing on what the realtor had said. Instead his mind kept coming back to Lisa and her behavior. Looking at the situation in a more objective light he found himself wondering if Lisa had changed her attitude toward him because she wanted to build a relationship of the "if you can't have the uncle, get the nephew" kind.

And that idea, whether true or not, cut him to the core. He'd seen it before in a relationship he believed was real, only to discover that it was not a relationship at all. He'd even gone so far as to marry that woman, a disastrous move as it turned out. What started off exciting and romantic had ended up with both he and his wife unable to trust each other.

Maybe he was too suspicious, but he had to get to the truth. He slammed the car door and strode toward her. As he approached she eased off the swing seat and walked toward him. The light caught her hair, creating a bright flame around her face, but he didn't care. Likely it was all part of her plan; show off her physical attributes.

As much as he wanted to confront her, he'd decided to let her do the talking; that way he'd know exactly what tack she was taking. He stopped several feet from her, and stared down into her uncertain eyes.

"Sam, I want to apologize to you. I didn't mean to deceive you." Lisa wrung her hands—a different move than what Sam had expected, but he'd learned Lisa was a lady full of surprises.

"Let's hear it," he said, keeping his expression neutral.

"Sam, when you asked, I should have been completely clear about my relationship with Herbert." She glanced around as if searching for help from someone. "When you came here and said you were selling the farm, I thought you were trying to get out of Herbert's obligation to give the farm to the Nature Trust."

"That's hardly news. And there is no legal obligation." He whipped the words at her, and she cringed.

"And when you alluded to me being Herbert's girlfriend I didn't correct you because it was shocking and so far out of my experience I just didn't know what to say."

"Really? Is this true confessions time, or is total honesty your new policy? A little late, I might add."

Anger flared in her eyes, quickly extinguished by a look of complete remorse. "I got so caught up trying to make sure that you did what your uncle wanted, I behaved badly..."

Sam waited for the crocodile tears. "I'm sure you have more you want to tell me."

Lisa looked away, and Sam could see the long expanse of her creamy throat.

"Sam, I have never had a relationship with your uncle except as his friend."

He gave an exaggerated shrug. "If that's what you want me to believe."

"Can we go and sit in the rose arbor?" she asked, her cheeks red, her eyes dark.

"After you," he said.

He followed her to the arbor and watched in fascination as she eased down onto the old bench. For a few minutes, Sam was tempted to stand up and let her talk up to him. He knew from experience just how intimidating that could be. But she didn't need a prompt to start talking and that was obvious as she swallowed before beginning.

"So, let's hear what you have to say," he muttered as he slid onto the bench beside her. Sam stretched his long legs in front of him and leaned back against the ancient seat.

Lisa looked straight ahead and inhaled deeply. "I loved your uncle."

Well, well, well. He'd been right all along. She had been having an affair with Uncle Herbert. He supposed he couldn't blame his uncle. A woman as attractive and full of life as Lisa would appeal to any man. "It would seem so."

She swung a scathing glance in his direction, and then went back to staring at the cobblestones around the bench. "It wasn't like that. I want you to believe me. Your uncle was a kind and wonderful man who took the place of my father for a while and helped me through my grief."

She rubbed her palms together. "I was devastated

when Dad died. I couldn't find a job and your uncle let me have the apartment."

"Uncle Herbert was a generous man."

"Don't you think I know that? That's why I would have done anything to help him." She gave him a shaky smile, and for half a second, Sam wanted to return it.

"And what would 'anything' include?" Sam tucked his hands into the pocket of his pants and waited.

"Your uncle and I shared one thing: his dream about making Harmony Farm a nature conservancy for future generations to enjoy."

"So when I came along, all you wanted was for me to do what you wanted. To break the terms of the will and pass over the farm."

"I hoped you'd locate a newer will and do what your uncle wanted." She shook her head as she reached down and picked up a wilted rose petal. "I don't know why he didn't change his will to include his plan for the farm, and for a while I had trouble accepting that he hadn't."

"You're telling me!" he blurted out and regretted letting her see that she could get to him.

"You hardly helped with your superior attitude."

"And so you did all these things for the right reasons?"

"If I could go back and undo the damage I've done, I would. I want you to believe that."

She lowered her head, and a mass of red curls curtained her face. "I felt that my relationship with Herbert was none of your business. You'd only be here for a few weeks, and I was still grieving the loss of my dear friend, a man you seemed almost indifferent toward."

"And a man you'd had a very close relationship with, and for whom you'd do anything. What was I supposed to think? Why weren't you honest and why didn't you tell me how you felt?"

Lisa whirled around, hurt and pain spilling from her eyes. "Being honest? How dare you talk like that?" Her eyes brimmed with tears. "You don't remember me at all, do you?"

"What do you mean? Remember you? From where and when?"

"Remember at the memorial service, I asked you if you remembered me and you said you didn't?"

"*Remember you?* Why should I remember you? Where is this coming from Lisa? I'd never met you until I came to the memorial service that day."

"Well, I remember. I remember a date I was supposed to have with Sam Jackson. I'm the girl you were supposed to take to the dance in high school. I'm the one that said I was sick so you could go to the dance with the one you really wanted to date—Samantha Mitchell."

"You had—" He reached for her hair and stopped. "You had blond hair, straight blond hair."

"Yeah, I had dyed my hair blond hoping you'd notice me."

"I did. You were beautiful. You still are."

"Please don't pretend with me. You can't go from anger to awe so easily. It's so phony."

He remembered the day she'd asked him out, and how pleased he had been. "I'm sorry about not recognizing you. But you have to admit you look different than you did back then." He saw the vulnerability in her eyes and realized she had been very hurt, and she was holding him responsible for her pain. And she was the one who broke the date... Still she looked so forlorn.

Wanting to make amends, he said, "But I did want to go to the dance with you. It wasn't until you said you were sick and couldn't go that I went with Samantha. She was beautiful, but that was about all. And you. You didn't speak to me the rest of the summer. I was hurt."

She stared at him.

He shook his head slowly in disbelief. "So you de-cided to get your revenge by deceiving me, holding back the truth about you and my uncle. I hope that's not your way of making a man jealous." Hell, if it was, it worked, Sam thought.

"I figured that if you didn't remember me, you wouldn't care about anything else I did. By not recogniz-ing me you made me feel invisible. You wouldn't listen to my concerns about the farm, you treated me like I was insignificant, not worthy of an intelligent conversation, and your plan to sell was going to make it impossible to keep my promise to Herbert."

"You did all that to teach me a lesson?"

"In the beginning, I did. But I regretted it the mi-nute I realized that you and I might be friends."

"So, you consider us friends?"

The expression on her face was an odd mix of dis-belief mixed with uncertainty. "I'd like to be friends with you."

"And I suppose you think I'm stubborn for not lis-tening to you, not waiting around for you and the Nature Trust to put in an offer on the farm?"

Lisa's gaze was assessing. "Now that you mention it. Yes, you're very stubborn."

"Well, never let it be said that Lisa O'Neill spared anyone's feelings," he replied.

He didn't want to give in to the annoyance her words caused, nor did he want to admit that she might be right. Lisa O'Neill had the ability to make him feel things even when he didn't want to feel.

Lisa O'Neill loved Harmony Farm. She'd done eve-rything she could think of to save it from the lumber company, even at the expense of alienating him. How far would she go for something or someone she loved? How long had it been since he'd loved anything or anyone with the intensity that Lisa did? Had he become a jaded man who's only currency was getting others to do what *he* wanted? Sam didn't like the thoughts he was having any more than he liked watching Lisa so close to tears.

Giving in to his need to comfort her, he touched her arm. "You may have a point. I do tend to see things one way."

The soft smile on her face swept the air from his lungs. "Sam, you have to know I wouldn't intentionally do anything to hurt you—"

"I would never have guessed that, given how you've been behaving." But the idea warmed him.

She touched her lips with her fingers, a movement carrying so much vulnerability that Sam nearly wrapped her in his arms. Yet, he couldn't do that, not with all the unanswered questions between them. "Lisa, I have to settle my uncle's estate and get back to work. Giving the farm to the Nature Trust is out of the question—for financial reasons. There are people out there that deserve to be paid. I think you know that."

"I do," she whispered against her fingers still pressed firmly to her lips. "I promise not to become involved in what you're doing, ever again…unless you ask me."

Her smile, the coaxing look in her eyes, and the way she watched his face for any sign of hope—all these things teamed up to make him want to kiss her and blot out the exasperated words that he'd used in his earlier response to her plea.

She was the most bewitching female he'd ever met, totally focused, yet totally unpredictable in ways that left him struggling to keep his emotional balance. "Lisa O'Neill, what am I going to do with you?"

She gave a deep shivering sigh. "I don't know, but I hope you do it soon. The suspense is killing me."

Laughter spilled from his lips and excitement swirled around him, leaving him feeling happier than he'd felt in his entire life. "You have an answer for everything."

Throwing caution to the wind, he worked his hands into the torrent of curls along her neck and pulled her to him. He brushed his fingers over her ripe, red lips and leaned closer.

It would be so easy to kiss her. So easy. But he cared enough for Lisa that he wouldn't toy with her. He knew when a woman had fallen for him. And that meant it was time to distance himself, to set the record straight.

Lisa was the kind of woman who loved passionately and he wasn't ready for love. He had to remember that whatever happened from here on in would simply be complicating his plans for leaving. He took a deep breath as he searched for a way to ease away from whatever it was that was going on between them.

CHAPTER SEVENTEEN

Love sometimes looks like a road full of potholes.

S am sighed out the words: "One thing I'm not going to do. I'm not going to kiss you, so you can un-pucker your lips and open your eyes. We have business to discuss."

Lisa opened her eyes and stared at him. She had been so sure he was going to kiss her.

"I was just resting my eyes," she fibbed. To think he had the nerve to play fast and loose with her. "You're mistaken," she added. Daintily, but pointedly, she plucked his long fingers from her curly locks.

"Yeah, right," Sam muttered. "Trust me. I know when a woman expects to be kissed, and you, lady, expected me to kiss you."

"Believe whatever fantasy you want. Not every woman lusts after you."

His gaze was electric and aimed at the butterflies dancing a jig in her stomach. "You planned to bring me into the rose garden and entice me by batting your eyes. So, of course, you expected a kiss."

"You are so full of yourself!" Lisa choked out the words, as she struggled to control the wave of longing and disappointment washing through her. Everything about him drew her, while his whole purpose in life seemed designed to drive her crazy and keep her at a distance. "Your ego is exceeded only by your arrogance."

She had wanted him to kiss her breathless. To hear music again. To have him say he loved her as she loved him. She could no longer deny her feelings.

And it appeared Sam was aware of that, and her only hope to deny it was to stop him from reading it in her eyes. She glanced away, and busied her hands with a rose bush, pushing its shiny green leaves over the back of the bench. She planned to continue the discussion on her terms once she gained control of her emotions.

"*Tsk. Tsk.* Let's not argue over whether or not you wanted me to kiss you. It's moot now." He leaned forward and rested his forearms on his thighs. "We have more important things to discuss."

Lisa cocked her head, and stared at the sky, struggling to tame her pulse. "I'm listening."

"We haven't finished our discussion about what you were to Herbert."

"I told you. He was like a father to me." She gave him her best mocking tone, in the hope that he didn't catch on that she was so attracted to him she could hardly speak. What a mess. History was repeating itself right before her eyes. She was the same love struck teenager waiting for the same man to finally notice her. Nothing ever seemed to change in her life.

"I'm not convinced," he said, glancing over at her.

"Well, while we're on the subject of who knows what. Why didn't you remember me? I stood right beside you at the service for heaven's sake."

"I didn't remember you because you looked entirely different. I told you that. Remember your hair was blonde when I knew you that summer. How was I supposed to connect your beautiful red hair with the bleached blonde from years before? And it's been what? Five years?"

Five years and three months, but she'd never admit

to knowing that, given the size of the man's ego. "It was a while ago."

"Look, let's just put it down to an adventure. I accept that I hurt you. I didn't mean to. You deceived me. You didn't mean to."

"I've already told you how sorry I am." She crossed her fingers, pursed her lips, and squinted in his direction. Having him so close to her suddenly made her unequivocally aware that he'd be gone in a few days. She and Harmony Farm would become a distant memory.

It was she who stood to lose everything—the farm, the life she loved, and most important, Sam. Watching his gaze move along her face, she had never been more certain of anything in her life. She loved Sam Jackson, as complicated and impossible as that seemed.

"I'll consider dropping the whole thing, if you'll tell me one thing," he said, his voice a soft caress.

Dreading what would come next, Lisa faked a nonchalant sigh. "If it will make you happy..."

Sam leaned back on the bench, moving his muscle-hardened thigh against hers. "It will make me very happy."

Excitement, like warm silk, flushed her senses. "I'll try. Then, can we let all of this go?"

"It depends on your answer to my question." His teasing tone gave her an unsettling feeling.

"Fire away," she said with as much bravado as she could muster.

"Why does it matter what I think of you?"

Lisa ached to kiss the man sitting next to her, if only to stop questions like that. "It didn't at first."

"And now?"

"I like you. You were kind to the dogs. And I think, if you were able, you would help with Herbert's plan for Harmony Farm—but you can't."

"And you know why," he prodded.

"I do, but it doesn't change how I feel about it. When those big tree-cutting machines come in here and start tearing up the ground and destroying the trees, a whole eco system will be lost. Your uncle wanted to save it, and I failed him."

She heard his sudden intake of breath. *Was he beginning to see what was at stake?*

"Lisa, there is no point in going back over the sale of the farm. I have no choice."

The tone of his voice, his words, his lack of understanding, gathered around her, forcing her to admit that there was no point in hoping for a relationship with him.

She would have settled for him understanding why the farm mattered so much to her. With his dismissal of her concern any thought of continuing with him was over for her. As much as she loved him, he didn't share her beliefs, nor did he seem to care about the pain she was going through.

There was only one issue she wanted to finally put to rest before she accepted defeat. "As for inviting you to the dance, I found you…interesting," she admitted.

"Are we back to that? Why does a silly dance matter so much to you?" Sam scrubbed his face in frustration.

"I pretended to be sick because Samantha was telling everyone that you and she were…" She shrugged to shake off the memory of that moment in the locker room after volleyball practice.

"Telling them what?"

"That if I hadn't asked you, you would have gone with her. That I was an obligation you wished you didn't have. That you and she were starting to date and I was in the way." Her cheeks flaming, she forced her eyes away from his.

"And you thought that I wanted to go with Samantha?"

"Of course. She was the most popular girl in the school," she said, feeling stupid for even bringing up the whole Samantha thing when she knew that a relationship with Sam had no future.

"I was not, and never have been, interested in Samantha. She's beautiful but that's about all. Why did you give up so easily? Why didn't you have a little faith in yourself, in the fact that you're a beautiful, interesting woman?"

She sat perfectly still, taking in his words. "I never imagined that someone like you would want someone like me."

"Someone like you. Someone warm and passionate, funny and bright." His finger lingered on her cheek, making her skin tingle.

She wanted to melt into his arms, stroke his chest, and kiss his impossibly gorgeous lips.

"No one's ever said those words to me before."

"I'm saying them now." His hand moved to cup her chin. "And you *are* beautiful, Lisa."

She yearned to turn her lips to the soft skin of his palm, to forget that Sam would be gone soon, out of her life for good. She fought the impulse to fold into his arms, and let the whole world fall apart around them. It would be so much easier than juggling her attraction to him with what she knew had to be done. "It's nice to know you think so highly of me, but the way things are going, I will soon be out of a job. I may need to change careers."

"Maybe you could become a dog whisperer," he said, his breath hot on her cheek. Her body trembled at his nearness.

Fighting for control she pretended to check a nail. Sam might be out of her life soon, and he might take the chance to save Harmony Farm with him. She had to focus on that, not on the need roiling through her. She peeked at him and was unnerved by the dark, almost wistful look in his eyes. "How about I promise to teach you how to train a dog?"

With quiet grace, he slipped his fingers under her chin, and gave her a long, lazy smile. "I'd like that, as long as you keep your other skills."

"And which ones would you be referring to?" He was barely a nose length away and closing fast.

"These." He pulled her to him and lowered his lips to hers.

Lisa had been prepared for the inevitable—losing Sam. But with his lips about to touch down on hers, she knew she was being given another chance. A chance she wouldn't pass up for the world.

As Lisa waited for Sam's kiss, heat spread upward through her tummy, knocking her heart on its end, and spilling all her pent-up need into her chest. Breathless, she anticipated the feel of him as he pulled her tighter to him, answering her need in the only way possible.

When she had first seen him get out of his car, she knew there was little hope for them. Sam's anger had been hot and visceral, and she had known the most frightening sense of loss when faced with the coldness in his eyes. Now his eyes searched her face, filling the air between them with an intimacy she had no intention of letting slip away.

"Kiss me, please," she whispered as she entwined her hands in the dark curls at the base of his neck.

"And if I do?" Sam whispered back. "What happens then?"

She angled her head closer; his male scent surrounded her, making her spine tingle. "You have to ask?"

He kissed her upper lip, ran his tongue along her cupid's bow, and drove her nearly crazy with need. "We can't go on this way," he said, against her eager lips.

"I know." Oh God, how she knew. The man with his arms wrapped around her meant everything to her. She closed her eyes and drank in the delicious sensation of his lips toying with hers. Wild with desire, Lisa kissed him, hungry for every part of him as she curled her fingers around his neck. "I want you."

He touched her cheek as if he were studying her profile. "And I want you. But, I'll be leaving here soon," he reminded her.

"I know," she murmured against the firm flesh of his chin as her lips made their way down into the male-scented warmth of his neck.

She had to have him, one way, or the other. It was as simple as that. "That's why we have to move fast." She ran her tongue over the soft skin of his throat, across his Adam's apple, and was delighted to hear his sudden intake of breath.

"Lisa, Lisa, Lisa," he sighed as he lifted her chin and gazed into her eyes. "If only things were different, if we had more time."

"How much time do we need?" she pleaded as she reveled in the heat of his gaze. Eager for more of him, she ran her hands up into his hair and toyed with the curl tucked along his forehead. She had all the time in the world.

"More time than I have." His fingers followed the line of her cheek. "If only—" He kissed her hard, making her lips hum with his intensity.

With a quick intake of breath, she pulled him to her and opened her mouth, anxious to take everything he offered. Wanting to feel his body on hers, she pressed closer, feeling the heated pressure of his erection as it probed the soft spaces of her pelvis.

Her heart soared as his tongue sought hers. She answered his every move. The pressure of his hands against her bottom made the blood roar in her ears as he ground his pelvis against hers. Nothing could stop them now. Music flooded her, filled her heart.

Sam lifted his face from hers. "Lisa"—he gasped—"we have to talk."

Lisa's heart yo-yoed around her chest as she stared up into his eyes. His expression was serious, his gaze intense. "I'm listening," she said as a long sigh started in her lungs.

"Let's go inside," he said, releasing her. "I have something to tell you."

She didn't want to talk about anything, but Sam had one arm around her and was moving her toward the house. With Sam's guidance, she made it to the kitchen, so in need of him she was barely aware of her surroundings as she slid onto one of the kitchen chairs.

Somewhere, a clock chimed, but Lisa couldn't have cared less. All she wanted was to hear whatever he had to say, and fall blissfully into his arms.

"Lisa, there's no easy way to say this." Sam worked his hands over the smooth wood of the table, his eyes downcast. "This isn't going to work. I just found out I'll be leaving Harmony Farm sooner than I planned."

CHAPTER EIGHTEEN

When life gives you lemons take it as an omen.

From the look on Lisa's face, she was expecting bad news. The last thing in the world he wanted to do was hurt her, but he wanted her to know what had happened, how his choice had been made for him.

"Leaving? But I thought you had things to do here, estate things..."

He'd seen that look in her eyes before, the longing mingled with anxious appraisal followed by her sudden cool withdrawal from words that hurt her. This time, there was a difference. What he had to tell her would hurt both of them. "I do have things to do, and they're coming together faster than I planned."

Standing with Lisa, feeling a connection he'd never felt before, and having to leave this woman was the last thing he wanted to do—and the only thing he could do.

"Faster than you planned. What does that mean?" Lisa's voice had a tremor in it he hadn't heard before.

As much as Sam wanted to take her in his arms and carry her off upstairs, he knew that would be wrong. The old Sam would have had sex with her to answer his physical needs without giving a thought to the consequences. But that was back when he had no emotional stake in what was happening. "I don't want—" He stopped. *What didn't he want? And why didn't he know?*

He saw the excitement and warmth drain from her

face and he cursed himself. He was responsible for the shattered emotions he saw there. Yet, he knew there was little point in prolonging her pain. "Things have changed, and now I have to make other plans."

He struggled to think of another way to break the news. *Was there any way of telling her that would soften the blow?* The sales contract needing his signature would be here early this afternoon...

With gentle words of endearment on his lips, he reached for her hand. She met his gaze, and the tension of unrelieved desire arced between them like lightning burning through the night sky. She was his for the taking, and he wanted her more than he had ever wanted a woman.

"I need to be fair to you," he said, his voice barely above a whisper. He realized the woman sitting across from him meant more to him than casual sex and half lies. He held her hand gently in his as he searched for the least painful way to tell her what he had to say.

"I've had another offer for the farm, a better one, and they want the farm as soon as possible."

He couldn't look at her, knowing the distress his words would cause. Her complete silence made him feel like a traitor. "My real estate agent says this is a much better offer than Morgan Lumber, and that there is a good chance that the trees with nesting sites can be saved."

He forced himself to look at her while his heart thundered awkwardly in his chest.

She saw the sincerity in his eyes, the caring, and her spirits rose. *Was the offer from the Nature Trust? Had Samantha's father come through with the money they needed?*

If the Nature Trust had made a higher offer, it would mean that she and Sam would be able to pursue their relationship, at least while they closed the deal and made arrangements for the Nature Trust to take over. Anticipation filled all the anxious spaces left empty in the past few weeks, reviving her dreams of a life with the man sitting across from her.

Yet, Sam's intense gaze unnerved her a little. Why didn't he just tell her what was going on? He seemed to expect her to say something, but if the farm was safe, any other problem could be worked out between them. "You said you were leaving earlier than you planned. Why?"

"I never expected this offer to be so generous. I had hoped to have a little money left over from the sale of the farm to cover some of Uncle Herbert's other bills."

"That's good, isn't it?" *How much money had Samantha's father come up with?* He was usually pretty stingy with the local charities. Maybe the new offer wasn't from the Nature Trust...

Yet if the trees were saved from being destroyed, that was important. The Naturalist Club had started making a plan for the farm that included the eagles, the beavers that dammed Willow Brook farther upstream, and of course all the migrating birds looking for food and sanctuary. Feeling suddenly hopeful she said, "Sam, you don't know what this means to me."

Sam reached for her hands, and she offered them eagerly. "Lisa, I want you to know the truth. Cascade Lumber made me a more than generous offer." He glanced at his watch. "I'm expecting to hear from my agent any minute."

Disbelief pin-balled back and forth across her mind; over to Sam and what he'd said, back to the heartbreak tumbling through her. "You mean you've sold out—" She swallowed over a boulder-sized lump in her throat.

"I didn't want it to happen this way." He pulled her hands tighter. "If I could have done anything differently, I would have. I just didn't have a choice—"

To stop the sob pressing against her lips, she wiggled her fingers free of his and covered her mouth with her hands. He mustn't know how much pain she was in. It was too humiliating to believe that she'd once again let her heart be involved, only this time her regret and embarrassment was a lot more serious than involving a date that didn't happen.

To think that over this time she'd come to know Sam in a deeper way and believed that she and Sam were a team working together. She'd convinced herself that he cared for her, all based on some crazy notion about love for Sam, for a man who lived life in the passing lane. Cold defeat filled her, blocking out the room around her, and the man sitting so near.

She wouldn't make a fool of herself trying to fight him anymore. It was pointless. She had lost the battle. There was nothing she could do. Harmony Farm was as good as gone. Forcing tears back, she managed to get up from the table, and walk away from Sam.

CHAPTER NINETEEN

Confession does nothing for the soul.

Something warm and hopeful slipped from Sam as he watched Lisa leave the table and hurry toward the door. An ache he'd never known before, knifed through him. "Lisa, don't go. We need to talk."

The door slammed, leaving his words suspended in the empty room.

He didn't go to the window to watch her. He knew where she was going, and he knew by the set of her shoulders she might as well be headed for Antarctica.

There would be square dancing in hell before Lisa O'Neill would have anything more to do with him. He couldn't say he blamed her for how she felt, but he had hoped they might have a chance to discuss it a little.

Yet, what difference did it really make? With so many differences between them, wasn't he simply kidding himself about a potential relationship? A firebrand like Lisa would never fit in with the smooth-talking elegance of his friends. She had too much life, passion, strength, and far too much capacity for caring...

Yet, his heart churned in his chest at the thought of leaving her. *Why hadn't he seen this before now?* He wanted Lisa—veggie burgers and all—any old way he could have her, and that left him facing a dangerous dilemma.

Lisa had occupied his thoughts during the day, and

clung to his dreams at night. The whole thing couldn't be worse. Lisa wanted a life he couldn't live; a life far removed from the hustle of big city lights. And Lisa was the kind of woman who would shrivel up inside without the open spaces and the warming earth found in a place like this.

She belonged right where she was, and he was about to take it all away from her.

He rose and stared out the window at the open field sloping toward the brook, a lovely shade of green—a water colorist's dream—and he knew he'd die of boredom in a place like this.

He felt tense and vulnerable, and wished he could leave now instead of waiting to sign the papers. He scooped a beer from the fridge and went back to the table. If the real estate agent would hurry up, he'd be out of here, back in his own world, one he understood and appreciated.

He rolled the edges of the sunflower placemat resting under his fingers as he drained the ale. A soft scratching sound at the door had him jumping for joy, until he remembered the canine troop. What would he do with the four of them? He couldn't take four dogs with him, and he'd forgotten to ask Lisa if she'd found homes for any of them. He sighed as he opened the door. "Come in you guys," he muttered to the foursome arranged like hairy stair steps at the back door.

No wagging tails; not one hair moved; not one eye twitched as each dog gave him a mournful stare. "What are you waiting for?"

Scotch hung his head and whimpered as he sidled past Sam. The other three followed, each giving him an accusatory look.

"What's the matter? You'd think you'd lost your best friend."

The four of them arranged themselves in front of

the sliding glass doors, and not one of them offered Sam so much as a sidelong glance.

"So, you blame me, do you?"

No response. Not even a melodramatic moan from Scotch.

"Well, go ahead and blame me. See if I care." *Damn.* He was at it again—alone in the house holding a one-way conversation with four dogs. He'd be a standing joke on the flight deck for months if anyone found out. He had come to Harmony Farm a sane, reasonable man with a plan. Now, he was talking to the animals.

He needed to get away from here, from the farm, the life style, and from Lisa. Nothing worked for him here, and it was time he admitted that it never would. He didn't belong here, never had. Even when his mother was alive, and she brought him here for summer holidays, he was always the city kid trying to make it in the country. As hard as his Uncle Herbert had tried, Sam hadn't learned to enjoy it. Sure, he'd loved the great big draft horses, but even those, from a safe distance.

Lisa was right. He was a confirmed city slicker.

So why postpone the inevitable? He had papers to sign, calls to make, and his supervisor was waiting for him to confirm his arrival time in New York.

A surge of adrenaline flushed through his body at the thought of a warm flight deck, brimming with noise, and the controlled excitement of taking off. Happy with his thoughts for the first time today, he picked up his cell phone and headed upstairs. He had to call the rental place and arrange for the return of the exercise equipment.

In the meantime, he'd pack up his uncle's personal things and take them with him. The contents of the house would be sold at an auction. He hadn't asked the representative from Cascade Lumber what they planned to do with the house...or the apartment.

He shook off a funny ache that threatened his peace of mind as he thought about the house, and his summers spent with his uncle. Herbert had sold his Percheron draft horses to help Sam pay for flying school instead of paying down some of his own debts...

The musty silence of the upstairs hall threatened to smother him. He caught a glimpse of the brass umbrella in the umbrella stand through the half-opened door of Herbert's bedroom. It had belonged to his grandfather, and now it was his if he wanted it. Everything in this house was his if he wanted it...

Dusty antiques and lace doilies were not his thing. He breathed in the cloying, still air and forced his mind back to the present. The past was gone—and with little to recommend it—as far as Sam was concerned. Yet, half-formed old memories swirled through his head, making him edgy. Memories of his mother and his uncle sitting at the kitchen table as they shared a beer and a laugh. The easy way they included him in their circle. Uncle Herbert said he always looked forward to the summers when Sam was around.

He needed a distraction from the guilt bubbling through his mind, something pleasant, like going out to dinner to celebrate. Selling the farm for top dollar was worth celebrating, but who could he celebrate with?

Not Lisa. He ignored the nagging sense of loss nesting in his stomach at the thought of no longer having her in his life. Glancing around the bedroom he'd called home for less than two weeks, Sam considered the possibilities. *What about celebrating with his real estate agent?* It was a win for her too.

He called and got her voicemail. He pulled the phone book from under the night table and searched the yellow pages for a restaurant. Nothing appealed to him. He shrugged. It didn't really matter what he ate, as long as he got out of the house for a while. He'd have the real celebration when he got back to New York.

What could be keeping the real estate agent? She had told him to expect her with the papers any minute.

After leaving Sam at the house Lisa had spent the past few hours working at the Wildlife Refuge, trying to contain her feelings by checking on the injured Merlin falcon they'd rescued a week ago. The distraction had done nothing to help her forget what might have been, and in a few minutes she was headed back to Harmony Farm alone. With the farm being sold, she'd have to find somewhere else to live. The lumber company would use the house and the garage for their own purposes.

Lost in her thoughts, she nearly missed the driveway to Harmony Farm. Braking hard, she headed up the driveway toward the house, checking for Sam's car as she went. She didn't want to see him, at least not right now. So she was surprised at how disappointed she was when she saw his car wasn't in the driveway.

He was probably in town signing his name all over the place, and sealing the fate of this beautiful place. She shook her head in disgust at herself for even thinking of the man. He hadn't wasted very many thoughts on her, or he would have worked harder to find another buyer other than the lumber company. After she left Sam she'd talked to Ed Chambers, and they were still well short of the money they'd need to make a competitive bid.

She glanced around as she hopped out of the pickup. The last rays of sun cut across the open fields in long shafts of golden light. A breeze whispered its way across the flagstone walk circling the statuesque sunflower plants, making them nod farewell to the fading light.

Longing filled her to overflowing when she looked

at the beauty around her. A beauty that was lost on the one person in a position to save it. *Would Sam ever regret what he'd done? Would he ever know a moment of anguish or indecision over the effects of his actions?*

Not likely. What Sam had done today stood in silent testament to the gulf that separated them. She had been wrong about him, so wrong.

Out of habit, she trudged over to the house to get the dogs. She and Herbert had had an unwritten rule between them. Whoever got home first walked the dogs. She opened the door and was greeted by four wagging, thrashing dog bodies, all bent on coming through the door at once. "Easy, guys. One at a time." She closed the door, and started across the field with them, each dog leaping and barking their happiness at seeing her.

With no enthusiasm whatsoever, Lisa managed to make it over the field and along the brook and then headed back toward the house.

She had decided she would keep the dogs. One way or the other, she'd find a way to provide them a home with her. That ruled out an apartment in town. No apartment owner in his right mind would allow her to keep four dogs, but she wasn't going to worry. She'd been pretty desperate the day she'd come back to Middleborough without a job or a place to live, and she'd found Herbert.

If she could do it once, she could do it again.

With that, she walked up the slope to the house. She'd put the dogs in and then check the newspaper for ads. Maybe someone needed a house sitter for a few months...

The dogs rustled around her legs as she opened the door. "Chow time, guys."

Trying to block the idea that this might be the last time she did this simple task in this house, she dug deeper into the bag and put far too much food into each bowl.

She glanced at the overflowing bowls in wry amusement. What difference did it make if the dogs put on a pound or two? "Join the majority," she said, planting the scoop in the bag.

She was about to leave when she heard the sound of crunching gravel. She peeked out the window. *Sam.*

Not wanting to face him, and to hear him brag about his big deal, she rushed to the back door and yanked it open. She walked right into him. "Sorry," she muttered, bracing her hand on the door jam to steady herself before making good her escape.

"Wait a minute." His hand touched hers where it rested, and the contact had her heart leaping in her chest. She stared into his eyes and was sure he saw the proof of her thoughts. Try as she might, the man held her in his grip with the slightest touch. She lowered her gaze, and ordered her heated thoughts to cool down. "I'm in a bit of a hurry," she said to his hand.

"Got a hot date?"

She sighed, gave in and looked at him. "With the bath tub."

"Uncle Herbert's antique tub holds two."

Was he teasing her? No. Teasing meant he cared, and he didn't. "I have things to do."

Sam took her hand. "What a coincidence. So have I. Our tub date can come later. Right now, I need to talk to you, Lisa. I haven't signed the sales agreement for Harmony Farm."

Lisa's gaze focused on his face. "You haven't? Why not?"

He lifted his shoulders, and shoved his hands in the pockets of his pants. "Come in and sit down."

Lisa nearly collapsed in her eagerness. "Does that mean you've changed your mind?"

"No." He settled at the table and fixed his assessing gaze on her. "It means I want a chance to think about it."

Lisa refused to sit until she knew what he was up to. "What do you need to think about?"

"I'm not sure. My real estate agent was very upset that I changed my mind, but after all, it's only money to her."

Was Sam Jackson developing a conscience? "That's true. But what made you reconsider?"

"My gut instinct tells me to take my time. Besides, the lumber people really want this place which means they'll wait."

She slid into the chair across the table from him, letting the captured air in her lungs escape as she marshaled her case.

"I agree with you. Your uncle was practically beating the lumber companies off with a stick, but they never stopped coming back for more. You don't have to worry about their offer, it will always be there."

"And maybe for more money, if I wait." Sam tapped the table. "But that's not what's bothering me."

Hope bloomed in Lisa's heart. "Can I help?"

"You might..." He leaned forward, his gaze studying her as he moved. "Can you meet me here tomorrow morning?"

CHAPTER TWENTY

Sometimes life is simply putting one foot in front of the other.

Sam's sleepy mind didn't seem to be working. He'd come back to the house last evening, deciding that he needed to work on clearing out his uncle's papers. He'd found so many bits of information, things he didn't know about his uncle's life. He went to bed filled with regret that he hadn't stayed in touch. He hadn't been able to get to sleep until daylight began its slow shifting into the room.

He opened one eye to the slit of light angling around the bedroom drapes. The room reeked of…dog breath. Sam put his arm up to ward off the smell and rolled over, only to run smack into a furry body. He opened the other eye and squinted around the room.

Chocolate was zeroing in on his face for another slurp when Sam heard pounding on the door downstairs. Dogs barked, the bed bounced, dog feet thumped down the stairs, leaving Sam alone with his thoughts, such as they were.

There was a sudden thudding sound downstairs and then silence. "Sam, are you awake? You said you wanted to talk to me this morning."

"Yeah." He scratched the back of his head and stretched. "Are you coming up, Lisa? We could start up here." After the look she gave him last night after he shared his news, he knew she'd be all business this morning, but it was fun to tease her.

"Let's try a little coffee and breakfast down here. I always think better on a full stomach."

"I'll be down in a few minutes. After I wash the dog saliva off my face." Minutes later the aroma of perked coffee and something cinnamon met him as he descended the stairs. "What smells so good?"

"Cinnamon toast."

"I'll take it." He poured a cup of coffee and sat down at the table. Lisa's gaze never left his face as he took a couple of pieces of toast.

Sam didn't know where to start. He didn't want to get Lisa's hopes up about there being any change of plans. "Lisa, you know I have no choice but to sell the farm. We've been through this before, and I want to be clear about that."

Her eyebrows tipped up. "Then what is it?"

"I had a little time last evening. I went up to my uncle's room to start packing his personal effects." Loneliness burst over him as he remembered the words written by his Uncle Herbert. "My uncle wrote a letter to my mother. I don't know how it ended up here, but the letter made me think..."

"What about?"

Lisa's earnestness, and the hope in her eyes made Sam feel foolish and guilty at the same time. "You must wonder what I'm doing, telling you this."

"No. I understand that something happened, and you want to tell me about it." Lisa put her coffee cup down and reached across the table to him.

The gesture made him feel appreciated and cared for; both were feelings he wasn't familiar with. Impulsively, he took her hand and played with her fingers. Her hands were warm, rough in spots, and strong. "Let's go upstairs. I want you to see this."

Lisa, Sam and the four dogs trekked up the stairs, and went to Herbert's bedroom. On the duvet was a large family album with a letter resting on its brown leather cover. "I think you should read this, and after that you'll understand why I need to think about what I'm doing."

Lisa glanced at him, her face radiating concern. "Sam, what is it?"

Sam couldn't voice the thoughts his uncle expressed without feeling the kind of pain he couldn't share. "Just read it and tell me what you think."

He watched as she sat cross-legged on the bed, her head bent in concentration, and the four dogs sitting in a line beside the bed. The dogs' attention never wavered as they rested their chins on the edge of the bed and stared intently at her. He had a sudden irrational wish that the dogs loved him as much as they loved Lisa.

Silly notion.

Instead he focused his attention on the window, and the lovely old maple tree standing so straight and strong outside. And the way the cedar hedge seemed to wrap itself around the old herb garden his mother had spent so many hours working in. Funny, he'd never seen something so common as a tree or a shrub with such clarity before.

What would his mother have thought of him standing here taking in the pastoral scene outside the window? She would have wanted him to find a way to keep the farm, of that he was certain. It hurt him to think that he was not going to be able to do it for her, or for Herbert. Or Lisa.

Sam heard it first, the gentle sniffling sound. Then a page turning, and more sniffling. He resisted the urge to climb up on the bed beside her. "Lisa, are you all right?"

"I'm fine." She sniffed and smiled at him.

It was the smile that did it—the sweetness, the vulnerability of it that made his heart lift to meet hers. Cautiously, he moved to the side of the bed, and eased onto the bed beside her.

She didn't seem to notice him, so he edged closer and breathed in the strawberry scent of her hair. He eyed the red curly strands flowing over her cheek like silk.

She turned to him. "Sam, this is lovely. How can you even consider selling this farm knowing how much this place meant to your uncle and your mother?" She bent further over the letter. "It says here that your uncle dreamed that one day you'd come back to Harmony Farm and claim your inheritance, to run the farm in the way nature intended."

"I know what it says."

"But to sell something that's been in your family for three generations, and has so many wonderful memories..."

"Not always for me."

"But your uncle talks about you being here, and learning to fish." She pointed at the page open in her lap. "He says here that you were always pestering him to be allowed to practice with the bow and arrow, to follow the team of draft horses."

It had been a mistake to show her the letter. He should have known that. He couldn't tell her he'd never be able to stay here, to fulfill his uncle's dream. It wasn't in him. It was nobody's fault, and there was no point in discussing it. "I know what it says there. And I know I have to sell the farm."

"Sam, is that really all this farm means to you?"

If she didn't stop watching him in that wrap-you-in-a-blanket-and-cuddle-you way of hers...he couldn't be held responsible for what he might do. "It's just that I'd never given a thought to what this place really meant to my uncle. And when I did think about it, I concentrated on the present and the problems involved in settling his estate."

"And reading this forced you to see things your uncle's way." Lisa moved over a bit, making more room for Sam. "Do you see why I was so sure about your uncle's wishes? He says the things here that I tried to tell you."

"But I wasn't listening. I don't know what to do about this. I don't want to throw it all away. I stayed up late and went through the filing cabinet in the den. Did you know my Uncle Herbert wrote his life story in journals?"

"No I didn't."

Sam pointed to a stack of binders on a table near the window. "It's all there. His memories of Harmony Farm, the plans he'd had for a family, the loss of the woman he loved, even details of the rose arbor and a sketch of it. Can you imagine? He describes what it was like here during the Vietnam War; the struggle to keep the farm going and then his involvement with the environmental movement."

In that instant Lisa had never looked more beautiful.

"Do you ever wonder why you and I didn't hang out together when I came here in the summer?"

She looked at him in surprise. "I wasn't part of the inner circle around Middleborough.".

"I wasn't either." He tweaked a strand of her hair. "But it might have been fun."

"I doubt it. You and I wouldn't have gotten along. My disastrous attempt to invite you out on a date proved that…"

"In your rush to play ill and get out of our date, did you ever consider that maybe I really wanted to go with you? That going with Samantha was not what I wanted?"

"Are you serious?" she asked, her eyes wide with surprise.

The sweetness of her smile sent Sam's heart tripping along his ribs. "I'm serious."

The room stilled. Her eyes grew rounder. "I just assumed that you wanted to go with the beautiful one, the beauty queen."

"You are beautiful in so many more ways. I would have preferred to go with you."

"When did you learn to be so charming?" Lisa touched his cheek, her fingers moving gently as she kissed his mouth, sending his heart into overdrive, his body straining for hers.

"It's in the genes I guess." He held her, snuggled her close and drew her scent into his lungs, into his memory to be stored there when he thought of her over the long months ahead.

The dogs nuzzled his hip. Scotch groaned. Lisa pulled away from him, leaving an empty space he hadn't known existed.

"What are you going to do with all this?" She fanned her trembling fingers over the material scattered around her on the bed.

"If I could afford to, I'd keep the farm, for at least a while longer."

"You would?"

Saying the words eased the tightness in his chest. How long had he wanted to say those words? Had he been holding back, unwilling to admit what the place meant to him, or the effect his memories of a long ago time were having on his plan to leave? Or was it the intimacy of the moment, with Lisa so caring and open to him?

"Yes, I would. I'd find a way to have the world remember my uncle—"

Her arms were around him, her lips pressed to his before he could draw a breath. "I can't believe I'm hearing this. I can't." She held his face snugly in her hands. "Sam Jackson, there's hope for you yet."

"Do you want to come up to the attic with me while I do some more cleaning out of Herbert's things? There might be something you'd like to have," he said, struggling to maintain his equilibrium. A part of him wanted to take her to bed. The other part wanted to simply get to know her better, to be part of her life, to spend time with her.

"I would love that. I was only in the attic to find a few things for the apartment. I would like to be with you when you go through your uncle's things."

CHAPTER TWENTY-ONE

Believe in the power of memories.

Two hours later Lisa sneezed and two large dust bunnies whirled off the old trunk and onto the painted brown floor of the attic. She'd been working in Herbert's attic, boxing up all kinds of books, papers and assorted folders that overflowed with everything from old receipts to old photos.

"Bless you," Sam said, glancing in her direction, his arms full of old books. They'd been working together in the attic of the farmhouse, trying to sort what would go into piles of purpose: a throw-out pile, a pile for Goodwill, an auction pile, a flea market pile, and a pile to offer friends of Herbert's. Sam had found some things he wanted for himself, and he'd given Lisa several old photo albums of the farm she'd asked for.

Lisa rubbed her nose to relieve another tickle building there. She'd expected the time to be long and boring, but being with Sam and hearing his comments on various items they'd found had made the whole thing easier and more interesting. Lisa suddenly became aware of how different Sam had been in the past few hours. She stretched her legs out in front of her as she settled deeper into the rickety wooden chair with the rush seat.

Thinking of him no longer provoked feelings of distrust the way it once had. A sense of camaraderie had grown between them, a feeling of togetherness that grew with each idea shared, each discovery made in the old attic. She watched as Sam lifted an old hat stand out of his way—the sudden movement creating a halo of dust around him.

"Your uncle didn't throw anything out, did he?"

"I guess not. Uncle Herbert must have taken great delight in saving things he thought would have pleasant memories for him," Sam said, surveying a tall stack of old *National Geographic* magazines.

"And great foraging for the antique dealers," Lisa said as she fixed her gaze on an old trunk standing to one side under the eaves.

"I'm going to take these boxes downstairs and..." He glanced across the space at her, his smile warming her tummy. "I guess since my car is so small, maybe we can load the boxes that are going to Goodwill into your truck."

"Absolutely. Do you want me to come with you?" she asked, wishing suddenly that he'd invite her to go to Goodwill with him.

"Why don't you keep working, maybe get to that trunk over there..." He nodded toward the old trunk along one wall.

"Okay..." She sighed, not keen on tackling the trunk.

Lisa watched Sam make his way to the stairs, stepping carefully around all the boxes they'd filled and piles they'd made. The single bulb that dangled from the wooden ceiling beams shone on him, exposing his muscled shoulders and a thin film of perspiration glistening on his brow. "Maybe we should quit for a while," she said.

Sam eased onto the first step and stopped, his load of boxes teetering precariously in his arms, his chin pressed against the top box to steady them. "Good idea. But before we do, I'm going to take these down and bring up some more empty boxes."

She glanced ruefully at the trunk. "Well, I'll open this while you're gone."

Three wide bands of dried leather stretched over the curved top of the trunk. A scarred brass lock hung off the front. Lisa pried the lid open to the squealing tune of old hinges that hadn't been oiled in a long time.

The trunk was filled to the top with old boxes, a vase, pieces of cloth and an assortment of knitting needles and yarn. Reaching into the trunk she lifted out a box made of some sort of heavy cardboard or wood. Curious, she balanced it on the corner of the open trunk and tugged at the lid, but the rusty edges resisted her efforts.

Determined to see the contents, she sat down on the floor and pulled the box onto her lap. One hefty yank and the lid pulled free, spilling a bundle of letters tied with rose-colored ribbon and a muslin-wrapped parcel over Lisa's legs. Gently, she lifted the heavy muslin, releasing its folded edges. The scent of lavender floated around her.

Lisa stared in amazement as an ivory satin wedding gown shimmering in the half-light of the attic. Silence filled the dusty space as she continued to stare at the most beautiful wedding dress she'd ever seen. Cradling the dress in her arms, Lisa rose to her feet. Carefully, she lifted the silken shoulders of the dress, allowing the satin to drape down over her in undulating waves. Tiny pearls, like dew drops, were sewn into the bodice. She held the dress up against her, letting the satin flow around her.

Who could have worn this beautiful creation?

Tentatively, she raised the folds of the skirt and swayed to the rustling sound of the sensuous fabric. *What would it be like to wear something so lovely; to walk down the aisle in a billowing skirt like this?* She stared down at the satin fullness and a thought struck her.

Gently Lisa draped the dress over the edge of the trunk. Would anyone care if she slid it on for a few minutes? She peeked around, half expecting the owner of the creation to appear wagging her finger.

If she was going to do this, it had to be done before Sam returned. She pealed off her jeans and sweater. With infinite care, Lisa eased the dress over her head, and down over her body. She soaked in the sensation of the dress hugging her form as if every stitch had been sewn for her. She slipped her arms into the sleeves and eased the dress up over her shoulders. The smooth silk felt like rose petals caressing her body; the sleeves warmed her skin where the antique lace points touched her hands.

Lisa closed her eyes and imagined coming down the aisle, moving to the sounds of an organ playing the wedding march. A handsome man waiting for her at the end of the aisle...

A creak on the stairs startled her.

"Lisa, what are you doing?"

She whirled around. "I... I couldn't resist."

Sam dumped the load of boxes he carried as he came toward her. "Where did you find that?"

"I... In the trunk—" She pointed self-consciously.

"You look beautiful, ravishing," he said, his voice husky, his eyes shining with pleasure.

Lisa touched the rounded neckline of the dress, her fingers fluttering over the beaded edge. No one had ever told her she looked ravishing before. "I hope you don't mind me trying it on."

"Why should I? It looks as if it were made for you." Sam glanced around. "But what's a beautiful wedding dress doing in Uncle Herbert's attic? I wonder where it came from..."

"And whose dress it could be." Lisa touched the shimmering folds of the skirt as she waited for Sam to say something to match the look of adoration in his eyes. No man had ever looked at her that way before, but of course no man had seen her parading half naked in a wedding dress before either.

"What's this?" Sam knelt down and picked up the letters tied with the pink ribbon.

Lisa sighed as she stared at the top of Sam's head. She should have known that any further flowery compliments were not in her forecast. Shoving aside her disappointment, she said, "I don't know. They were in the box with the dress."

"Should we?" He glanced up at her with an expectant, conspiratorial look on his face.

"What if they're love letters?"

"They might be, given that they were with the dress."

Lisa chewed her lip. "What if they're letters for the woman your uncle built the rose arbor for? Likely your aunt Elsa."

Sam gave her one of those knee-shaking smiles of his. "Then we solve the mystery."

"I don't know if we should pry into his life this way."

Sam sniffed the packet. "Joy Perfume, a very uncommon and expensive woman's fragrance."

Lisa noted Sam's quick identification of the expensive perfume for future reference. The man was obviously very much at home with the finer things in life. "So, Sherlock, you think they're letters to your uncle?"

"From the mystery woman." Sam loosened the ribbon and opened the first letter.

"May 10, 1988," he read aloud.

"The year the arbor was built."

"It's post marked Middleborough." Sam scanned the letter for a moment.

"Dear Cassandra..."

"That's my mother's name," Lisa said.

"This will be my last letter to you as a single man. I know you've loved your time in Washington, and I did too. If it hadn't been for Washington we probably would never have met, and now it's time for us to start our new life together. You made me the happiest man alive when you agreed to move here and marry me.

We belong here in Middleborough. We'll raise a family here. You'll love it. I promise. I've told you all about it here, the lovely scenery, the people, and the happiness we'll share. You know I'm not much for writing letters, but I wanted you to know how happy you've made me, and I am blessed.

This time next week, you'll be here with me. I love you so very much, but you already know that.

The rose arbor is finished. The stone wall is being put in place this weekend. Your dress arrived today. Don't worry. I didn't look at it. It's upstairs in the closet waiting for you.

Sam turned the page and a letter postmarked Washington slipped from the crease of the letter. Lisa grabbed it.

"This one is dated June 15th, 1988...." She began to read aloud.

Dear Herbert,

This will be short because I'm a coward and I can't bear to hurt you. I want you to know that I wanted to marry you and move to your farm, but when it came time to leave Washington I couldn't do it. At first I made excuses about leaving and postponed the wedding on you. But I can't go on lying to you any longer. I've met a wonderful man. He's a member of the Marines, stationed in Washington. His name is Timothy O'Neill—

"My father was a marine." A searing pain settled vice-like around Lisa's ribs, blocking the air from her lungs. "He was posted to the marine base at Quantico and decided to move there to be handy to his job in 1988."

"Are you sure? This could simply be a crazy coincidence."

In total disbelief, Lisa read the rest of the note. Her mother went on to explain that she would live her life in the big city with her new love.

"I'm sure it's my mother. She left your uncle for the big city life, just like she left Dad and me."

"It can't be."

"But it is. It fits. Dad worked in Washington DC. Mum met him there. After Mom left my father told me that she'd been engaged to a man who lived on a farm in Virginia. I never guessed…"

"She sent this letter to my Uncle Herbert."

"What an awful thing to do. How could she?" Lisa choked on the words. "When they moved here for Dad's work in the marines Mom was angry for so long. I know from the fights my parents had that she loved her life in Washington."

"And being moved here to the place where my uncle Herbert lived must have really upset her."

"I wonder if your Aunt Elsa knew anything about their relationship?"

"I doubt it. They were very much in love with each other. Aunt Elsa wasn't the kind to go digging around in the past. She was the only person I've ever known who was completely content with her life. They didn't socialize very much."

"And Mom wouldn't have wanted any reminders of the past. She was too busy trying to figure out a way to escape her life here with Dad." Lisa touched the beads along the neckline of the dress trying to imagine the pain her mother had caused so many people, not just her dad and her. "When she left Dad and me it was for a man who lived in Chicago." Lisa touched the gossamer folds of the skirt billowing below the fitted bodice—a dress meant for her mother, a woman who tossed men aside like used tissue.

"My uncle must have loved your mother very much to keep her wedding dress."

"Maybe that explains why Herbert was so kind to me when I came back after college. He saw how much I looked like his Cassandra."

"And he wanted to help the young woman who had just buried her father not so many months before."

A shudder started in Lisa's stomach and made its way through her body. "I can't believe this. Why didn't Herbert say something? How painful it must have been for him. Why would he put himself through such a difficult thing?"

"Maybe for him, it wasn't painful. Or maybe he needed to be kind to you for his own reasons. We'll never know, will we?" Sam's arms went around her, shielding her from the outside world, and all Lisa wanted was to hide out in his arms.

Her mother had never been happy in Middleborough. All her life she'd wanted the excitement of a big city, even if it meant losing her only daughter. And to learn that she'd hurt Herbert… "If only I had known my mother had caused Herbert so much pain, we might have been able to talk about it. Things would have been different between us if I'd known."

"You would have been able to share some of your pain, you mean?"

"Yes. Dad wouldn't talk about it after Mum left. Aunt Clara was kind, but I couldn't confide in her."

"Maybe talking to Uncle Herbert would have helped."

"At least I could have apologized for my mother's cruelty."

"Uncle Herbert would have talked to you if he'd

wanted to. He never was afraid of speaking his mind, or sharing his thoughts. Knowing him, he probably enjoyed having you here," he said, his voice tender.

"For a long time I thought her leaving had something to do with me. But maybe she was escaping Dad and Herbert. It must have been really awkward living so near to each other. I wonder if either of them told anyone else?"

"Does it matter now?"

"No, I guess not."

"And doesn't it help just a little to know you're not responsible for what happened, that it was something inside your mother that made her do what she did repeatedly?"

She nodded against his chest. Sam held her close.

"I'm sorry. I didn't mean to turn you into my weeping pillow." She sniffed.

"We all need a shoulder at one time or another." He held her at arm's length and gave her a look that sent her blood thundering through her.

"It's sweet of you to be so kind." Lisa wanted to slip back into the warm circle of his arms.

His eyebrows lifted slightly. "Maybe someone else will wear the dress some day."

"I doubt that your uncle would want that."

Sam didn't move, but something changed in his eyes and suddenly Lisa felt foolish standing there in someone else's wedding dress. "I'd better take this off."

"Yeah, maybe you should." He took his hands away and Lisa yearned to pull him to her, to bury her face in his shoulder again, to be comforted. She eased the dress off her shoulders, her body trembling. Sam was so close and she was so nearly naked. Lisa bunched the fabric in her hands. "Turn around will you?"

His glance tracked over her bare shoulders. The air sizzled between them. "Sure," he said before turning away.

Lisa hadn't felt this mixed up in a long time. It had to be the closed in space of the attic and the forced intimacy created by the revelation about the intended owner of the wedding dress. She lifted the dress up and in one fluid movement pulled it over her head. "Hold this, please."

She passed the cloud of silk to him then pulled on her clothes and smoothed her hair. Gently she replaced the dress in its box and closed the trunk. A sense of sadness flooded her, a sadness filled with longing and compassion for Herbert and her father and what they'd endured at the hands of her mother. She swiped the tears from her cheeks. "You can turn around now," she said, standing straight to face him.

He touched her cheek with a gentleness that made her ache with need for him. "We're both tired. Let's quit for now."

Her eyes followed the curve of his jaw, his high cheekbones and dark hair. He was the most gorgeous man she'd ever known. How could she want someone so much, knowing he could never be hers? Why couldn't she just walk away with her head held high and a sophisticated pout out on her lips, like one of Sam's other women would do in this situation?

Sam's hands were shaking as he slipped them into the pockets of his gray chinos. A war raged in him; on one side was the promise he'd made to himself to keep Lisa at arm's length until he escaped back to the city; on the other was his overwhelming need to make love to the woman standing so close he could feel her body heat.

While the battle continued, he forced his thoughts back to reality. "Before we go, I want you to realize that this doesn't have anything to do with you. Your mother made her choice back then, and Uncle Herbert paid the price. Your mother probably regretted her decision at some point."

"We'll never know."

"Sometimes people can't bring themselves to admit their mistakes, no matter how much they'd like to."

"I don't think that was the case with my mother. She's had lots of time to make amends and hasn't."

"Maybe it's not always that simple," Sam said and saw the puzzled look in Lisa's eyes.

"Meaning?"

Sam had a senseless and overpowering need to confide in Lisa. "I understand where you're coming from, but I was talking about how hard it is to make amends sometimes."

"In what way? How hard can it be?"

Not knowing what to do to bridge the gap between them, he let the words flow. "I was remembering another wedding."

"Whose?"

"Mine."

There was a sharp intake of breath. "You're married?"

"Was. For all of a month," he said, trying to keep the self-pity out of his voice. *Why had he brought that up? What difference did it make now?*

"You were married." Lisa's words sounded like a chant.

"For better or worse, mostly worse as it turned out."

"I had no idea."

"No one did. We decided to get married while we were on vacation in the Bahamas. I called Mum and she came to the wedding, completely shocked but trying desperately to be supportive of her only son. It was a wild and wonderful time that should never have happened, except that I mistook lust on a tropical island for love."

Lisa's eyes were warm pools of concern. "It must have been very difficult for you."

Dismissive words were on his lips, words he'd used with everyone when they asked about his feelings. But he wanted Lisa to know the truth. His truth. "It was really hard. I believed she loved me. We'd dated for a few weeks. She seemed perfect for me in so many ways. I loved her, or thought... Hell, what did I know about love?"

Slowly he became aware that he was telling someone he planned to leave behind, how he felt about what he'd done. *What had he done?* He pulled back from her. His feelings had been brought on by the moment, a moment that would pass quickly into obscurity.

Let it go. Don't start something you can't finish.

He looked into her eyes and that was his undoing. Warmth and something deeper cascaded from her, rocking his soul. "Like I said, we've all done things we've regretted."

"Like my mother?" she asked.

"Sure. Your mother had to have regretted leaving you."

"I spent a lot of time hoping she'd feel guilty enough to come back. A lot of wasted time, as it turned out."

"She never did?"

"Well, if you count Dad's funeral." Lisa shrugged and looked away, but not before Sam saw the raw hurt in her eyes.

"Nothing before that?"

"She wrote long letters of explanation, but explaining something that painful just didn't cut it."

"You wanted some sign—"

"You're damned right!" Lisa jammed her hands into

her jean pockets and glared at the ceiling.

"Maybe it's not too late." Sam touched her shoulders and felt the tightness of the muscles there.

Her face flushed, her eyes bright with tears, she asked, "How can you be so forgiving? She hurt your uncle the same way she hurt my father."

Wanting physical contact, he touched her cheek and saw her lips quiver. "Because I've been there. I've made the kind of mistake that changed another person's life, deeply and permanently. A mistake that can't be revoked."

"So what are you saying?"

"I'm saying it would help you if you forgave your mother. Forgiving her will make room in your life for other...relationships. Room for you to grow away from the hurt."

〜

Sam's words echoed through Lisa, leaving her fraught with indecision. She realized that the hurt she felt had permeated every part of her life. It made her afraid that once again she'd be left behind. Whatever she felt for him, or whatever he felt for her would be trapped inside her fear of being abandoned. But the idea of changing, of forgiving her mother seemed so difficult.

"Thank you for that," she told him.

"No thanks needed, but think about what I said."

What he just said to her would stay with her the rest of her life. "Yeah, I will. I don't want to spend any more time being angry with my mother."

"And ruin the chance for good things coming into your life." He grinned and tweaked her nose.

Lisa suddenly felt lighter, somehow relieved... Freed. Just saying the words had released some of her pent-up anger. Anger that had become so much a part of her she hadn't noticed it. She was a long way from over-coming those feelings, but Sam had shown her a different perspective. And because she admired his ability to face his mistakes, she'd work on her feelings where her mother was concerned. "Thank you."

"For what?"

"For being so kind and caring," she said.

He gave her that old familiar smile that sent her heart thudding against her ribs. "You're welcome," he whispered, his lips light as feathers on her neck.

What she wouldn't give to have him make love to her right this minute. But making love was too danger-ous; too difficult to forget once he'd left her and made his way back to New York. "Come on," she urged as she eased away from him.

"You're dragging me away to some lust-filled island paradise?" he teased.

"Not exactly. I'm dragging you downstairs so we can get comfortable and talk."

"I'm all for that," he said, pulling her back toward him and lifting her into his arms.

"Put me down, you brute!" she kidded as her body melded with his.

"I think the cavemen had the right idea. Behave woman, or I'll sling you over my shoulder fireman style."

He went down the narrow attic steps carrying her in his arms, and Lisa couldn't remember a time in her life when she'd been happier. He settled her on the sofa in the den, and sat down next to her.

"Cavemen must have had better stamina," he huffed.

"Or lighter women," she added, remembering her unwanted ten pounds.

He touched her nose. "Don't you change one thing about you. Understand? I like you just the way you are."

There was another reason for loving Sam Jackson—as if she needed any more. "And to think we would never have met if it hadn't been for Herbert," she said.

"Yeah... When I think how I felt when I arrived here the day of the memorial service—"

"With your determination to breeze out of here at the first opportunity. And I was so ticked at you and your superior attitude, and the notion that your uncle and I had been having an affair. For that alone, you deserved to be deceived." The man sitting next to her was so different from the man she'd met that day at the funeral.

"I was pretty determined, for sure."

"You're telling me!" A quiet happiness settled around her, easing the physical need brewing in her. For now it seemed so right that they take pleasure in simply being together, whatever happened in the future.

Sam smiled as he pulled her into the crook of his arm. "My uncle was a man who took his beliefs seriously."

"Herbert taught me a lot, and it wasn't just about birds and conservation," Lisa agreed.

"Uncle Herbert was an all round good Samaritan. He always had someone staying in the apartment over the garage. Someone who needed his help in some way, but I think you were the first woman."

"Yeah, and you put your own spin on that," she said, ruefully.

"I did, and I apologize. I know you were not having an affair with my uncle."

His disarming smile strengthened the growing trust she felt for him. Before, she would never have associated the word trust with Sam. Having discovered this new feeling, she wanted to hold on to it, nourish it in the hopes that it would lead to more. "I had no idea he was sick. I didn't see that there was anything wrong with him. Just like my dad. I didn't see anything wrong..."

Sam took her hand in his and massaged her palm. "Tell me about your dad."

"I knew my father wasn't feeling well when I came home at Christmas. I should have done something then. Instead, I went back to my life, leaving him alone when he needed me most. He'd been there for me ever since Mom left, and when I could have helped him, I—"

"Lisa, don't beat yourself up this way." His arms formed a safe haven as he pulled her closer. She rested her head against the solidness of his chest. The heavy thudding of his heart was the most comforting sound Lisa could remember.

CHAPTER TWENTY-TWO

Where's an off ramp when you need one?

S am rocked her gently back and forth in his arms, offering her soothing words to ease her pain. Holding her seemed so natural. He no longer wondered what had changed, or how he'd gotten to this place. It was enough that they were together as friends.

Underneath the gentleness of the moment was the knowledge that he had to get back to work. Being with Lisa was wonderful, great and more than he could ever hope for, but reality ruled his life. A life that took place far from the whispering pines of Harmony Farm and the warmth and caring of the beautiful woman beside him.

As much as he liked to entertain the thought that they might have something special going on between them, Sam knew that his life would never fit into the narrow confines of a farming community. And Lisa would never be happy in his high-rise apartment with the hothouse raised potted plants in the foyer and the cacophony of city traffic just outside the door.

Although he'd come to understand what the farm had meant to his mother and Uncle Herbert, he wasn't prepared to stay in a place just because of the memories. Memories didn't make a life—enriched it maybe, but it wasn't what he was looking for.

But they could enjoy each other's company without getting too serious. "It's been a long day. Why don't I cook supper?" he asked.

She sat up, a startled expression on her face as she stared at her watch. "Supper? It's only four o'clock."

"We've done about all we can do for today. I'm tired, and so are you. We could go into town and get some groceries, buy a bottle of wine, and toast the fact that you and I are officially getting along. What do you say?"

"Lead on, dear man." She gave him the kind of smile that would usually have him pulling the clothes off another woman. Yet... A part of him wanted more than just sex with Lisa. The same part of him that knew the risks involved: Anything more than friendship would only cause both of them a lot of heartache and pain.

Later, after they'd gone into town for groceries, Sam leaned against the counter and watched as Lisa opened the cupboards, set the narrow table, lit candles, and moved about the kitchen with a natural ease. Sam liked the way her casual cotton pants displayed her well-muscled body, the way her coppery silk top set fire to her hair.

Lisa didn't dress the way other women in his life did: no expensive earrings, cloying perfume, or wreaths of gold bracelets jangling on her arms. He liked the way Lisa could pass in front of a mirror without checking her appearance, something every other woman he'd ever known did without fail. Lisa dressed to be comfortable and Sam liked her all the more for it.

Funny how he'd always taken the sophisticated facade of the women in his life as the norm, the natural order of things. But now he realized that was about as natural as plastic cups and TV dinners.

One of the things he liked most about Lisa was the

absence of a perfume cloud that surrounded so many of the women he knew. He'd always suspected they drank the damned stuff just to have it ooze from their pores. Lisa smelled of strawberries and fresh air.

He met her inquiring glance as she came around the corner of the table, clutching a handful of bright yellow napkins. "You look like you're waiting for something," she said, her expression softening.

"Just enjoying the moment." The thought struck him. He had been waiting all his life for someone—a special person who matched his need to live life just as they found it. He thought he'd found the special someone when he took his marriage vows. It had seemed so right at the time. He'd believed his new wife was "the one" because she'd been different and exciting.

The wrong kind of different, as it turned out. He could still feel the sting of failure over what had happened. His friends had welcomed him back into the singles set with glee, happy that he'd seen the light. He blamed himself because he knew, deep down, he had never bothered to learn more than the superficial things about the woman he'd married...and divorced.

He put aside his painful thoughts. Lisa stood near him, a hesitant expression on her face, and a steely glint to her eyes. It could only mean trouble.

"What's going on with you?" she asked.

"Nothing. Can I help you with that?" he asked.

"You did the cooking. I'm setting the table." She gave him a half smile as she turned her attention to the yellow napkins.

Lisa had been very quiet since they'd returned from town with their wine and groceries, but he'd put it down to being fatigued after their time in the attic. It had been a shock to learn about her mother and his uncle. He was pretty sure that when Lisa was ready she would talk about it. And if she decided to confide in him, anything at all, he'd listen.

Beef Burgundy bubbled in the oven, filling the air with the tangy scent of red wine and spices. A comfortable silence settled between them, hiding the fact that he'd be gone in a day, and things would never be this way between them again.

He'd miss her; there was no doubt in his mind. He'd miss the warmth, the challenge, the open way she treated him. He'd missed women before and gotten over them. But with Lisa all this was different, maybe too different for him. There was this niggling sense that if he had sex with her, everything would change, including his control over the situation, the relationship.

He drew in a deep breath of air. There would be no sex with Lisa. Sex was too risky. There was only tonight as a dinner between friends.

"Sam, I want you to know I really appreciate you letting me have the photo albums of Harmony Farm and the pictures of your uncle."

There was an odd stiffness in her tone. He glanced at her and saw the sincerity in her eyes, and something else; he wasn't sure what. "You're welcome."

"I... Those pictures mean a lot to me," she said.

"And what about finding out that your mother and my uncle loved each other?"

She shot him a look as she busied herself with the roses she'd picked from the garden. "It hurt me to learn that my mother had hurt my friend that way." She placed the last brilliantly pink rose in the silver vase, touching a shimmering petal as she did so. "Thank heavens my mother didn't get a chance to do any more damage to your uncle—"

Needing to shield her from her negative thoughts, he moved around the table to where she stood.

"I'll never leave my children. If I ever have any," Lisa said, her fingers gently touching the rose petals.

"You will have children. You'll meet the right man and have a great life, a house filled with laughter, love and a menagerie of kids and animals."

"Thanks for the vote of support." She gave him a wry smile, and for one long moment, he wished they could stay close, see each other often...

"Just think, if things had been different, you and I might have shared the same family reunion," he said, to cover the sudden sense of loss filling his chest.

"Like kissing cousins?" Her teasing glance made him feel ridiculously happy.

"Yeah, kissing cousins..." His gaze inched down to her mouth, to the perfect cupid's bow that framed her upper lip. Easing closer, Sam reached for her hand. Her luminous gray-green eyes were fixed on his face, drawing him into her space.

He nudged a shiny auburn curl from her forehead with his fingertips and saw the awareness in her eyes. He let his fingers play along her cheek, coming to rest on her lips.

A soft gasp escaped her as she straightened, bringing her perfectly shaped body closer to his chest. "I don't know if this is such a good idea."

"Kissing you?"

Her eyes did a chameleon-like shift to green. "I mean, we have our dinner just about ready, and I know that look in your eyes."

"And you don't like it?"

"That's not the point. I'm hungry."

Forgetting his earlier resolve, he pulled her into his arms. "So am I." He growled the words into the hollow space at the base of her throat. Heat flooded him as he caressed her jaw and moved to her waiting mouth.

She ran her fingers into the hair at his neck, her lips answering his kiss in a way that had his body taut and ready. "Sam." There was sadness in her tone when she whispered his name.

"What is it?" He kissed the frown line between her eyes.

She pulled away from him as her eyes focused on his shirtfront. "Let's stick to our plan."

"I didn't know we had one."

She pressed her lips together in a snug line. "We agreed to have dinner. And that's all."

He stared at the ceiling, willing his body to relax. His attraction to Lisa was in danger of getting out of control. And like Lisa, he didn't want complications in his life, especially now that he was close to getting back to New York where he belonged. "You're right."

He reached around her and picked up the open bottle of wine.

Lisa's heart fell like a stone. She had wanted him to make mad passionate love to her right there on the kitchen floor, minus the dogs of course. Silly idea in light of the fact that he'd said nothing about how he felt or even whether he'd miss her. Yet the sense that somehow they'd missed the best part, the chance to be more than friends, filtered through her, filling her with sadness.

All her life she'd avoided men who swept her off her feet. They were dangerous, painful people. Now, she stood toe to toe with a man who did it all for her, from the music to the deepest need she'd ever known. Lisa stepped out of his reach and carefully smoothed a placemat. "You're right. We have the whole evening to enjoy ourselves."

Sam poured wine into the heavy goblets and passed one to her. "To you, Lisa."

Raising her glass and keeping her eyes on a spot over his shoulder, she murmured, "To both of us."

The red wine slid down her throat, trailing warmth to every part of her body and spreading a sense of well being through her. She slipped into the chair offered by Sam and tucked her feet close to the rungs for support. "Nice wine."

"One of my favorites." Pulling out the chair across from her, Sam sat down and placed his glass close to hers.

As the wine washed over her edginess, she let her gaze move to Sam's face. Only days ago she'd wanted to run him out of town, and now she would give anything to have him stay. She couldn't let herself think about what it would be like when he was gone. She had no claim on Sam, and she never would.

It was also daunting to think that when the lumber company took over Harmony Farm, she'd have to leave the apartment. In a few months, no one would remember Herbert, his dream or the natural beauty that once was...

Letting her thoughts drift, she took another sip of her wine and closed her eyes. She wanted to hold this moment forever, soaking up the pleasant sensation of Sam's cologne, his closeness, a closeness she craved.

As foolish as she knew it to be, she let herself imagine what it would be like if they were living in this house, just the two of them. She listened to the familiar sounds of the kitchen: the clock ticking, the water from the tap plunking into the stainless steel sink, the growling lament of Scotch as he slept.

"You're not going to nod off on me, are you?" he asked.

She opened her eyes and found Sam staring at her, his quizzical smile making her feel giddy. "No, of course not."

"Taking a cat nap?"

She laughed at his words. Yet she couldn't tell him what she'd been thinking. If he knew that she had been mooning over him like a lovesick teenager, he'd make light of it, embarrassing her. "*Hmm*. Taking stock is more like it."

"Well, I have something I wanted to tell you, and I think now is as good a time as any."

Lisa's heart lurched in her chest. *Had he changed his mind about leaving?* "I hope it's good news."

"It is. I've decided not to sign the sales agreement until my next days off."

Lisa couldn't decide whether she should kiss him or whack him for letting her live on the edge like that. She studied his expression for any sign that he might be kidding. If there was a chance, however small, that the farm could be saved... "Why are you doing this? What's changed? And why didn't you tell me this earlier?"

"Because I just thought of it now. I want the Nature Trust to have—"

Lisa moved the two glasses of wine, reached across the table and pulled Sam to her, opening her lips and drawing him to the warmth of her mouth.

Sam's hands slid over her shoulders, as his tongue mingled with hers.

"Lisa," he sighed against her lips.

She heard the gentleness in his voice, felt the caress of his finger tips, and dreamed, however hopelessly, that he was beginning to feel a little of what she felt. Desperate to claim their last hours as her own, she linked her arms around his neck. "Please, don't say anything."

"Only that I want you..." He held her shoulders in his grasp as he came around the narrow table. He took her face in his hands and rubbed his fingers along her mouth, sending sparks of heat over her skin.

Her gaze met his as her heart soared. "Are we ruining a good thing?" she asked.

"We're making it better. Come here," he said as he took her hands and pulled her back into his chair.

She slid into his arms, her lips seeking his as her heart pounded. She wanted to say something smart, funny. Something that one of his other women would say at a time like this. But she wasn't one of his women, and she never would be. And for now, she let that go.

Raw, reason-defying need tore through her as she sank into his embrace. She'd had enough of pretending she didn't want him. Her fingers worked their way into the cotton fabric of his shirt, unfastening the buttons.

"Lisa," Sam whispered against her lips as his hands slid under her shirt and began their slow caress of her heated skin, "I need you." He pulled her silk shirt free as his fingers continued to weave over her taut skin. The heated challenge of his dark eyes held her captive. "I'm tired of fighting this."

"Oh…" she whispered, pressing her body into his.

In one easy movement, he freed her trembling body from the confines of her clothing, leaving her exposed.

She gasped in pleasure.

"We're taking this upstairs," he whispered into her throat as he pulled her to her feet.

CHAPTER TWENTY-THREE

Just when everything seemed so perfect...

Hours later Lisa refused to open her eyes, believing that if she did she'd end the dream. Sam's muscled body curled around hers, cradling her, his breath warm and sweet against her cheek. The lace curtain rustled as the breeze fluttered against its folds. Somewhere off in the distance Lisa heard the throaty whirr of a tractor, and just a few feet away she heard Scotch's muted sighs.

Lisa hadn't planned to stay the night. But all that changed when Sam carried her upstairs and made love to her. She sighed and snuggled closer to him, her heart full to overflowing at the memory. Sam had been warm and passionate and everything she needed... She touched Sam's hand where it rested so contentedly on her tummy. There was such a feeling of intimacy in the way his fingers made contact with her skin, as if he was meant to sleep with her every night...

What would a future be like with Sam beside her, wrapped around her every night as he was now?

Heaven: It would be heaven. She edged closer, feeling every point of contact, every curve of his muscled chest against her back. They may only have a couple of days before he left, but she would make every minute count.

The sound of heavy breathing close to her nose

snapped her from her reverie. She opened her eyes to see Scotch's nose edging toward hers. She reached out a hand and rubbed the dog's muzzle, hoping to postpone the inevitable lolling tongue.

The furry foursome wanted to go out. If she moved carefully, she might be able to slip out of bed without waking Sam. She'd take the dogs out and let him sleep a little longer. Carefully, she slid one leg toward the side of the bed.

Sam stirred, his hand moving up her body, coming to rest on the curve of her breast. She muffled the sound of her sudden intake of breath. Sex with Sam held more appeal than walking the dogs, but four impatient dogs would be a ribald audience unless they were locked in the bathroom. Their howling chorus from the toilet would probably put an end to any amorous moment.

She continued to ease away from the delicious comfort of Sam's body.

Scotch, his brown eyes watching with anticipation, moved toward the door where the other three stood on full alert. "I'm coming," she whispered.

"Not without me," Sam said as he pulled her back into bed and wrapped his arms snugly around her, "and not before we finish what we started last night."

Lisa turned in his arms, her heart beating a tattoo in her chest as she met his gaze.

"What's a girl to do? I'm wanted on both sides of the bed. The boys are waiting for me to take them for a walk."

"And I have something waiting for you as well." His erection nuzzled her hip as he pulled her onto her side and angled her closer.

Lisa moaned and arched her body toward his, the heat rising deep in her abdomen, her body tightening with expectation.

"I'm so glad you slept in the nude," he said.

The bleating mechanical sound of a cell phone punctured the air.

"Let it ring," she whispered against his throat.

He sighed in resignation. Rolling away from her, Sam glanced at his watch on the table as he picked up his phone. "It's my lawyer in New York."

Lisa listened to his half of the conversation as she played with the black curls of hair matting Sam's chest, and watched his face.

Surprise, followed by excitement flashed across his features as he talked. Whatever was going on had made Sam very pleased.

"Al, you know I want it. We need it. I'll be there as soon as I can." Sam's voice was eager as he spoke to the person on the other end of the call.

Lisa waited with a sinking feeling in her stomach.

Sam clicked the phone closed. "I can't believe it."

"Believe what?"

"My company has just been offered the contract we've been waiting for. I had bid on the contract months ago, and just about given up on getting it. I guess I'll have to be more patient in the future. With this new freight contract, my company will be financially secure."

Lisa was too surprised to make much sense of it all. "That's nice."

"Nice. It's a lot more than nice. I'll be able to cover my loans and think about expanding my company. It's the chance I've been waiting for. You don't know how much I've wanted my company to succeed. Ever since I qualified as a pilot, I've waited and planned for the day that I would have an air freight company with the potential for success that I have now." He kissed her, his mouth demanding, searching hers.

Warning bells clanged in Lisa's head and she pulled away from him. "I'm so pleased for you," she said.

"Thanks. I'll have to finish up here before I go. I

don't know when I'll be able to get back. If by any chance you and Ed find the money to match the offer, I'd be willing to wait a couple of weeks before signing the agreement. If you do find the money, call me. In the meantime I'll let my real estate agent know I'll be back in touch with her later."

Lisa felt a terrible pain in her chest as if her heart were being pulled from her. "Are you serious?"

Sam wrapped his arms around her. "Uncle Herbert had debts that I have to pay, which meant that I had to clear off as much of his debt as possible, which meant selling to the highest bidder. I didn't have money to even pay any of my uncle's outstanding credit cards. With some of the financial pressures in my life easing a little, I will be able to give you and your friends a chance to come up with the money."

If Lisa could save Harmony Farm from the logging company, that would fulfill her promise to Herbert. But she would lose Sam back to his old life without a chance to know how he felt about her. Funny how something that seemed so simple before could be so devastating now.

She glanced at Sam's face. His eyes were filled with excitement, his smile confident and open. She wanted to tell him she loved him, to have him hold her close and say the words back to her. She wanted to tell him he couldn't leave her.

If he did, she'd die of loneliness.

She couldn't tell him anything remotely close to what she felt. He was leaving for good. He wouldn't be back to Harmony Farm. "I wish the Trust could find the money, but it not likely," she said, feeling lost and alone all over again.

"It's the best I can do. Even with my business prospects improving I can't pay off his mortgage."

Suddenly feeling naked and exposed she snugged

the sheet around her body.

"I wish I could do better," he whispered as he touched her lips, and cuddled her closer.

Lisa's heart wasn't in it. She could hide her feelings of loss at his leaving, but she couldn't bear to have him make love to her knowing for certain that he never planned to return. It would feel too much like sealing a deal.

She would find a way to survive his leaving. She'd had lots of practice with people leaving her. She just couldn't have sex with him again. "You don't want to be late getting back to New York," she said, as she kissed him lightly on the lips, as though kissing him meant nothing.

Yet knowing it meant everything.

CHAPTER TWENTY-FOUR

Happiness needs to be cultivated like roses.

Something was very wrong. The loving woman of a few moments ago had become a cool, distant person. *Where was the fight? The passion? Wasn't she going to argue with him?*

"Are you all right with this?"

"Why shouldn't I be?"

Sam sat up and leaned back against the antique wooden headboard. "Come here," he said, reaching for her.

Lisa shifted to her side of the bed, her face hidden from him by a veil of curls. "I think I'd better take the dogs out for their morning walk."

"Don't change the subject, Lisa."

"I'm not. I heard you when you said you have to get back to New York as soon as possible. That you have a great new opportunity waiting for you."

"One I've wanted for a long time."

"Congratulations. So, what's your problem? You have what you want."

"And what about you?"

She shook her head and hunched her shoulders. "Don't worry about me. I'll manage. I always do."

The excitement over his news had evaporated, leaving him feeling empty. "I know this is a little sudden."

"No. You've gone back and forth about leaving so many times my head's spinning, is all. And you deserve good results for all your hard work. You say you've waited a long time for this opportunity," she countered.

Sam was certain he heard a sniffing sound coming from behind Lisa's curtain of hair, but he wouldn't mention it and chance embarrassing her. Really, he wasn't the least bit sad about leaving Harmony Farm, and there was no point in pretending. "Yes, I've waited for a long time and it's everything I've ever wanted, but I feel I'm letting you down somehow."

"Why? Because you changed plans again and have to leave earlier than you expected yesterday?" She reached for her clothes scattered on the floor.

"Yes...partly."

She dressed with amazing speed, never once looking in his direction.

"Lisa, I hope you and the Nature Trust can raise the money to match the lumber company." Or even a little less if it meant he could make Lisa happy.

"That's sweet of you, I'm sure." She tucked her shirt into her pants and strode to the door. "And Sam, thanks for the chance you're giving us. We'll find a way to raise our bid. Count on it."

Without looking back, she went out the door with the four dogs chasing along behind her. Sam listened to the sounds of the dogs: their barking and half growls of excitement as their nails clicked and clacked over the wooden floors and to the closing of the back door, and for the first time in Sam's life he felt completely alone.

Lisa stumbled along the path leading to Willow Brook, her hair sticking to the tears washing her cheeks. She wanted to be angry with him, to say so much more than she said. But she couldn't. Her heart was breaking, her mind reeling at his words—all so sudden, so unexpected after the night they'd spent together.

How could he feel so little while she felt so much? She stopped. Who did she think she was kidding? Hadn't he made it painfully clear that he didn't want a permanent relationship? And who could blame him when he loved his single life and after the disastrous marriage he'd had?

The dogs spotted a rabbit and were off in a howl and a rush, leaving Lisa alone with her thoughts. She stood on the knoll where less than two weeks ago she'd stood and surveyed Sam Jackson with suspicion. She had known he was dangerous back then. She should have stayed clear of him and let him do as he pleased. He had done what he wanted to do anyway, and she had little or nothing to show for her efforts, except the pain of loving someone who didn't love her in return.

She scuffed the crumbled earth as she watched the dogs gamboling over the open field. At least she hadn't made a total fool of herself by confessing her love to him. Her pride was intact and that had to be worth something.

There was only one thing she could do if she didn't want to end up making a bigger fool of herself: She'd stay away from Sam until she knew he had left for New York. She'd load the dogs into her pickup and go out the line road to the back of the property and bury herself in work. She hadn't checked on the eagles in a day or two. She shoved her hair behind her ears and started back toward the house, determination dogging her every step.

Later as the darkness gathered around Lisa she sat in the rose arbor, her mood somber. She had stayed away from the farm all day until she was certain Sam had left, but it hadn't been easy. She had invented a dozen reasons why she should go back to the house, all of them totally transparent to anybody with half a brain.

She'd wanted to see Sam one last time. But seeing Sam would only reinforce her feelings of loss. He had his high-flying life and said he was happy going back to it, while she had an empty sensation in her soul that nothing could fill.

If he cared for her even a tenth as much as she cared for him, he wouldn't have been able to leave so easily. She would have recognized a struggle in his eyes, a moment of indecision. But there hadn't been anything like that. That realization carried more pain than even she could admit to. Her desire and overactive hormones had gotten in the way of her seeing what was right in front of her: There had been no chance of a relationship with Sam from the very beginning.

She stared at the pattern of light and dark created by the setting sun across the narrow space. The patterns merged with her tears. If only he'd revealed that he cared even a little for her. Lisa knew he trusted her and liked her, but that was a long way from love.

She shifted on the rustic bench as she peered out over the darkening fields. She loved this place like no other. She'd get over the pain of knowing that her mother had caused such grief for Herbert by doing everything she could to find more money to save it.

The garden suddenly reminded her of her Grandmother O'Neill, a "renaissance woman," as her Aunt Clara used to say. Educated in Europe, she'd returned to her roots to marry her childhood sweetheart, Calum O'Neill. She'd lived a full and productive life except for the disappointment of having only two children.

How she wished her grandmother were with her today. She'd know exactly how to handle a man like Sam.

Why was she thinking this way? This wasn't like her at all. The last couple of days had clearly fogged her reasoning. Sam might be gone, but she couldn't let the farm go without a fight.

Lisa scrambled out of the seat and began to pace. Any activity was better than sitting around moping over the loss of someone who hadn't been hers to begin with. She had to find a way to turn this situation around. If she didn't, she'd have no one to blame but herself. And she was through blaming herself.

There had to be someone the Nature Trust hadn't approached, someone who might be convinced to help...

She'd go into town tomorrow and talk to Ed Chambers. Between them they should be able to think of someone they hadn't canvassed. Or they might be able to get the bank to finance the rest, if they could prove they had the money for half the asking price even.

But first she'd have to put the dogs in the house. Lisa forced herself toward the back door, her heart set on ignoring anything she saw that reminded her of Sam. She opened the door and peeked in. The dogs raced ahead of her to their bowls. As she turned, she spotted an envelope resting on the corner of the counter. It bore her name in big bold print.

It had to be from Sam. Her heart pounding, she picked it up and tore it open.

Dear Lisa,

I waited for you to return, and I'm sorry I couldn't wait any longer. I wanted you to know how much I appreciated getting to know you and spending time with you.

I know we had our differences, but I hope you won't think ill of me when I say it's better this way. I know you'll do your best to meet Cascade Lumber's offer and I wish you all the luck in the world.

Pat the dogs for me.

Sam

Tears welled up in her eyes, blurring her vision. *What did he mean by it being better this way? Had she been so obvious about her feelings that he knew she loved him, and he wanted to escape?* Lisa swallowed against the pain rising through her. *Sam couldn't be that cold, could he?*

No. Sam might not love her, but they'd agreed they were friends, and he wouldn't do anything intentionally to hurt her.

Sam had just been nice to her; it was as simple as that. And nice didn't have to have anything to do with love.

CHAPTER TWENTY-FIVE

Sometimes you have to leave in order to come back.

The past two weeks had been the longest of Sam's life. He couldn't pinpoint what was different. He'd had two runs to Tokyo and loved every minute of those. At least that part of his life hadn't changed. He'd finalized the deal that would put his air-freight company on solid financial footing, something he'd dreamed of happening. Yet, something was definitely different...odd...unsettled. A restlessness he'd never known dogged his every step. He felt out of sync, somehow. As if he didn't fit in his old life, and that was totally ridiculous.

He'd taken the shuttle from the airport to downtown Manhattan thinking that what he needed was a night out. Maria Bennett was having one of her parties and Sam looked forward to the evening and the chance to get back with his friends.

He had been out of touch with them and his life for weeks. That had to be the reason he was feeling so weird.

On top of that he'd let thoughts of Lisa meddle with his mind. She hadn't come back to the house the day he'd left and that still bugged the hell out of him. He had wanted to say good-bye, not just leave her a note.

Her disappearing act had left him no choice. She hadn't called or contacted him since he'd left. He had really wanted to be friends with her after their night together. Most women wanted to stay in touch, at least in the first few weeks.

It bothered him that Lisa hadn't let him know what was going on with the Trust's hoped-for proposal to purchase the farm. The Nature Trust hadn't contacted him with an offer, meaning that he'd have no choice but to contact his real estate person and have her fax the sales agreement to him for his signature. With the deal made he'd be through with Harmony Farm. No more difficult women, no more dogs, no more reminders of a life that wasn't his.

He should be happy, and yet he didn't feel happy. Satisfied maybe, in one way, but not happy...

He strolled through Central Park, aware of the admiring glances of women he passed. Yet, a stranger's admiration didn't lift his spirits in the way it usually did. Maybe he was coming down with something...

Ahead of him a short, older gentleman sauntered along toward him while a large black dog followed on a leash. Sam gave the dog a cursory glance. The beast looked a lot like Scotch: same floppy ears, same coloring, same loping gait.

If the canines back at the farm followed their usual routine, they'd be cross-piled and sound asleep at this time of the day. A sudden pang of longing shot through Sam. He pushed it away. Missing a bunch of mutts made about as much sense as missing an itch.

The dog sprinkled a low shrub while the man stared myopically at Sam. "I see you admiring my Andy," he said, his face crinkling into a smile.

Sam watched as the dog scratched the ground, tossing a fine spray of dirt out behind him. "He's a big dog," Sam said as the dog moved toward him.

"He's an old Gordon Setter. My wife doesn't like Andy, but I enjoy being outside with him. We have a great time, don't we old fella?"

Remembering how much the foursome at the farm enjoyed a solid round of patting, Sam reached out to touch the dog's head. Andy nudged Sam's leg as he pushed his muzzle into the palm of Sam's hand. The silky smoothness of the dog's face reminded Sam of Scotch and the gang in spite of his best efforts to keep his thoughts on his plans for the evening.

The older gentleman reached for Andy. "Oh my gosh! I'm so sorry. Don't let him rub against you. He'll shed all over your dress pants." The man looked worried as he pulled on Andy's leash. But the dog had other ideas and pulled closer to Sam.

"It's okay. I'm used to it."

"Do you have a dog?"

"No. I know one like yours, though."

"You do? Gordon Setters are very rare, especially in a city. They're highland dogs, bred to hunt. Can I ask where you got yours?"

"He's not really mine. He belonged to my uncle—" Sam stopped himself. He didn't want to share anything with this man. For some unfathomable reason he couldn't talk about his uncle or Scotch.

"You lost your dog, didn't you?"

"Lost him?" The question confused Sam.

"Yeah, he died, didn't he?"

Somehow the thought of Scotch dying depressed Sam. God knew why. After all, he wasn't really good with dogs. Sam stared into Andy's liquid brown eyes, and could have sworn the dog understood... "No. He didn't die. He's back on the farm."

"A farm." The old man sighed and sank onto the nearby bench. "I had a farm one time. Up in Maine. Pamela and I worked on it all our lives. Until she died, that is."

"I'm sorry to hear that," Sam said, and was surprised to know how much he meant the words.

"I am too. Andy here's all I got left. After Pamela died, I married a woman who spent her summers in Maine... Thought I could handle being in New York the rest of the year..."

Sam saw tears glistening in the man's eyes and looked away, embarrassed by the raw feelings of loss surging through him, taking his breath.

The weight of sadness settled around Sam. Why did he feel he'd lost something? He had his life back the way he wanted it. And missing a farm was stupid. Sam wanted to move on, but Andy still had his face buried in his hand while the older gentleman sat looking up at him as if he'd lost his best friend.

"You enjoyed your farm?" Sam asked.

The older man rubbed his cheek with the back of his hand. "Oh yes. I never tired of the open land, the trees. I even had a brook with an old gristmill, once used for grinding wheat. Didn't work anymore—the gristmill, I mean. But the old stone walls were as sound as the day they were built. Have you ever lived on a farm?"

"Yes. Yes, I have."

"Recently?"

"As a matter of fact, yes."

"Are you going back?"

An anvil-sized weight shifted in Sam's chest. "Probably not."

Clutching the dog's leash tighter, the older man shook his head back and forth slowly. "Then, I guess we're both in the same boat."

"Oh, no. You don't understand," Sam said, meeting the older man's gaze.

"Oh, but I do understand. I see it in your eyes. And a man's eyes don't lie."

They met one another's gaze for a few moments, and then the older man stood up. "Have a nice day," he said.

Shoring up her courage with a few short, sharp breaths, Lisa pushed open the door of the bank and strode over to the secretary guarding Mr. Mitchell's inner sanctum. Lisa had this feeling that what she was about to do was an exercise in frustration and futility, but she'd try anything to save Harmony Farm and honor the memory of Herbert Stackhouse.

After finding out what her mother had done to Herbert, Lisa was even more determined to succeed in her plan to have the Nature Trust purchase the farm.

"Good afternoon," the secretary said in a starched voice, tucking an imaginary stray strand of hair into the knot at the back of her head.

"Good afternoon. I'm here to see Mr. Mitchell."

Muriel Hanson's gaze moved over Lisa, resulting in just the slightest sneer forming on her heavily lined lips. "You're Miss O'Neill."

And you know it. I've been in here a half a dozen times about my university loan. "I am."

"Go right in," she said, her back, steel-rod straight.

Lisa walked past her without looking back. She didn't need such impersonal treatment from a witch like Muriel when she was trying her best to gather her courage for the ordeal ahead.

If only she believed that Tom Mitchell would listen. She cleared her throat and tried not to think about what lay ahead as he greeted her. "Mr. Mitchell, I'll come straight to the point. I'm here to see if you might be interested in making a donation to the Nature Trust."

"Sit down, young lady," he said as if he hadn't heard a word.

As Lisa made her way to the chair, she glanced

around the room and saw a gold-framed photo of Samantha, looking every inch a Barbie Doll in a black skin-tight dress and pearl earrings. Lisa bit back the envy coming to a gentle simmer inside her. Samantha's father would do anything for his little girl, and Lisa was desperate enough to use any approach necessary.

"Now, what can I do for you?" Tom Mitchell's tone was all business.

"I am here on behalf of Harmony Farm."

"Oh yes, the farm that belongs to Sam Jackson." Tom Mitchell rubbed his chin.

How did he know? Had someone already talked to him?

"Yes. The Nature Trust would like to buy it and keep it as a nature—"

"There's a lot of money owing on the property. You'd have to cover the mortgage on it."

"I know..." The hard look in Tom's eyes was disheartening. *What was she doing here alone on such an important mission?* At the very least, Ed Chambers should have come with her. He'd have a better chance of making the case with a banker. She was sure Ed didn't owe the bank any money *he* couldn't pay.

Tom Mitchell leaned back in his chair, making it squeal in protest. "I'm considering a donation, but I want to talk to Sam Jackson first. He and I have some mutual business to discuss. Do you know when he'll be back?"

Lisa gulped in surprise. "No, I don't know for certain. He had to leave sooner than he'd planned, but I'm sure he'll be in touch. I'd be happy to tell him you're looking for him."

"Do that. In the meantime, I'll think about the whole project."

"You will?"

"Yes, I will." His gaze roamed over her, making her feel like a poorly wrapped pot roast. He brought his heavy-lidded glance to meet hers again. "I'll think about it."

He picked up the phone the split second it rang, letting Lisa know by the preoccupied expression on his face that their meeting was over.

The lilting melody pouring from Kenny G's saxophone filled the huge loft room with its towering windows and its black and white decor. Every object in the room held an angled beauty, not unlike some of the women Sam recognized. All glitz and hard edges, not a gentle curve in sight.

A ripple of anticipation raced through him as he eyed the elegant mix of well-heeled men, and well-toned women. A tall brunette, with the kind of backless dress that made a man want to run his fingers down her spine, moved slightly to let him close to the bar. She gave him a quick, clinical once over, and he knew by the smile of appreciation in her eyes that she liked what she saw.

He ordered his vodka straight, returning her smile with one of his own. The night was going to turn out just fine. He could feel it through his entire body. No point in rushing things, he thought idly as he checked the room for the hostess.

Maria was one hell of an attractive woman, and her parties were designed with people like herself in mind. She spared no expense, as was evidenced by the delectable choices on the buffet table over in the corner of the room, and the magnums of champagne cooling on the counter at the back of the bar.

Something equally delectable was standing next to the buffet table: a voluptuous redhead, her eyes wide in amusement, her hand resting lightly on her companion's arm. Sam was about to go back to scanning the room when the redhead caught his glance and smiled, an open invitation in her eyes. When the man she was standing with reached for something on the buffet table, the red-head gave Sam a questioning shrug of her shoulders, a signal Sam knew only too well.

Sam smiled back, his interest rising as she held his gaze.

Her tongue moved, slowing along the inner edges of her pouty lips.

He knew they were probably surgically enhanced as was most of her body, but he didn't care. She was showing a keen interest in him and he planned to return the compliment in full measure.

He'd missed the game, every slinking, suggestive innuendo in the dance of mutual attraction. Tonight he'd make up for all the time he'd wasted playing dog master, and general plan spoiler at Harmony Farm. An image of Lisa flashed across his mind but he ignored it as he honed in on the redhead. He smoothed the silk of his shirt against his body as he watched her play out her game of tantalizing him while she chatted with the man next to her.

"Well, hello there." Maria Bennett let her fingers linger on Sam's arm as she gazed a little too rapturously into his face. "It's been a while."

Amused by Maria and interested in the redhead, Sam wrapped his arm around his hostess and gave her an enthusiastic hug. "Yeah, too long." He kissed both her cheeks.

"You really did miss me," she said with just the ti-niest hint of surprise in her deep blue eyes.

"More than you'll ever know," Sam said, holding Maria a little longer than was necessary. It wasn't as if he wanted anything from her. To the contrary, they'd had their day, and she'd offered something more permanent. An offer he'd politely refused.

"Well, what a pleasant surprise," Maria nearly purred as she tongued Sam's ear.

Had he been away that long? Or was Maria desperate? They'd said their farewells months ago, and both moved on to other people. "Great party," Sam said.

She slid closer, her hands working up his silk-clad chest. "Glad you like it. But I've always known what you like, haven't I, Sam?"

Sam was about to say something entirely uncomplimentary to get her to take her hands off him when a man appeared at her side.

"Oh, Sam, let me introduce you to Harry, my...my companion," Maria purred.

Sam glanced at Maria's flavor-of-the-month boyfriend, a man with shoulders that blocked the light and hands like bricks. Sam gave the usual pleasantries and made his mind up to escape to the other side of the room and the waiting redhead.

"Sam has his eye on the redhead over there." Maria gave a short, sharp laugh as she pointed.

Seeing his chance to make a getaway, Sam grinned. "If you'll excuse me..." He nodded at both of them and scooted out of range of Maria's overpowering perfume that was marketed as unisex, but was "no sex" as far as Sam was concerned.

"Tell you what. I'll introduce you"—Maria nodded in the direction of the redhead as she grabbed his arm— "if you'll promise to come to brunch on Sunday."

"Brunch on Sunday." Sam watched the redhead pat her companion's arm affectionately as she hitched the micro-thin strap of her black bag over her bare shoulder, and gave her skin-tight black spandex skirt just the slightest tug.

Sunday was a long way off. And if the redhead brayed like a donkey when she spoke, Sam could make his escape by rejoining Maria and big paws. If things went the way he hoped, he'd be in bed with the redhead before the night was out.

"Brunch on Sunday sounds fantastic."

Sam had been the target of all the redhead's moves in the past few minutes and he loved it. Aggressive women who knew what they wanted turned him on. He waited for the casual tightening in his loins, the good old "call to action" as his father liked to refer to it.

"Can I bring a guest to brunch?" he said to Maria. He kept his eyes on the redhead as she rounded the last group of people separating them.

"You have to be introduced to her before you can bring her to brunch," Maria said with a snort of displeasure.

"Only a matter of minutes from now," Sam said, waiting for the warmth of first contact to spread through his body. The old bod seemed to be slow off the launch pad tonight, but it might have something to do with the reptilian stare aimed at him by Maria.

The redhead strode across the silk carpet, her long legs below her skin-tight skirt showed off the twin masterpieces of toned muscle. Sam mentally calculated the upkeep costs on such a lady. More than he could afford, but then again, he wasn't buying. Her eyes were on him, her expression confident.

The moment of mutual assessment.

He waited for the jolt of anticipation deep in his gut.

"Sam Jackson, so nice to meet you at last," she purred.

"Let me introduce you two." Maria glanced from one to the other. "Sam, this is Pauline Simpson."

"It's a pleasure," he said, taking her hand just for the rush he'd feel when their palms touched.

Nothing.

"No, the pleasure's all mine, Sam. I've been waiting

242

for you."

"You have?" Sam said, noting there was still no response from his body.

Pauline moved closer, her well-tanned skin shining under her flimsy T-strap top. "Why don't we go someplace quiet? Maria has a huge collection of books. Let's go to her library."

Maria's book collection was news to Sam, but he didn't care one way or the other. All he wanted was a night of unbridled lust. And Pauline Simpson fit the bill. "After you."

The air in the library was cool, the room dark with just one lamp burning in the corner. They slid onto the white leather sofa as Pauline's hands snaked inside Sam's jacket and loosened his silk shirt.

"What do you think?" she whispered against his chin, her heavy perfume marking the air around him.

Sam's hands found their way over Pauline's bare back, along the edge of the open space just above her hips. No rush of adrenaline, not so much as a lift from his buddy down below.

Pauline moaned and moved closer.

He had to be tired. Or maybe he had an illness of some sort, something affecting his libido...

Have a little faith. Old buddy will come through. He always has.

Sam met Pauline's hungry gaze. With grim determination, he buried both hands in her mane of red hair.

Her eager lips were on his, like two squirming pieces of bread dough. "I want you," Pauline hissed against his mouth.

There was something really wrong with the gladiator. Not a flicker of interest, no tension, no hardness. Nothing.

While Pauline's tongue darted between his lips, he closed his eyes and concentrated on the luscious curves, the heat of her body, the scent of musk on her skin.

Then, unbidden, a picture of the rose arbor and the woman whose smile he wanted to forget filled him.

CHAPTER TWENTY-SIX

Trust your heart.

The next morning Sam gunned his Corvette and raced down the highway toward Middleborough. He'd lain awake most of the night after his disastrous evening. He cringed as he thought about how phony his flu story sounded. When his body refused to perform, leaving him no choice but to fabricate a story, he got out of there as fast as he could and went home. Alone.

He didn't have the flu. He had a bad case of heartache for a woman who'd probably forgotten all about him and who would probably tell him to get lost when she saw him.

Yet, he couldn't wait to see the smile of happiness on her face when he told her his news about the farm.

Maybe she didn't love him, maybe she never would, but he needed to go back and find out where he stood. After last night, he knew he was doing the right thing.

And, it felt so good. So right.

How had he been so dumb? What a self-absorbed cad he was. Well, he had learned his lesson, and all he wanted to do was make things right with Lisa.

He saw the exit ramp ahead and flicked on his signal light. In a few hours, he and Lisa would be talking, or he would for sure. He would tell her about his change of heart, his realization about what life was really all about. A part of Sam knew he could charm away any resistance Lisa had to his plan, but another part of him wanted to start fresh with her. Charming Lisa would always be a fun part of their relationship, but complete honesty was what he wanted right now.

The ribbon of asphalt looped around houses, over bridges and through wooded areas as Sam made his way across the open countryside. The closer he got to Middleborough, the more it felt like he was going home.

Everything he was doing felt so right, so much the way it should be. Now, all he needed was to find Lisa and talk to her. He wanted to make a quick stop in town. In his haste he'd forgotten to buy the one thing that would make the moment perfect—a bottle of champagne. The Corvette's purr changed to a rumble as he pulled into the parking lot. He eased out of the form-fitting seat and went through the sliding glass doors of the gourmet food store. Feeling pleased and at the same time excited, he reached for a bottle of bubbly.

"Hi there." A female voice that reminded him of last night caught him off guard. Slim, well-manicured fingers wrapped around his arm as the exotic scent of yet another sophisticated perfume filled his nostrils. He glanced at the upturned face of Samantha Mitchell.

"Hello, yourself," he said, struggling to sound upbeat against the disappointment flipping around inside him.

"Well, if you aren't just the man I'm looking for." Samantha's voice floated around him in a cool, sensual way. "My daddy's been looking all over for you, Sam." She ran her fingers over Sam's arm in a familiar, cloying way, as if she had some claim to him.

Annoyance bubbled to the surface, but Sam buried it. He didn't want to ruin a perfect day. "Well, here I am."

"I know. I know." Her gaze traveled over his face.

Sam saw the flutter of her eyelids and nearly laughed out loud. If she only knew...

"Daddy and I want you to come to dinner this evening."

"I wish I could, but I have other plans." He sure as hell did, and nothing was going to get in his way.

"Would you consider changing them? I'd make it worth your while." Samantha's voice was on low simmer, its softness grating on Sam's impatience.

"No can do," he said, careful to keep control of his annoyance. From long experience, Sam knew it wouldn't do to antagonize someone like Samantha Mitchell.

"Well, in that case, sweetie, maybe you'd give a girl a lift to Mac's Garage. I left my car there."

"Sure." By the way her fingers were working on his arm, and the not-so-gentle sway of her body as she moved closer, Sam could tell that Samantha had a lot more on her mind than a drive to the garage. He'd seen it so many times before, and there was a time when he would have risen to the bait. He could see why Lisa considered him a womanizer. He had been that and more. Now he didn't really care what Samantha wanted from him. She wasn't going to get it. A drive over to the garage was all he'd provide.

Samantha settled into the seat beside him and traced her fingers lightly over his as he rested his hand on the stick shift. "Daddy wants to talk to you. Just a little business..." She gave a sigh and curled her fingers over his.

"It'll have to wait. I have some business of my own to attend to."

"Trust me. You'll want to hear what Daddy has to say." She leaned toward him, her silk shirt gaping just enough to afford Sam an excellent view of her lace-covered breasts.

Already regretting his offer of a drive, Sam kept his

eyes on the road as he edged into the traffic.

Lisa stared unseeing out the window. "So, even if we count a possible contribution from Tom Mitchell we won't make it?" she asked Ed Chambers. She was in his office to discuss the chance of finding enough additional money to make an offer.

"Short of a miracle, no." Ed moved a pile of papers from one side of his desk to the other.

"Maybe we could ask Tom for more money, and maybe get him to help us line up new contributors. He might consider it, you know. If we put his name on a plaque or something. He might be more willing to donate if the request came from you—" Lisa said, feeling a sense of hopelessness about it all.

"I talked to him. Tom's offer of a donation is conditional on him talking to Sam first. Sam isn't going to help us. He's perfectly happy with the lumber company's offer. You said so yourself. Sam Jackson has no reason to do anything more than what he's already done by giving us some additional time."

Lisa's first thought was to defend Sam. He wasn't the cruel, mean person she'd thought he was a few weeks ago. He could be very kind and funny, and he did have a very strong reason for wanting a good price for the farm. But defending Sam to Ed would require an explanation—one she couldn't give without giving away her secret. She'd fallen in love with Sam.

"Why would Tom want to talk to Sam? It doesn't make any sense at all..." Lisa chewed her bottom lip while she considered the angles. "Tom Mitchell was not the giving kind, and yet he was willing to consider a donation if Sam talked to him."

Deep inside, Lisa had a suspicion that "Daddy" was

trying to please his daughter. Samantha couldn't have been happy about Sam's response to her that night at the barbecue. Lisa didn't think that Samantha handled rejection well, when most of her life she got what she wanted.

Ed rubbed his bald spot. "Beats me. Unless he thinks he can gain some sort of advantage. Tom Mitchell only deals when he's assured he'll get something in return."

"You know, Ed, this thing is getting more suspicious by the minute. Tom Mitchell has never so much as bought a raffle ticket from us to support the Nature Trust. So why would he consider it now?" Lisa's voice trailed off as her eyes focused on the garage across the street. A bright red Corvette with the top down had just pulled into Mac's. A handsome man was behind the wheel and the woman sitting next to him, laughing and flipping her hair off her shoulders looked an awful lot like...

Lisa looked closer.

Sam Jackson. "It can't be!" she said without thinking.

"It can't be what?"

Even from across the street, Lisa could see that Sam was enjoying himself. He had a grin on his face, as Samantha touched his cheek. There was a familiarity between them that was unmistakable.

Hurt, like hot lava, flowed over Lisa, sealing her lungs shut and making her eyes sting with tears. Her desire for Sam, that had haunted her every night since his departure, gave way to shock and an overpowering need to protect herself from what she saw across the street.

"What is it Lisa?" Ed came around his desk and stood beside her as she stared out between the slats of the blind at the scene across the street.

Lisa watched with a sinking heart as Samantha kissed Sam, patted his cheek and got out of the car. All

Lisa could see were her long, slim legs finished off with a pair of sling-backs that Lisa could never wear. Envy piled on top of the hurt. "It's trouble. That's what it is."

"That's Sam, isn't it?"

"In all his glory."

"And Samantha Mitchell. So now we know why her daddy wanted to see Sam." Ed parted the blind to get a better look.

"Don't!" Lisa glared a warning at Ed.

"What difference does it make if he sees us? We need to talk with him. If Sam's back in town, it means only one thing. He's here to finalize the sale. Why don't you go over and see what you can do? You know him better than I do. See if you can find a way to get him to wait just a little longer."

"No," she croaked. She'd fry in hell before she'd have a conversation with someone who could betray her like this.

"Then, I'll go."

"No. Let's wait and see..."

Lisa could feel Ed's gaze hanging over her face like a spider's web. He knew something was wrong, but he was too much of a gentleman to ask. And darn him; she wanted him to ask. She wanted to tell him about the traitor across the street. About the man who'd said he had to go to New York. For all she knew he hadn't left Samantha's bed.

CHAPTER TWENTY-SEVEN

There are few things in life that faith can't fix.

Lisa pushed her pickup to its limits as she drove out of town on her way to Aunt Clara's house. Not knowing who else to turn to, she had decided to talk to her aunt. It was probably a bad idea, but she was out of good ideas when it came to Sam. And she needed a different perspective on the man if she was to help convince Sam to give the Nature Trust a bit more time. Seeing Sam with Samantha had mobilized her to take action.

The old farm house stood nestled at the end of a shaded lane just south of town. The back of the house looked out over Harper's Lake, a summer swimming place for Lisa and her friends when they were growing up.

Aunt Clara had devoted her life to her grown children who now lived out of state. But Aunt Clara still baked as if they were living at home: ginger sugar cookies that melted in your mouth; chocolate cake with boiled icing; homemade pralines; and not to mention donuts that made Lisa's mouth water whenever she thought of them.

Her Uncle Angus was a crusty gentleman of the old school who believed that women belonged at home raising babies and doing housework, while men were responsible for all the interesting experiences of life. It irked Lisa to see the way her uncle always seemed to do as he pleased with his time and money, leaving her Aunt Clara to be satisfied with the house and garden and her Thursday evening bridge club.

Lisa drove her truck into their driveway, relieved to see that Uncle Angus's Explorer was not in its usual spot. Aunt Clara waved from the kitchen window as Lisa got out of the truck and walked toward the back door.

"Well, hello honey. It's so good to see you. I'm just taking a batch of brownies out of the oven. I'll put the kettle on and make us a cup of tea."

"That would be great, Aunt Clara," Lisa said, hugging her aunt and soaking up the comforting scent of baked chocolate.

With obvious pleasure, Aunt Clara wiped her hands on the corner of her apron overflowing with embroidered roses and ivy. "I was hoping you'd come by and see me."

"I should have done it sooner," Lisa mumbled around her second brownie.

On the way over there she'd accepted the fact that she'd been a fool to believe that Sam needed to leave early for New York when it was clear that he'd spent his time with his favorite Barbie Doll. No wonder Tom Mitchell wanted to talk to Sam. He had plans. He likely wanted an engagement or promise of marriage for his daughter, in exchange for his contribution to the Nature Trust.

To think that Sam had spent the night with Lisa, knowing that he was headed straight to another woman's arms, filled her with pain and anger. He was a cad of the worst kind. She'd fallen for his line and now it hurt to remember how she'd spent all those hours after he'd left imagining how she'd feel if he changed his mind and came back. She'd wasted all her emotional energy on the doomed belief that Sam cared.

She gritted her teeth in fury as the truth hit her.

She'd show him once and for all that tangling with Lisa O'Neill had consequences. "Aunt Clara, I need to talk to you."

"Anything, honey. You know that." Her aunt popped two tea bags into the blue teapot and filled it with boiling water. A satisfied smile wreathed her face as she settled her rounded frame on one of the sturdy kitchen chairs and rested her arms on the table.

Aunt Clara's expression was open and loving and Lisa's heart squeezed in her chest. If it hadn't been for her Aunt Clara she would never have been able to survive her mother's leaving.

"Don't you ever get tired of me crying on your shoulder?" Lisa asked.

"Never. You're like a daughter to me. You know that."

Searching for something to do with her hands, Lisa poured each of them a cup of tea. Funny how difficult and pointless the whole thing about Sam seemed now when she tried to put it into words.

"I'm listening," her aunt said as her gaze followed Lisa.

She took the chair across from her aunt. "I need to know if you can help me."

"I'll try."

Suddenly, Lisa couldn't tell her aunt how foolish she'd been about a man who didn't care. It was too humiliating to admit just how dumb and naive she'd been. She suddenly regretted coming to her aunt's, but it was too late to leave without explaining. "I'm trying to raise enough money to stop Sam Jackson from selling Harmony Farm to Cascade Lumber."

Her eyes wide with surprise, her aunt said, "But how can I help? Angus is the one you should be talking to about that sort of thing."

"But you know lots of people. People who might be

willing to contribute if they knew you were in favor of saving the farm."

"Yes, I suppose..." Her aunt sipped her tea, her expression thoughtful. "I might know lots of people, but not those with the money to spend. Have you talked to Angus? He belongs to several fundraising clubs."

Lisa shook her head. "Ed Chambers has covered most of those."

Her aunt smiled. "I'll see what I can do. Why didn't you come to me earlier?"

"I guess I thought I could do this on my own. I mean with the Naturalist Club."

"But it's not working?"

"No. We need more help than we can get through our members and so we're trying others in the community."

"Like Angus and me."

Lisa nodded. "I'll need to know soon if you can drum up any extra support."

"It's that urgent?"

"Yes." Lisa chewed her lip.

Her aunt leaned across the table and affectionately rubbed the back of Lisa's hand. "I've known you all your life, Lisa O'Neill, and I know there's more to this story than you're telling me."

Lisa fought the blush rising in her cheeks as she studied the wood grain of the tabletop.

"So. This young man has caught your attention in more ways than one."

Her aunt knew her well. "Aunt Clara. I don't want to talk about this."

"Well honey, I do. I've waited a long while to see that look in your eyes."

Lisa's heart thumped in her chest as she avoided her aunt's searching gaze. "Aunt Clara, I can't—"

"Honey, I'm going to tell you something. You're not

going to like it, but it needs to be said."

Lisa braced herself and tried for a defiant stare. She didn't want any advice from her aunt, because there wasn't anything going on in her life that her advice could help. What she needed was to escape Sam and the feelings he provoked in her. "What's that?"

"I know how much you've tried to prove how independent and capable you are. I guess you saw it as something you needed to do to free yourself from the pain of your mother's behavior. But don't let that pain rule your life."

"I don't know what you're talking about."

Lisa started to speak and her aunt squeezed her fingers. "Let me finish. After your mother left, I watched a lonely young woman struggle to make sense of her world. I watched your father fumble in his attempts as well, and I watched the way you shielded yourself from the pain by pretending you didn't need anybody."

Fighting to keep the tears from flooding over her cheeks, Lisa looked at the ceiling. "Why need someone who doesn't care?"

"Oh, Lisa, honey. We all need someone. Leave the past behind and reach out to people."

"I've tried, but it's so hard." Lisa sniffed and her aunt pulled an embroidered hanky from her pocket and pressed it into Lisa's hand.

Encouraged by her aunt, Lisa slowly opened up about what had gone on since Herbert passed away.

"I knew all along that Sam never wanted to be here, that it was inevitable that he would leave."

"So you tell yourself." Clara's eyes narrowed as she stared at Lisa.

"It doesn't matter what I tell myself. Sam's not interested in me, or he wouldn't have agreed to sell to the lumber company."

"Then, why did he not close the deal right away and

be done with it?"

"Greed, I guess. I don't know." And she didn't care. Right now, all she wanted to do was get away from her aunt and her unnerving way of getting to the bottom of things.

"I think you've got a lot of thinking to do."

"I can't let him hurt me like this. He's wrong for me."

"Lisa darling, he's the right one, or you wouldn't be struggling with this. You would have let go of him a long time ago."

"I had to stay involved, if I wanted to save Harmony Farm," Lisa protested.

"Even if it breaks your heart?"

The pain of talking like this was nearly unbearable. Her aunt was right about so many things but at the moment Lisa felt smothered by her emotions. "My heart's fine."

Her aunt's voice grew stern. "No, it's not. You're in love with him and you're letting your own fear and inability to forgive him stand in the way of your happiness."

Sam breathed a sigh of relief as he pulled out of Mac's Garage. It didn't take much to figure out that Tom Mitchell's little girl wasn't through trying to manipulate him into a relationship. Sam had known she was a willful woman the first time he'd spent the summer there. Thinking back to that fateful dance that summer, he should have just stayed home that night.

Yet, he didn't care about any of that now. All he cared about was finding Lisa. She was probably out observing the eagles' nests this time of day. He planned to go to the farmhouse and set the scene, chill the champagne...

He was bumped out of his reverie by a car that honked as it passed: a beat-up Volkswagen with racing stripes and driven by a young kid with a gleam of satisfaction in his eye as he passed. Sam remembered the days when passing a Corvette in a beat-up old clunker you'd bought for a song would give you an adrenaline high.

Sam smiled and waved. The kid could have the whole damned road as far as he was concerned. He drove on toward the farm, rehearsing what he planned to say to Lisa. He'd have to take it slowly at first, test her mood a little. Telling her his plans would be a disaster if she wasn't ready to listen.

Maybe a quick call... He rounded a curve in the road and slowed as the realization hit him. He should have called her while he was away. *What had he been thinking?*

He whizzed around the next turn and the white frame house with its long, flowing driveway came into view. He geared down and turned in, his heart pressing into his throat. He could see her truck in the yard, and there she was watching the dogs as they romped around her. The sight of Lisa made him smile for the first time in days.

They had so much to talk about, so many things to work through.

He had never been happier in his life.

He slid the sports car into the lane in front of the house. Jumping out of the car, he ran up the gently sloping lawn separating the lane from the graveled driveway. "Lisa!"

The dogs broke and ran toward him. He opened his arms and the foursome barreled into him, nearly knocking him over. He patted and rubbed and talked dog talk for a few minutes as he waited for her to move toward him. "Easy guys," he said as he continued to pat heads while he smiled at Lisa.

She didn't return the smile.

"It's so nice to be back," he said, his voice sounding anxious in his ears.

"Really? You could have fooled me." She placed her hands on her hips in a way he remembered—a warning of dark clouds ahead of an impending storm.

Sam's spirits fizzled in his gut. "Lisa, I'm back."

"This is your farm, you can do as you please and be where you want."

"Lisa, what's wrong?"

"Nothing is wrong, and nothing has changed. You can take your Barbie Doll girlfriend Samantha and get lost."

CHAPTER TWENTY-EIGHT

Happy endings make sad beginnings worthwhile.

Lisa saw the confusion in Sam's eyes, and her heart fluttered against her ribs like a bird trapped in a cage. Despite everything, she still wanted to comfort him, to feel his arms around her as she whispered words of apology.

But she had nothing more to apologize for and an apology was out of the question.

Her crack about Samantha was nasty, hateful even, but it was true and expressed how she felt. She had thought about what her Aunt Clara said all the way back to the farm, about being willing to risk letting go and trusting someone. Under ordinary circumstances she might be right... But Sam's betrayal had cut too deep.

"Samantha? What has she got to do with anything? Did something happen while I was away?"

Samantha in all her feral beauty rose like a specter between them. Lisa had always felt inferior around women like Samantha. And when she'd felt forced to fake an illness to protect herself from being the laughing stock at the dance... But now she felt even worse. Sam had broken her heart by carrying on yet again with Samantha.

"The problem is you. And I don't want to waste any more time on anything involving you or Harmony Farm."

Sam waded through the sea of dogs and reached for her. "Lisa, I don't understand what's wrong. Can we talk?"

She fought the urge to move toward him, narrowly convincing her eager body to back away. But not before she came under the spell of his overwhelming male scent. His closeness engulfed her, nearly wiping out her determination. Her body ached for him even as she moved out of his reach.

"What do we have to talk about, Sam? You're here now, and thanks, by the way, for letting me know you were coming back today. If you even left at all…" She dumped as much sarcasm into her words as her constricted throat would allow.

"I'm sorry. It was a last-minute decision and I should have called you, but I wanted to get here as soon as I could."

She knew he was a cad, but she hadn't known he could lie so easily. How had she spent time with him, loved him and not seen this side of him? "Please don't pretend to me."

"Pretend what?"

"About where you were or why you didn't call. Your false interest in me and in being here is a little hard to take under the circumstances."

"Circumstances? What circumstances?"

Lisa, her heart pushing into her throat, took a deep breath. A pain stronger than any she'd ever experienced in her life, surrounded her, choking the air from her lungs. Sam Jackson didn't want her. He wanted someone else. Someone who so clearly would fit into his world.

Anyway, she'd be gone from Harmony Farm for good in a few days. "It doesn't matter anymore."

"What doesn't matter anymore? I don't understand what's going on. When I left here I thought we were friends. You were going to work on the Nature Trust deal and let me know if you could meet the price. I didn't hear a word from you. Is that what this is about? Are you upset because you couldn't raise the money?"

She met his concerned gaze, feeling defeated and embarrassed at how easily she'd fallen into the trap of believing that Sam had changed after the time they'd shared together.

"Lisa, it'll work out. You'll see. I've done something to make sure that Harmony Farm is safe."

So her suspicions were true. Sam and Tom Mitchell had cut a deal. Sam would marry Samantha and Harmony Farm would be saved. And it made a lot of sense in a sick sort of way. Sam was no stranger to the flash wedding concept. He'd done it once for lust, this time he could do it for money. The reasons didn't matter and the results were the same. "Too bad," she murmured.

He frowned. "I'm sorry?"

For the second time in a few hours, Lisa struggled to hold the tears back. It wasn't working, and she couldn't face the idea that Sam might see her cry. He'd taken everything else from her. He didn't deserve to see how much he'd hurt her. "You and I have nothing to talk about. However, I'd appreciate it if you'd make arrangements for the dogs."

Sam reached toward her, and before she knew what had happened, he'd tucked his hand into hers. "Lisa, listen to me. We need to talk."

His touch reverberated through her, sending rivers of need coursing through her body, and making her knees shake. "Why now, when you have what you want?"

She tried to free her fingers, but he held fast. "That's the whole point. I don't have what I want. I came here to see you, to tell you what a stupid fool I've been."

"The Barbie Doll dumped you, did she?" Lisa tried for a wry lift of her eyebrows, but only succeeded in releasing the tears clinging to her lashes.

"Oh God, Lisa, don't cry. I never meant to make you cry. I care a great deal for you." He dipped his head, and she felt the warmth of his breath on her cheek.

"And that should matter to me? You're out of here and back to your old life. You don't have to pretend with me. If you'll remember, I predicted this from the very beginning."

"Lisa O'Neill, I've had just about all of this I'm going to take." With one quick swoop, he picked her up and carried her toward the house.

"You put me down!"

"Not unless you agree to act like an adult and let me explain."

She wiggled and twisted her way free of his arms, landing hard on her butt in the grass along the drive. "I want you out of my life, you and Samantha," she gasped as the air fled from her lungs with the resounding bump on the ground.

He sat down next to her, pulling a strand of curls off her cheek. "*Samantha?* Is Samantha the reason for all this?"

"Don't act dumb! I saw the two of you at Mac's Garage a while ago."

Sam placed his arm gently around her shoulders. "You're jealous of Miss Mitchell."

Lisa turned her face to his. "I am not jealous." She ground out the words.

Now that he knew what caused this, Sam wasn't surprised at Lisa's resistance. Her pride and independent streak were doing the talking for her. "Lisa, dearest, I love the look you're giving me right this minute. The way your eyes do that funny chameleon thing. You know, where they turn from green to a green-yellow."

"I don't believe you. I don't believe anything you

say."

He pulled her up with him. "You will," he whispered as he snuggled her ripe body against his and kissed her mouth.

At first, she resisted, her lips firmly closed. He pulled her tighter, nibbling along the edge of her lips, and had the satisfaction of hearing her deep moan. He pressed his advantage and eased her lips open with his tongue. She tasted warm, sweet, and in that moment he knew beyond any doubt he'd made the right decision. He ran his lips along her cheek, rejoicing in the way her breath was coming in short spurts, and the way he could feel the pounding of her heart through the wall of his chest.

Sam watched the struggle in Lisa's eyes and wanted to yelp with joy. She wanted him as much as he wanted her, and he was so damned glad.

"Lisa, there's only one thing I'd like to do right now, but I think we might do it better somewhere a little more private." He gave the foursome, lined up on the knoll, a sweeping glance and eased his grip on her hands as he did so.

Lisa's pulled free, moved her arms into the limited space between them and pushed him away. "I meant it, Sam. You can't have me. You had your chance and you blew it."

"And now you think I have Samantha?"

"It doesn't matter what I think; but yeah, something like that."

"What if I told you I didn't want Samantha? Never did, in fact."

"And I'd say you were lying. I'd say you had quite a little time with her, and I wouldn't even have known about the two of you if I hadn't seen you at Mac's Garage."

Sam had no intention of letting go of Lisa until he'd

set her straight about a few things. "I was buying a bottle of champagne when Samantha appeared. She wanted a drive to pick up her car. End of the story."

"Yeah, right. Tell that to someone who believes you. Samantha and her daddy want to see you. He'll make a contribution to the Nature Trust on the condition that he talk to you first. I don't need a college degree in math to put that particular two and two together."

"Well, believe this. I'm through with the Samantha Mitchells of this world. I don't care what her father wants. I'm back here to make things right, with your help. I've learned my lesson."

"And what lesson would that be?"

"That I love you, and I want us to make our home here on Harmony Farm. If you'll have me."

"What?" she asked, surprise knocking the air from her lungs. "What are you saying?"

"I'm going to set the record straight, and from here on in, things will be different."

"In what way?" She gave him a suspicious glance.

"First you have to choose where we will discuss our future, the house or the apartment?"

Future? Was she hearing things? "The apartment," she said in disbelief, her head swimming, her heart dipping into her tummy.

He smiled as he put his arm around her shoulder. "Good choice."

Once in the apartment, Sam sat down at the table, his hands resting on the scarred wood.

"It's this simple. I love you. I realized that when I tried to go back to my old life. I discovered I didn't fit there anymore. I belong here with you."

"I… I don't know what to say." It was as if she'd

entered some weird parallel universe where everything seemed reversed. She wanted to tell him she loved him, but it was all too sudden, too unexpected for her to trust what was happening. His coming back here to live on the farm didn't make any sense at all. Sam had made it very clear: His life was in New York.

"You've made me see things I never understood. I went back to New York with every intention of going back to my old life. Turns out I couldn't do it. Didn't want to do it."

Wanting to believe him so much, yet so afraid, she whispered, "But how can you be so sure in such a short time? How can you give up something you've been working on for years? Did something happen?"

"I wasn't very happy in spite of having the job of my dreams, and my business doing well. Something was missing. It took an old man and a dog to point the way for me."

"You missed the dogs?"

"That was part of it. But I missed you a whole lot more," he said so gently and so softy, with so much heart she found his words irresistible.

Yet it was his smile that truly melted her resolve. If she were willing to take the risk and trust in his love for her, and her love for him, they could work things out... Wasn't that what Aunt Clara had said? She had to risk letting go, take a chance on love.

It all seemed too easy now... "And all those sophisticated women just fell by the wayside in your moment of truth?" she said, trying to remain aloof.

"All those sophisticated women couldn't hold a candle to you. I'm hooked on you, Lisa. All the time I was away, I didn't really see another woman. And when I tried to return to the singles' scene, the whole thing felt phony and unfeeling."

He came around the table, taking her hand in his.

"There's only one woman who does it for me, and that's you."

His words were mushy, sentimental, and just what she needed to hear.

But what if this didn't work and he walked out again? Yet she knew if she didn't take a chance she would never know if she and Sam could work it out. And given how she'd always felt about Sam, if she didn't give this a shot she would regret it for a very long time.

"You'd better not be toying with me," she warned, searching for a way to protect herself from this man who had been her dream for so long.

"I promise you, Lisa. I'm completely serious. I want you, and no one else. It's that simple."

Seeing the truth of his words in his eyes, she whispered, "Then come with me, Sam Jackson. I want to show you my etchings."

"Your etchings?"

She stood up, pulling him with her.

Needing to reassure herself, she locked her arms around his waist and pressed her body to his. "I have a scratched-up, thoroughly gouged, old four poster bed. It came from your uncle's attic..."

The next morning Lisa woke to the most obnoxious pounding sound she'd ever heard. The dogs set up a chorus of yelping and barking that made it almost impossible for Lisa to collect her wits enough to realize where she was.

Slowly, she became aware of Sam's warm, muscled body lying next to her. He was stirring, but not awake. She had plans for that gorgeous body, but first she'd dispense with whoever was making such a racket at the door. Pulling on an oversized shirt and a pair of leggings, she tumbled down the stairs followed by the swirling mass of dog flesh.

She yanked open the door and saw Ed Chambers standing there with more excitement on his face than she'd seen in all the time she'd known him. "Lisa, I have to talk to you. Can I come in?"

"Sure." She opened the door wider and pointed the way up the stairs to her apartment.

"You're not going to believe what happened."

"I'm not?" Fear mingled with expectation.

Ed walked into Lisa's tiny living room and turned to face her. "Sam Jackson is going to keep the house and ten acres. If he does that, the Nature Trust will be able to buy the rest of the land."

"What about the lumber company? Won't they have something to say about this? After all, they made a bid—"

"You leave the lumber company to me," Sam said as he came up behind her, wrapping his arms around her, and pulling her snugly against him.

"Good morning, Ed," Sam said as he nuzzled Lisa's neck.

"Good morning. I guess you know how pleased the Nature Trust is with this new development."

"No more pleased than I am to make the offer." Sam turned Lisa in his arms and tilted her chin up. "What do you say?"

"I'm thrilled," she said, loving the way their bodies snugged together, the heat of him, the look of desire in his eyes.

"Then that's settled," Ed said. "I'm off to tell the rest of the group." With that he went down the stairs to a rush of dogs following along behind him.

"When did you do that?" she asked.

"Yesterday."

"Why didn't you tell me?" Lisa asked.

"If you hadn't been after my body, I might have found a moment to explain—" He laughed as she pretended to slap him.

"Seriously I wanted you to accept another proposal first, but we got side tracked," he whispered against her neck.

"May I remind you it takes two," she said, loving the look in his dark eyes.

"Something else takes two as well."

"Meaning?"

"Will you marry me and live with me on Harmony Farm?"

Her heart rose in her chest at the thought that she would get to live the rest of her life with the only man she'd ever loved. She could hardly believe this was happening, but she wasn't going to let it slip away from her, not now after all the time she'd waited for him. "I'll marry you, Sam Jackson, on the condition that we get married in the rose arbor."

"With the dogs as witnesses?" he asked, a smile spreading across his handsome face.

"You got it." Lisa wrapped her arms around his neck and kissed him. She felt the tightening of his body and the rounded pressure against her pelvis.

The world receded as she clung to his warm body, her heart filling with the kind of happiness she could only have imagined. The man she'd spent her life waiting for had made her dream come true

The End

Dear Reader,

I am thrilled that you have chosen to read my book. Thank you so much.

Finding Mr. Gorgeous is the second book in my Liberated Ladies series, books about women facing huge challenges in their lives while they search for love.

In **Finding Mr. Gorgeous** I've included four dogs, central to the story and so much fun to write about. I love dogs, and for years my husband and I had a Gordon Setter named Woody who ruled our lives with a gentle paw.

If you like dogs you will find the story of Chocolate, Scotch, Soda, and Peanuts endearing. But the love story between Lisa and Sam will make you smile as you cheer them on to their happy ending.

Please let me know what you think of this story, and if you have a dog I would love to hear about the antics of your pet.

I can be reached at stella@stellamaclean.com.

Or you can visit my website and sign up for my newsletter at:

www.stellamaclean.com

Or on twitter: @Stella_MacLean

Or on Facebook: facebook.com/**stella.maclean.3**

I hope this letter finds you in good health and enjoying your everyday of your life.

Sincerely,
Stella

Here's a quick look at what to expect in the next book:

Finding Mr. Fix-it

Cookie Carmichael has spent her life being the perfect wife and mother, and taken her husband's philandering ways in stride to keep what the rest of the world thinks is the perfect marriage. She's taken care of her grandmother, taken her mother's advice even when it was wrong, taken her turn knitting scarves and mittens for the school fundraisers. She's taken so much in her life, including the arrival of her husband's latest squeeze on her front doorstep.

Now it's Cookie's turn to take back her life, take back her respectability, and take up a relationship with the man of her choice. Shane is not sure he wants to be taken, given how much he enjoys the smorgasbord of women who pass through his life. In fact, Shane sees himself as a man who takes control of any situation. That is until the day Cookie shows him her secret weapon—her caring and support during the greatest crisis of his life.

Finding Mr. Fix-it is due out in September 2018.

OTHER BOOKS BY STELLA MACLEAN

Heart of My Heart, Harlequin Superromance

Baby in Her Arms, Harlequin Superromance

A Child Changes Everything, Harlequin Superromance

The Christmas Inn, Harlequin Superromance

The Doctor Returns, Harlequin Superromance

To Protect Her Son, Harlequin Superromance

Sweet On Peggy, Harlequin Superromance

Unexpected Attraction, Harlequin Superromance

Bringing Emma Home, Harlequin Superromance

Finding Mr. Wrong, Contemporary Romance

Desperate Memories, Romantic Suspense

Desperate Acts, Romantic Suspense

Unimaginable, Romantic Suspense

ABOUT STELLA MACLEAN

Stella MacLean has been writing for years. She likes the close relationship she has with her computer, and her furry friends, Jethro and Sully. Stella also enjoys the hours she spends hiding out in her office writing stories about the lives of very ordinary people doing extraordinary things. Stella believes that love and laughter bring out the best in us.

Finding Mr. Gorgeous was inspired by living in Port Greville, Nova Scotia.

Stella loves to hear from her readers, to have discussions about writing and reading and anything else that is of interest to those people who enjoy her books.

She can be reached at her website: **www.stellamaclean.com**

Or you can find her on Twitter: @Stella_MacLean

Or on Facebook: facebook.com/**stella.maclean.3**

50059059R00170

Made in the USA
Lexington, KY
25 August 2019